A high-velocity bullet whined off the blacktop, making the horses buck and rear

Abe stayed up on the box, fighting for control. He looked over his shoulder, watching as the Armorer unlatched the rear door of the hearse, and, helped by Ryan, heaved Trader inside.

"Leave it open," the older man yelled. "I can slow the bastards down from here."

"Whip them up, Abe!" Ryan shouted. He fired several carefully placed rounds at the advancing mob, putting down at least three men, sending others scattering for cover among the trees.

J.B. climbed quickly onto the box alongside Abe, hanging on to the side rail, waiting for Ryan to join them. The little gunner was poised, whip in hand, watching as the one-eyed man swung onto the foot plate.

"Now!"

The whip cracked, ringing out into the bright morning like a dueling pistol. The horses whinnied and began to move, hooves slipping. Abe bellowed at them, lashing the animals unmercifully to get the hearse on the road and out of there.

Ryan hung on by his left hand, the toes of his boots only scant inches from the rolling wheel. The first hesitant members of the mob appeared, and he fired a couple of rounds among them.

"They're giving up!" J.B. called. "You did good, Abe!"

The team slowed as they approached an avenue of ancient yews. The attack came out of nowhere.

**Also available in the
Deathlands saga:**

JAMES AXLER

DEATH LANDS®

Trader Redux

A GOLD EAGLE BOOK FROM

WORLDWIDE®

TORONTO • NEW YORK • LONDON
AMSTERDAM • PARIS • SYDNEY • HAMBURG
STOCKHOLM • ATHENS • TOKYO • MILAN
MADRID • WARSAW • BUDAPEST • AUCKLAND

This one is dedicated to the beloved memory of the
ever-stylish Vincent Price. He gave us so many hours of
the richest pleasure and amusement. Nobody ever did it
better. May the earth lie lightly upon him.

First edition December 1994

ISBN 0-373-62524-3

TRADER REDUX

Copyright © 1994 by Worldwide Library.

During my too long life, I have often lost touch with good, good friends for a number of years and then contrived to meet up with them again. These meetings, which I always anticipated with great eagerness, were universally a great disappointment. It is one of the great truths in the world that you can never go back.

—From *The Gospel According to Me*,
by Bobo "Tinky" Finkelstein,
Showbiz Press, New York, 1937

PROLOGUE

The day was bitterly cold, with a dazzling sun hanging at the center of an untouched blue sky. From east to west and north to south, there wasn't even the hint of a cloud. All around it seemed that you could reach out and touch the perfection of the snow-covered mountains.

The cold air had the unmistakable scent of salt, from the Cific Ocean only a few miles away, beyond the ruins of old Seattle. Here and there it was possible to make out the thin tendrils of cooking fires, among the stumps of nuked city buildings. But whatever ate there, ate alone.

The oppressive wet weather of the past three days had vanished, and it had snowed during the previous night as the temperature dropped well below freezing.

Now, an hour after dawn, it was a heaven of morning.

Ryan and J.B. had found no cover, waking up to find their sleeping bags were crusted with frozen snow, which crackled when they moved.

"Last day of the last week," Ryan said as he stooped, trying to get a fire going to warm them up and dry their clothes and heat some oatmeal.

"Now we'll see." J.B. checked that the cold hadn't affected any of his blasters.

"Yeah, we'll see."

THEY HAD DECIDED that the best place to begin the final stage of their search would be to pick a high spot with a view over Seattle from the east. There was a particular hill that suited their purpose and they had been working their way toward it, occasionally slipping on the icy trail.

Apart from the scattered fires among the ruins, there didn't seem to be a living soul within fifty miles of them.

There had been a pair of white-pelted hares gamboling in a clearing among the pines, as they climbed higher, who'd totally ignored them.

In a valley to their right they spotted a small herd of deer picking its way delicately through the frosted grass. J.B. had nudged Ryan and pointed to the Steyr on his shoulder, but he'd shaken his head.

"Bullet on a still, cold morning like this might be heard twenty miles off. Could attract Abe and the Trader. If they're anywhere near. Could attract anyone else."

It was hard work, and both men were panting as they neared the crest of the small mountain.

"You can make out the sea from here," Ryan said, pausing for breath.

"Yeah. Look at the Cascades back yonder."

A few more paces brought them to the top, giving them the ultimate view, all the way around.

Now they could see the far side of the slope, bisected by a narrow hunting path. Two figures about a hundred yards below them, struggling upward through the deeper snow. The smaller man was sliding and falling, a little way to the rear.

The leader, using the butt of what looked like an old Armalite rifle to help himself, was gray-haired, tall and erect. He spotted the pair on the ridge above him immediately and stopped for a single heartbeat. Then he lifted his blaster above his head in an unmistakable gesture.

"There they are," Ryan breathed.

Chapter One

As soon as he spotted J. B. Dix and Ryan Cawdor on the top of the hill, Trader turned to call to Abe, then started to run toward them, his long legs ranging through the powdery snow.

"How old do you reckon he is?" J.B. asked, slinging his Uzi across his back, out of the way.

"No idea. I always figured that he never had a real childhood. Teethed on an implode gren. I never heard him say much about his early past. You?"

The Armorer shook his head. "Never. Lots of rumors, but nothing to support them."

Trader was closing fast, breath pluming from his open mouth. At his back, Abe was having difficulty with the steep ascent, slipping and falling twice in the rutted blanket of white.

Suddenly Trader was there, standing six feet away, panting with the effort of the climb, nodding as his eyes ranged over the two men. Finally he broke into something close to a smile.

"Ryan Cawdor and J. B. Dix," he said. "Never thought to meet up with you again."

The men clasped hands, Trader's grip as strong as ever. While they stood grinning at one another, Abe finally blundered over the crest.

Ryan turned to him, patting him on the back. "You did well, Abe. Real well."

"Thanks." Despite the cold and the exertion, the little man had a wide smile stretched across his face. Tiny icicles were crusted in his drooping mustache, making him look amazingly like a happily lugubrious walrus.

Trader simply stood there nodding. "Well, I'll be hung, quartered and dried for the crows," he said. "This truly is something."

"Ain't it just," J.B. agreed. "We heard you'd been having some trouble."

"Causing trouble, J.B., causing trouble. Man who admits to having some trouble is *in* real trouble."

Abe laughed. "If that wasn't real trouble we had a few days ago, Trader, then I sure as shit don't ever want to find myself in real trouble."

The older man turned sharply, the smile disappearing like dew off a summer meadow. "I told you..." He hesitated. "Abe. Told you before about arguing."

"Sure, sorry."

It was a prickly moment, and Ryan hurried to pass it over. "Listen, we got a lot of catching up to do. We could use a roof and some food. Any ideas?"

Trader glanced toward the distant ruins of the sprawling city. "Probably our best chance is to scout around the suburbs."

"Yeah, agreed," Ryan said.

"Skirmish line." Trader beckoned to Abe. "Take point. I'll go second. J.B., follow me and Ryan bring up the rearguard. Let's go, men."

The Armorer glanced across at Ryan, who shrugged. It wasn't that much of a surprise that the Trader had automatically assumed command of them, just as though no time had passed. No sand run through the glass. No water flowed beneath the bridge.

Just as though he were still leading the full, highly trained crews of the two war wags.

THEY DROPPED DOWN into a wide valley, following the path of an old blacktop. Abe twice managed to lead them into regions of swampy ground, where they all broke through thin ice into rank, stinking water.

They saw a solitary figure, accompanied by a dog, watching them from the hogback ridge to their left. Apart from that, their first hours together were uneventful—no threats from any kind of life.

"Muties in these parts, Trader?" J.B. asked when they stopped for a brief break after the first hour of steady walking.

"Haven't got a sniff of any. How about you?"

"Yeah. Way back."

Trader stopped suddenly. "Hey!"

"What?" Ryan queried, catching up, drawing the SIG-Sauer, suspecting that Trader might have seen some danger. In front of them, Abe turned so quickly he slipped on an iced puddle and nearly fell over.

"No danger, Ryan. Stand down from double red and relax a little. Just that I realized I never asked you where you were when you got the message."

"Down in New Mexico on the ranch of a friend. Krysty Wroth is there. Remember her?"

"Hair that was so hot it scorched your eyeballs? Course I remember her."

"And the old-timer, Doc Tanner. He got himself time-trawled with Operation Chronos."

"Chronos?"

"Sure. It was a section of Overproject Whisper. Cerberus was a bit of that. That lethal fog?"

Trader nodded. "Sure, sure. All bits of that fucking cosmic puzzle they called the Totality Concept. Abe here's been telling me plenty of that."

"Sure brought him up to date," Abe said, grinning eagerly and wiping moisture off his mustache. "How did the message get through to you? You get several copies of it?"

"Just one."

"Bet it was that big black guy with one ear missing," Trader said.

Ryan holstered his blaster. "No. Little ville called Patriarch Springs. Something like that. Drummer was called Friedman. Smoked the foulest cigars I ever smelled."

Abe punched his right fist into his left palm. "Damn it! He was about the last we asked to carry the message to you, Ryan. And he did it."

"What did you pay these packmen?" J.B. asked.

Trader laughed. "Pay! You been away from the war wags too long, Armorer! Trader doesn't pay for what he can trade."

"What did you trade?"

"His life, Ryan. All of them. Told them that I'd come down and pull their lungs out of their asses if they didn't do like they'd been asked."

"How're things back down in the Southwest?" Abe asked. "How's Jake and—"

"Button that up, gunner!" Trader snapped. "First thing is shelter, then food and then fire. After that we can spend the whole night talking about where we've been and what we've been doing."

Ryan glanced behind him, checking that the figure with the dog on the ridge hadn't reappeared. But the land was still deserted, the watery sun glinting off the snow.

THEY WERE ON WHAT LOOKED like an old blacktop that had been superseded some time in the late 1900s by a wide, elevated interstate. The newer highway had collapsed, its piers and bridges tumbling in the quakes that rumbled the land during the long winters.

But the ancient, lost road remained.

It writhed over the wooded country like a dog trying to rid itself of fleas, but it made for easier walking than the muddy, freezing trails that they'd begun on.

The skirmish line had reasserted itself, with Abe leading, followed by Trader, Ryan and J.B.

The skinny ex-gunner held up a hand, two fingers extended, and pointed ahead to the right.

"Company," Ryan said. "Couple of strangers."

Then he saw them. Less than a quarter mile away were two men, well wrapped in wolf-skin coats and

muffling scarfs. Each carried what looked like hunting rifles.

Trader gestured with his Armalite, beckoning Ryan
to one side of him, J.B. to the other, not noticing that
they were already moving. Abe fell back to join the
other three.

The pair was within eighty paces when they stopped,
both holding up a hand in a gesture of peace. "Hi,
there!" called the one on the left.

Ryan realized they were both quite young, probably in their early teens.

"Hi," the Trader replied, holding his beloved Armalite at his right hip, the barrel pointing in the general direction of the young men.

"Come far?"

"Been hunting back yonder," Trader told him,
hitching a thumb toward the eastern horizon.

The other teenager spoke. "Seen anyone?"

Abe answered. "Feller with a dog on the ridge.
Hour or so ago, I reckon."

"Ah, that'll be our pa. Went out after breakfast
with ol' Bess, finest coon dog in Deathlands. We figured to mebbe join up with him this afternoon."

"Live around here?" Trader asked.

"Small horse ranch, three miles west and then north
off a spur trail."

The other youth laid a hand on his brother's sleeve,
as if he were warning him about speaking too openly
to the quartet of outlanders.

Trader ignored the movement. "How far from here
to the skirts of Seattle?"

"Reach them by sunset, if you want to," the slightly taller teenager replied.

"Not many wants to go that close to the cannies and ghoulies livin' there."

"Cannibals?" J.B. asked.

"So they say."

It wasn't any surprise. The sprawling, nuked ruins of virtually every major American conurbation were a breeding ground for every kind of mutation and social perversion.

Ryan suddenly felt the short hairs raising on his nape. Something didn't set quite right here. The body language of the two youths was just that fraction out of kilter, a tenseness above and beyond meeting the potentially hazardous situation of four strangers on a snowy highway.

As if they were waiting for something.

Someone?

"You'd be welcome to stay the night at our place, if you don't take to the skirt of the ville," said the shorter teenager. "Have to be one of the barns, but it'd beat a lot of other places at a frosty time."

"Real kind," Trader replied.

His blaster had started life as one of the early AR-16 models, originally designed to deliver 7.62 mm rounds. But over the years the Armalite had seen a great number of reworks and changes. Now it had yet another flash-suppressor and had been rechambered to fire twenty rounds of the more common 9 mm ammo.

He leveled the rifle at the taller of the strangers and shot him through the chest, at the same moment yelling the single word "Ambush!"

A heartbeat after the sharp crack of the Armalite, Ryan heard the boom of a black-powder musket. But by then he was already moving, diving to his left. He felt the hot breath of buckshot close by his cheek.

Out of the corner of his eye he watched as the teenager shot by Trader took a few staggering steps backward, slipped on the frosty ground and went down on his back, sliding and leaving a smear of bright blood on the ice.

The second youth was alert enough to snap off a return shot at Trader, but not quick enough to allow for the speed of the gaunt figure. The hunting rifle snapped, but the bullet went a good yard wide.

J.B. had been ready for the attack as well, but he skidded as he moved to his right, falling badly and knocking the Uzi out of his grasp.

Abe was slowest to react. But he rolled forward, coming up in a crouch, realizing that nobody was actually shooting at him. He took his time with his Magnum and carefully placed a .357 bullet into the small of the back of the standing teenager, the powerful round exiting a handbreadth above the left hip in a fountain of dark blood and ribbons of torn flesh.

The youth screamed, his arms thrown wide, his blaster spinning from his fingers into the frozen ditch at the side of the old highway. His leg gave way under him and he stumbled, falling heavily onto his left side.

"Someone's behind us," Trader called, swiveling around to peer in the direction that the ambush had come from.

"Mine," Ryan said.

The shot had barely missed him, and it had given him a good idea of the angle. An antique billboard stood twenty yards away, with a pile of rubble behind it. His combat instinct told him that the attack had come from there.

He scuttled sideways, the SIG-Sauer pistol in his right hand, keeping low. His guess was a single-shot musket of some sort. The idea behind the ambush would have seen him blown away, while the other two opened up with their rifles. If it had worked, it was likely that all four of them would have been down and done for.

But Trader had gotten there firstest and fastest.

As he left the blacktop, Ryan heard the sound of hasty movement ahead of him, in the shadows behind the wreckage of the billboard. He glimpsed a dark shape and snapped off a quick shot at it, seeing a burst of icy mud just to the left. He adjusted his aim and fired a second round

This time he heard the unforgettable sound of a full-metal jacket striking flesh—a strangely wet yet solid noise—a gasp of pain and then a body falling.

Stillness.

Two spaced shots rang out behind him, as Trader and Abe propelled the wounded young men into the next world.

"Got him?" J.B. called.

"Yeah. Not sure if he's bought the farm yet."

"Go find out, Ryan!" Trader shouted with the old, familiar rasp of command in his voice.

For a moment he hesitated, feeling an odd mix of emotions. But there wasn't time to stop and analyze them. He went on, keeping low, ready for a second shot.

But the man was dead. A clean head shot had blown away most of the left side of his face, leaving him lying in a steaming puddle of his own brains. From the matted white hair, it looked like he could've been the father of the two teenagers. And he was wearing the same coat that Ryan had spotted up on the ridge. A single-shot smoothbore musket lay close by his corpse. There was no sign of the dog.

Ryan noticed that the dead man had been crippled, and wore a built-up boot on his left leg.

There was nothing worth taking off the body, so he turned on his heel and rejoined the others, finding Trader quickly going through the pockets of the teenagers.

"Was it the man off the ridge, Ryan?" Abe asked, reloading his Colt Python.

"Reckon so. Must've shown himself as a decoy. Set our minds at ease, then looped around behind us under the cover of the old interstate. Nice plan. It could've worked."

Trader straightened, wincing and holding the small of his back. "Bastard rheumatiz! Not a thing worth removing from these stupe kids."

J.B. had brushed himself down, taking off his spectacles and peering closely at the lenses, making sure they hadn't been muddied or scratched by his fall. He replaced them on the narrow bridge of his nose, then checked the action of the Uzi.

"I hear right?" Trader asked.

"What?" Ryan had also reloaded his SIG-Sauer P-226 with two more rounds of 9 mm ammo, slotting them into the mag with its push-button release.

"They say they ran a ranch?"

"They told us they had horses," Abe said excitedly. "Could use transport to get us down to New Mexico."

"If that's where we're going." Trader gazed at Ryan, his face showing no hint of any emotion.

The one-eyed man knew his old leader, knew that this was one of his typical tests. He was pushing to see what sort of a response he'd get from Ryan.

"It's where I'm going," he replied. "Not saying you have to come along."

Trader threw back his head and gave a short, barking laugh. "Haven't changed, you son of a bitch, Ryan! Let's go find this spread and then we can talk."

Chapter Two

By midafternoon they'd found the ranch, precisely where the two teenagers had described it.

Trader ordered a careful approach, in case of a further trap. He went around the back to the left, with Ryan doing the same from the north. J.B. and Abe worked their way up the main trail, past a stubbled field, a pair of barns, an empty corral and a neatly maintained vegetable garden to the white frame house that stood foursquare on the side of a gentle hill. Smoke seeped from its chimney.

But there was nobody home.

Trader kicked in the back door, Armalite at the ready, Ryan covering him from behind a water trough four inches thick in ice. The others waited for the shout, hunkered down at the side of the larger barn.

A rich stew simmered slowly on the stove, great chunks of meat, so sinewy that they all agreed it had to be buffalo, with carrots and pieces of unidentifiable root vegetables. There was fresh bread in the larder and a crock of butter. Jars of preserves and pickles lined the shelves in the cool walk-in pantry, and a smoked ham dangled from an iron hook.

"Never seen such a tidy house," Abe said. "Curtains are clean and there's spotless sheets on the beds. Everywhere polished so you can see your face."

There was a stripped-pine dresser that looked at least two hundred years old, with a set of matching crockery. A drawer in the kitchen table filled with silver-mounted cutlery. Glasses twinkled on another shelf, along with a row of sized copper pans.

"Dark night!" J.B. laid his fedora on one of the chairs, shaking his head as he looked around. "Just the neatest place I ever saw."

Ryan was admiring a row of rifles and shotguns, each on its own set of brackets, alongside a superb wall clock that he reckoned was even older than the dresser.

"Wish Krysty and the others were with us," he said. "And Doc. They'd all appreciate this."

Trader sat on a maroon chaise longue, resting his muddied boots on a fringed white cushion. "Could stay here a few days. Plenty of food."

"I want to get back to New Mexico as soon as we can," Ryan said.

"We'll see about that, Ryan."

"No. Best get this sorted now, Trader. I can't tell you what it means to me, and to J.B. here, to meet up with you again after all those long months. But the tide's been in and out a few times. No war wags with crews to back us up, parked around the last bend in the highway. Right here and now there's just the four of us."

The silence stretched on and on.

Ryan stared at Trader, unwilling to shift his gaze, knowing from long experience that the older man would interpret it as a sign of weakness.

"Ryan's right, Trader," J.B. added.

"Now which one is the bear and which one is tugging on the bear's chain?" Trader asked, nodding to himself. "Guess it never mattered much, and it doesn't matter much now." He stood and took two steps toward Ryan, then stopped and sniffed. "Likely we'll talk about this again, soon. But for now, I think I'm going to put a light to that pile of logs waiting in the hearth there."

THE EVENING PASSED all too quickly, with reminiscences from all four men, overlaid with bringing one another up to date with what had been happening during the missing times.

Ryan told about his relationship with Krysty, and the unexpected finding of his son, Dean. Trader had nodded at that particular story.

"I remember Sharona," he said. "That sort of bitch makes a young man come in his breeches and an old man wish that he was a young man again."

Ryan also told about Jak Lauren, how they'd met in the bayous, the way the lad had settled down with a wife and a little child. And how things had turned against him.

"Some men get snake eyes all their life," Trader commented, pouring himself another shot of the milky moonshine that he'd discovered in a closet in the main bedroom of the house, "and some don't."

As the darkness gathered around them and the fire burned with the brightness that told of a frost outside, Ryan began to realize that Trader wasn't all that interested in what had been happening when he wasn't there himself.

Nor was he keen to talk about what he'd been doing since he'd disappeared. He wouldn't elaborate on the mysterious Native American who'd been around the deep forest at the time that he'd taken the long walk.

Ryan had seen him clearly, could recreate him from his memory—elderly, shy of medium height; hair as bright as polished silver, tied back in two long braids with scraps of vermilion ribbon; wore a robe of animal skins, decorated with a fantastic and complicated pattern of multicolored silken threads. His eyes had been set deep in sockets of wind-washed bone, and there had been a single feather, white as snow, in his hair.

All Trader would say was that the old man had been a shaman. "Silver Light Feet was what they called him. He was the one first gave me an Indian name. Man Who Walks Without Friends. I went with him because I thought I was on the last stretch of my life's highway."

"You wrote a letter," J.B. said.

Trader grinned at the Armorer. "Know better than that, friend. I never rightly mastered the skill of putting little black scratches on paper. Got myself a scribbler out of Mocsin to do it for me."

"I can remember most of it," Abe said, barely stifling a belch from the rich stew. "Went on about how you were dying with that rad cancer eating out your guts."

Trader stared into the fire's glow, straining for the memory. "This is me saying goodbye and the best of luck. If it goes the way I want, I'll just walk away in the night. Don't come after me. I asked you not to follow me. Not anyone." He paused for a few moments. "And then I finished saying that you and J.B. were to look out for each other."

"We've done that," the Armorer said quietly.

"Then Abe here got the itch to come and start digging under the boulders."

The little gunner shrugged. "Too many whispers that you hadn't gotten on that last wag west. I even started to hear them in my sleep. So..."

"Close to midnight." Ryan had glanced at his chron, for something to do during the sudden silence. "Least you know now where we've been and what we've all been doing, Trader. Can't say the same about you."

"Shaman held a singing ceremony for me. Sweated in a kiva with peyote and sand paintings and all that shit." He laughed. "All that shit! All that shit saved my life. Said he found what was wrong in my heart that caused the rad cancer in my guts. I'd always figured it had been living too long in some pesthole rad hot spot in the deserts."

"You and Abe talked about what went down after you met up. The gang after you on the vengeance trail.

Way you got clear of them. Blood price. Nothing else you want to tell us about?'' J.B. asked. "Like where you wandered?''

"I been up the snow-tops of the Rockies and down the length of the old Sippi. From the great Lantic to the wide blue Cific. Highlands and lowlands. Came to a time when the hills didn't seem to get any taller. Just that the valleys were getting deeper and deeper.''

Ryan yawned. "Been the longest journey, Trader. Trouble is we can't just get us into a gateway and jump back to the others in New Mexico. Going to have to make it on foot, or with what we can find and steal.''

"There's the horses out back,'' Abe said. "Don't like riding much, but they could set us well on the way. And we won't need any gas for them.''

Ryan had already decided, within minutes of their arrival at the isolated ranch, that the animals in the barn and corral would be their passport onto the highway again. But he was still a country mile off understanding Trader. He knew what his former leader really wanted.

"Sooner we get moving, the better,'' J.B. said. "Could be the family we chilled have friends or kin around here. Don't want a posse after us.''

"Amen to that!'' Abe exclaimed with great intensity.

There was no argument about whether they needed to place a watch during the night, not even any discussion.

"I find sleep comes hard these times,'' Trader said. "I'll take now up to the mid of night.''

"I'll go until two," Abe offered, looking at the others, who both nodded.

"Two through four?" J.B. glanced at Ryan. "Okay with you?"

"Sure. I'll go until dawn."

RYAN SLEPT FITFULLY.

Usually, the first night after some tough times, such as a prolonged firefight, he dropped off without any trouble. Now, at the end of an odyssey that had taken them most of the way across Deathlands, the feeling that had swept over him was of bone weariness.

Despite that, he'd awakened five or six times, once going to the outhouse outside the back door to relieve himself. Abe had been sitting in a deep brocade armchair, cradling his blaster. The little man had been more than half asleep, jumping into startled life when he became aware of the shadowy figure of Ryan looming over him.

"Holy shit!"

"Not asleep on guard are you, Abe?"

"Course not. Just sitting and thinking a spell with my eyes closed."

"Good job it was me and not Trader who caught you. He might've snapped a finger or two to remind you about duty, Abe. Remember?"

"Course I do. Could be a bastard when he wants to." He was aware of the odd mix of tenses in what he'd just said. "I mean he sometimes was and sometimes is."

Ryan perched on the arm of the sofa, sticking his own SIG-Sauer into his belt. "He's changed."

"Older."

"Yeah. I should have guessed that. But somehow he never seemed to change, year in and year out. Always the same. Hacked from living granite."

Abe stood and walked to peer out from behind the curtains. "Bit of moon," he said. "I guess that when we all lived together, it wasn't easy to spot changes in each other. Then you go away for a year or more and you see the way time's been treating him. Yeah, he's changed."

"But, from your story, he's still tough as ever."

"Right, Ryan, right. Wouldn't want to give you any other impression about that. Harder than ever."

"Harder?" Ryan repeated disbelievingly.

"Yeah." Abe sniffed, fumbling for a kerchief to blow his nose. "Got a bastard cold. I sort of find a couple of changes. One is that his memory kind of comes and goes a bit. Keeps forgetting my name. And gets confused about what's past and what's present. What's been real and what's not."

"What's the second change, Abe?"

Both men were talking quietly to avoid disturbing the other two.

"I think . . . I don't know."

"Go on."

"Trader was always cold and hard. That was the way we loved him, I guess. But he was never mean. Never unfair. Since I met up with him I've seen, once or twice, the way he seems sometimes to like violence and chilling for its own sake.''

Abe quickly told the story of the young woman that Trader had butchered, during their escape from the posse.

Ryan listened in silence. ''I suppose that his time alone might have changed him some, Abe. Now we all have to try and sort of shuffle down together. But it isn't the same as it was. Never be the same as it was.''

BEFORE GOING ON WATCH, Ryan found himself slipping into a dream. In the background was the rhythmic beating of a slack-skinned drum, accompanied by chanting. But where he was sitting was pitchy dark, the high-walled canyons of the Colorado Plateau. A single flute was piping, above and behind him, slow and mournful.

His nostrils caught the elusive scent of wood smoke, far away, below and to the north, where he knew a narrow river trickled its slow way through the red rocks. There was a faint rustle of movement, farther along the ledge where he squatted and waited.

''Hey, Brother Eagle,'' he whispered, hearing the harsh scratch of claws on stone.

The sound wasn't repeated.

Without any change in his sensations, Ryan realized he now lay in soft, sun-warmed earth, in a vast prairie of swelling corn. He heard the angry buzzing of a gas engine, not far away, and he knew instinctively that it was hunting him. But if he kept very still, then he might be safe.

A baby rabbit limped trembling toward him, ears flattened along its skull, eyes wide and staring. Each movement brought a tiny puff of orange dust from beneath its paws.

"Dad? Where are you?"

The voice was Dean's, overlaid with desperation and terror, ragged and cracking. Ryan wanted to reply to his son, stand and look for him, take him in his arms and keep him safe from the evil that was darkening around them. But if he moved, then a great eye would seize upon him and he would be plucked from cowering safety to a hideous, rending death.

"Ryan."

He didn't move. Something touched him by the shoulder and he thought it was the brush of honed, brazen talons. Ryan moaned in his sleep.

"Ryan. Four o'clock. Nothing stirring out there. You all right?"

"Hi, J.B., yeah, fine. Locked into a bad dream. Thought I heard Dean calling for help."

The slight figure of the Armorer was silhouetted against the side window. "I've been thinking about Mildred for the past few days. Specially at night. You think they're all right down there, Ryan? Safe?"

"Who knows, old friend? Trader wants to visit the ruins of Seattle. I just want to get on home. But, well, today's another day."

Chapter Three

"Yesterday was the last day for their rendezvous," Mildred Wyeth said, peering at a handwritten calendar on the scrubbed wall of the kitchen.

The doors were open in the ranch house, allowing a cooling breeze to find its way through the building. Cooling was relative. Outside, the baking New Mexico sun was at its apogee and the old predark thermometer nailed to the shaded wall of the veranda was registering one hundred eighteen degrees.

Doc Tanner was snoring out on the porch, his cracked knee boots lying discarded by his bare feet, gnarled hands folded across his stomach.

Dean Cawdor and Jak Lauren had gone hunting together, just after dawn, looking for some small deer that the boy had spotted the previous evening in a narrow draw to the west of the spread.

Krysty sat at the table in the kitchen, fanning herself with a cloth.

"I've been checking off the days as well," she said. "Be so good to get some news."

"You don't 'feel' anything, Krysty?"

"You asked me before, Mildred."

"Sorry. But..."

Krysty smiled, brushing back a wisp of fiery hair from her pale forehead. "No, I'm the one should be saying 'sorry.' No need to snap at you. We're all edgy."

"You can't pick up vibrations over big distances. You told me that often enough."

"According to my mother, it's impossible, unless you're a true seer. But I still sometimes get feelings from a good distance. But nothing of J.B. and Ryan."

"Least we've had no real trouble since Jak picked up that splinter when he was replacing the broken fence."

Mildred poured herself a dipper of water from the galvanized bucket and sipped at it, pouring the last drops over her face, letting it run down her neck onto her breasts. "If he hadn't finally showed it to me, the stupe could easily have lost his arm."

The tiny splinter had worked its way down under the nail on the index finger of the teenager's right hand. Mildred had noticed the boy wince when he nearly dropped a plate, helping with the washing-up, and had asked him what was wrong.

Reluctantly he'd rolled up the sleeve of his shirt, showing the swelling, bright crimson against his parchment skin that ran from the back of the hand, over the wrist, past the elbow, up toward his shoulder. It looked like the aerial map of some red-etched river drainage system.

Mildred had immediately lanced the infection, cutting deep through the nail, to its root, using a pair of thin-bladed dressmaking scissors. Pus had spurted into her face as she pierced the core of the wound, some of it hissing on the hot top of the iron stove, filling the kitchen with its foul stench.

During her medical training she had once attended a bad car crash, and had to work under cramped and dangerous conditions, with no anesthetic available to her and without proper surgical instruments. But there both the injured had been deeply unconscious, and both had survived.

Jak had been very much conscious.

Krysty had offered to try to use her Earth Mother skills to send him into a trance that would have taken him away from the worst of the pain.

But he'd refused.

"Lose control and never know when get it back," he'd explained to her.

He chose to stand rather than sit at the table, laying his swollen hand flat on the grained pine. He closed his red eyes and took slow, deep breaths, the veins standing out in his forehead like whipcord.

But he never made a sound during what Mildred knew had been the most vicious pain.

She'd bandaged the finger, reassuring him with totally false confidence that he would be fine and that there was no risk of amputation. The teenager was a fast healer and didn't prove her wrong.

They'd also had a scare with a brace of lean coyotes that had managed to dig a hole in the back of the barn where they kept the horses.

But the scavengers had reckoned without the venomous spleen of Judas the mule.

Dean had heard the ruckus and rushed out, holding the Remington 580 that he'd snatched off the wall. He arrived in time to put a .22 slug through the angular skull of the surviving coyote, where it lay on its side, bleeding from the mouth, its ribs splintered from the kicking Judas had given it. The other was dead in a corner, its neck broken.

"WHAT DO WE DO if they don't come back?" Mildred asked.

"I figure that the chilling of Trader, Ryan and J.B. would be big news and we'd get word. Eventually. They got a reputation, for better or worse, all through Deathlands."

"What's he like?"

"Trader?"

"Yeah."

Krysty sniffed as she considered the question. "Got dust up my nose," she said. "Remember I only knew Trader for a very short time. J.B. and Ryan rode with him for most of their adult lives." She grinned. "For better or worse."

"You like him?"

"That's about the same as asking if you like a mountain or a river or the sky. Trader isn't a man you can compare with anyone else."

"I get the picture of someone . . . like a sort of colossus from ancient myths. Striding out across the land with that blaster of his."

"His Armalite."

Mildred nodded. ''Yeah. Sort of a person that you took care not to cross.''

''Sounds right. I think the nearest I can tell you is that Trader resembles a grizzled old wolf. Leader of the pack. Not a breath of doubt about that. Could be entering his last season before someone younger, stronger and faster comes along. But he hasn't come along yet.''

''When I ask John about him, he gets a real funny look in his eyes, like he's remembering a tough but fair father. Know what I mean?''

Krysty smiled. ''Course I know. Ryan's the same. Father he never had. And I think that Trader sees the two of them as the sons that he never had.''

Mildred looked out of the window, at the endless desert. ''And they're out there, someplace.''

''They'll come back. Mebbe not today. Not tomorrow. Could be weeks, I guess. But I know in my heart that they'll return safely to us.''

There was a sudden barking cough from the porch and a barely muffled oath.

Mildred shook her head. ''Sounds like our beloved and worthy time traveler's returned here from the land of Winken, Blinken and Nod.''

''Heavy on the 'nod,' isn't he?'' Krysty asked.

They could judge what was happening from the noises. There was much puffing and panting as the old man struggled to pull on his boots, a sharp exclamation and clatter as he dropped one of them. The springs creaked as he levered himself upright.

''Now he'll spit,'' Krysty predicted.

They heard a phlegmy hawking, followed by the explosive expectoration over the rail.

"Now he'll come in and he'll feel he has to offer some excuse for crashing out like that," Mildred stated.

The door opened, and a shaft of sunlight darted across the room, tiny motes of dust floating in its heart.

"By the Three Kennedys! The best of times to all in this house."

"Been sleeping, Doc?" Mildred asked.

"No, no. I was lying out there with my mind seeking the memory of the solution to the famed theorem of great Pythagoras. My eyes were probably closed for a few moments with the effort of my concentration."

"The one about the squaw on the hippopotamus being equal to the sons of the squaws on the other two hides?" Mildred grinned. "That the one, Doc?"

"There is nothing like a good joke, madam." He paused. "And that was nothing like a good joke."

Krysty looked puzzled. "I did a little math, but I don't know that one."

Doc bowed, his disheveled hair tumbling over his shoulders. "Pythagoras deduced that a square constructed on the longest side of a triangle would be equal in area to the two squares constructed on the two shorter sides."

"I see," Krysty said doubtfully. "Does that work for all the triangles, then?"

Mildred couldn't resist interrupting. "Yeah. For once Doc's been really exercising what passes for a brain."

He shrugged and turned away. "Devilish warm out there. I wonder what sort of climatic conditions our dear absent friends are experiencing?"

"Probably colder and wetter," Krysty replied. "Seattle's not the sun capital of the land."

"What are we having to eat?" He had wandered into the doorway of the kitchen.

"What would you fancy, Doc?" Krysty rested her hand on his arm. "Anything, anytime?"

"My own dear wife's mutton chops, with her special wow-wow sauce. Capers and fresh cauliflower. Baked potatoes with a honey glaze. Positively lashings of her thick, rich gravy. Ah, I can almost taste it now. Perchance, followed up with a steamed treacle pudding and cream. A decent Médoc with the main course and then a marsala for the dessert. An '82 port, properly decanted to go with the coffee and cigars."

"I'll join you in that, Doc," Krysty said.

"I fear that you and all the other chattering Amazons would have retired at a decent point, before the port and cigars, to gossip about babies and other women's talk."

Mildred gasped in outrage. "And fuck you, too, Doc Tanner! Maybe all things have changed, but some of them sure have changed for the better."

"What delicious repast would you have selected for yourself?" Doc asked, making a real effort to heal the sudden breach between them.

"None of that fancy-Dan stuff for me. I was in New York for a while, staying at the good old Chelsea Hotel on West Twenty-Third. I used to eat at a diner a few blocks away called the Galaxy, just a way south on Eighth."

"A fast-food greasy spoon!" Doc mimed disgust. "About the level of cuisine I would have expected from you, Dr. Wyeth. Definitely 'low' cuisine."

"No, no, not at all. The Galaxy had wonderful food and it was a real good deal, too." She licked her lips. "Their eggs, bacon and home fries set you up for the whole day. And Greek omelets with feta cheese. Cheese blintzes with sour cream. Chicken cutlet parmigiana. They did a Galaxy Platter with steak and sole and a whole mass of other goodies. I had it a couple of times, and I can still taste that great feeling of being so full with good food that you can hardly move."

Doc held up a hand. "All right, all right. But forgive me if I stick with Emily's home cooking."

"Have to agree to differ, Doc. Nothing unusual about that. We seem to spend most of our time together disagreeing about something or other."

He smiled, showing his full set of oddly perfect teeth. "Into every life a little rain must fall, my dear lady. Our occasional spats are one of the things that make this lonely life bearable for me."

The black woman turned, startled. She took a quick step to him and kissed him on the cheek. "Wouldn't be without you, Doc," she said, then laughed. "Now I've made you blush."

He turned away, standing and staring blankly for several seconds at the wall of the room. When he swung back, both of the women were surprised to see the brightness of unshed tears in his pale blue eyes. He tugged out his swallow's-eye kerchief and noisily blew his nose.

"By the..." he began, then blew hard again, examining the crumpled cloth. "I feared that I was likely to have one of my notorious bleeding noses. But I see I am not." He put away the kerchief.

"You all right, Doc?" Krysty asked.

"Affection has always unmanned me, my dear. I confess that your kindness, Dr. Wyeth, sent my thoughts racing back to my beloved lost wife."

LATER THAT AFTERNOON, when Krysty was strolling out in the yard, Doc came quietly up to her.

"I've been thinking."

"Yes?"

"When I was with you and Dr. Wyeth..."

"When Mildred kissed you and you gave your famed impersonation of ripe tomato?"

"Indeed."

"While Ryan and John Dix are away from us for a while, and as there appears to be no grave threat to our safety...I wondered whether I might venture on a small adventure of my own." He smiled. "I say! Venture on an adventure. Rather good that, wouldn't you say, Krysty?"

"Yeah. You mean go off on your own?"

"For a while."

"A while, Doc?"

"Two or three days. No more than a week. I doubt my survivalist qualities for any longer."

"You'd need to speak to Jak."

"Of course I would."

"He might not think it was a good idea. Lot of things could go wrong, specially if you're on your own."

"But that is the very nub, the kernel of my feelings. I know that I am all too often the lame duck on the good ship *Enterprise*. I know that."

"That's double crap, Doc. Gaia! I've lost count of the number of times you've saved our lives. You chilled three of those crazy fladgies on your own. Think if you'd failed us then."

"I had thought to increase my chances of survival by taking Judas along with me."

"If he doesn't chill you first, Doc."

She took his arm and the two friends walked together toward the house.

When Jak and Dean returned, Doc asked the albino teenager for his opinion of his plan.

Chapter Four

The dawn sky squatted, brooding, on the snowy tops of the mountains around them. The temperature had dropped further, leaving the sheen of gray ice on the water bucket within five minutes of Ryan drawing it up from the rattling depths of the well.

The fire had gone close to dying, until J.B. went to bring in some fresh kindling and hewn logs from one of the outbuildings.

Trader had awakened slowly and grudgingly, stretching and cursing. "Damned back and damned knees and damned shoulders and damned fingers. I say fuck them all!" He saw that the other three were looking at him. "Best you can hope for is to die before you get old," he said.

"I heard that already," Abe chirped brightly.

"Well, now you fucking heard it again!"

FLURRIES OF SNOW were carried in the teeth of the blue norther that came rampaging down through the Cascades, having started its life somewhere in the glittering white wilderness of the Arctic.

Ryan and Abe got breakfast crackling and spitting in the skillet, while J.B. went out to check on the ani-

mals available for them. Trader sat in the deep armchair, massaging his knees, mumbling to himself.

It struck Ryan yet again how much his old leader
had aged during the time that they'd been parted. But
he still sensed the mix of steel and whipcord, like before. And when the firefight began, Trader had ef-
fortlessly delivered the ace on the line, just like he
always had.

"You thought more about paying a visit to the out-
ers of Seattle, Ryan?"

The harsh voice made him jump. "Yeah. I thought
about it. Rather get started on the road home to New
Mexico, Trader. But I'll come along for a day or so."

"Not far," Abe said. "If the horses are— Sod and
buggery!" Some hot fat spat from the pan onto his
wrist. He splashed cold water on the burn. "Horses,"
he repeated. "One thing you gotta watch out for when
you're in them old mean streets, is that a horse isn't
just a way of moving. It's some food for a tribe of
thirty muties for a day."

They heard J.B. stamping snow off his boots on the
back porch.

"Cold as a gaudy slut's soul out there," he said,
rubbing a crust of ice from his eyelashes.

"Ryan's just agreed to spend some time in the ville."
Trader was grinning like a fox in the henhouse.

"For a day or so," Ryan added quickly. "Want
some bacon and grits?"

J.B. nodded. "Sure. Then we'll all go out into the
smallest of the barns."

"Why?" Trader asked suspiciously. "What you find out there? Gas wag?"

"No." J.B. took off his glasses, wiping away the smears of melting snow. "Wait and see."

"WELL, I'LL BE..." Trader's voice faded away into the freezing silence.

J.B. had thrown back the door with a gesture like a traveling magician revealing that his lovely assistant had mysteriously vanished. "Been locked in here for the best part of a hundred years," he said.

Ryan whistled, his breath hanging like ragged ribbons in the gloom. "That is something."

Abe was rubbing his hands together, his mouth slightly open because of his cold. "Yeah, but what the fuck use is that to us? Tell me that."

"We can carry plenty of supplies in it. Better than pack animals. And it's big enough for all of us to sleep in at night. Better than no shelter at all." J.B. turned to Ryan and Trader. "What do you reckon?"

It was a hearse. Not just any old hearse, but a beautiful Victorian horse-drawn vehicle.

It was covered in dust and bits of windblown straw, but they could all see its amazing state of preservation.

"Near perfect," J.B. said. "Got a full set of harness on the wall yonder."

The woodwork was ebony, the sides and back made from fine etched glass. It was ornamented all around the top with carved plumes and tiny turrets and crenellations. The large wheels were also painted black, with a fine line of crimson around the rim and along each of the hand-turned spokes.

The four friends moved in out of the wind, Abe pulling the door partly shut. But even in the poor light it was impossible to miss the quality of the rig.

"Take a team of four to pull it," the Armorer said, "plus another four saddle horses and a couple of pack animals. They're all out there, waiting for us. Could get them hitched up and be on the road in an hour. Or less."

Abe rubbed his sleeve over the glass, shading his eyes against the reflection from the doorway, and peered inside. "Hey! There's a coffin in there."

Ryan joined him. "Real pretty one, too. Brass handles and nice workmanship."

"I didn't see that," J.B. said. "Yeah, that *is* nice, isn't it?"

"Put in a blanket or two and I could travel in that." Trader tried the catch on the rear, which opened as easily and silently as if it had only been closed an hour before. "Keep out the chilly winds. Abe! Climb in and take a look. See if it's going to be big enough for me."

"Sure, Trader."

The little gunner hopped up, sliding inside the hearse, alongside the coffin. Ryan realized that the wag was amazingly roomy. Abe was able to crawl along on hands and knees with no risk of bumping his head on the high roof.

Ryan thought it wasn't a bad idea to take the rig along with them. "Get that little box of pine out of there and it's plenty big enough for us to bundle into."

The door behind them creaked in the wind, making all three men swing around.

"Nothing," Trader said. "Get a move on, Abe. You're too slow to catch a funeral."

The gunner's voice was muffled by the thick glass. "Gotta get the lid up."

J.B. had crouched, checking the springs and suspension of the hearse. "Looks in great shape," he said. "No worm in the wood anywhere, and the axles all greased. I reckon we could give her a try."

Trader sniffed. "Never rode a death wag before. Still, first time for everything."

Ryan was watching Abe's struggles with the polished lid. He heard the crack of a catch snapping, followed almost immediately by a deep-throated scream from Abe, who shuffled backward and fell awkwardly out of the rear door, twisting his knee as he landed. His face was as pale as a sun-bleached bone, and there was a small dark patch of damp at his crotch.

"In there..." he babbled. "In there someone there inside someone woman think inside..."

Trader grabbed at his shoulder, shaking the ex-gunner like a terrier with a rat. "Cool down, Abe! Is it someone living?"

"Yeah. No. No. Yeah. No. No. Don't think so."

"Well, I'll take a look," Ryan said.

He thought about drawing the SIG-Sauer, but kept it holstered. Just in case of trouble he unsheathed the eighteen-inch steel blade of his panga, then clambered inside the hearse, feeling it rock on the soft springs, aware of a strange, musty smell, like pepper and dog piss, salt and sugar.

The lid of the coffin had dropped back in place when Abe let it fall in his panic. Ryan positioned himself on hands and knees, feeling a passing frisson of something very close to fear. He held the panga tightly in his right hand and pushed back the lid of the coffin with his left.

"Fireblast." The word breathed very gently, misting the polish on the coffin lid for a triple heartbeat.

The smell was much stronger, like a spice box that had been hidden at the back of a dark larder.

It was almost certainly a woman, most likely the mother of the boys that they'd chilled down the trail. The lustrous silvery hair clinging to the grinning skull was a good clue, as was the long black organdy dress with a high collar of stained, yellowed lace, and the narrow golden ring on the shrunken bones of the left hand, folded across the flat bosom.

The eyes had long gone and the skin was leathery and brown, stretched so tight across the planes of the skull that the sharp-edged cheekbones had sliced through.

"Chilled woman," he called out. "Stopped breathing a good while ago."

Trader rapped the butt of his Armalite on the packed earth of the floor. "Well, don't just stand there, men. Get the box out and the corpse with it. Dump them in the corner and we can start bringing in some food and blankets from the house. You harness up the team, J.B., and look for saddles and packs. Be

good to be on the road for Seattle within the next
couple of hours or so. Come on, let's move it!''

As THEY ROLLED THE HEARSE out of the barn, Ryan's
eye was caught by the discarded body of the woman,
lying in a dusty corner, where Trader had thrown it. It
lay now like a bunch of broken sticks, wrapped in
rags.

The old man had never shown much respect for
corpses, unless they belonged to his crew. His people.
Ryan had seen a firefight against half the sec force of
a powerful ville in the Shens, where Trader had insisted on recovering the corpses of a young comm nav
and a cook from War Wag Two who'd accidentally
triggered an ambush, just so they could be buried
properly.

The two hours had already stretched to three.

All of the friends were reasonably familiar with
horses, but the rigging of the ancient hearse was un-
usually complicated. It wasn't like putting an ordinary pair of animals into the shafts of a wag. There
was an inordinate amount of tangled, pliable harness, chrome and brass trimmings. They had several
false starts, with a team of four matched black horses
that were skittish and uneasy with the sweating, cursing strangers.

Abe had bustled in and out of the house, pausing
only to clean his pants. He carried out blankets and
loaded them into the gaping space in the rear of the
empty hearse. Then came cans of food and canteens

of water, boxes of spare ammo and fruit and eggs. All was packed away.

Trader stamped around, getting in everyone's path and doing precious little of the fetching and carrying himself. Ryan and J.B. weren't at all surprised at this. It had always been the old man's way.

It was around noon, with a sun that hadn't chosen to show its face at all, that they were more or less ready to roll. J.B. had volunteered to drive the loaded hearse, while the other three rode along, leading the pair of placid pack animals and the spare saddle horse.

"Best fire the place first," Trader stated.

"Why?" Ryan was already astride a bay mare, trying to adjust to the discomfort of being in the saddle again. "Not doing any harm."

"Keep a posse off our trail."

"What posse?"

Trader gestured to Abe with his Armalite. "He said the same when that young stupe got hisself chilled. Said there wouldn't be a posse after us." Abe opened his mouth as though he were going to protest, then closed it again. "Those boys and their pa could have kin. Less clues we leave behind, the better. Locals'll likely think it was wolf's heads or Indians."

There was a kind of sense in what Trader was saying. Ryan shrugged. "All right. I'll fire it."

There were several earthenware pots of lamp oil stored in a closet off the kitchen. Ryan took them and sprinkled it liberally all over the first floor of the house, smashing the last two containers in the front hall.

"Why am I doing this?" he muttered. "Bastard nice place. Why destroy it?"

But he was already finding that the old, ingrained habits died hard.

IT WASN'T QUITE SO COLD, the wind having eased down, meaning that some of the lying snow was just beginning to thaw. The hearse handled easily once they got onto the blacktop toward the dark ruins of Seattle.

Ryan reined in his horse on top of the first ridge and stood in the stirrups, peering back to the column of thick black smoke that was soaring skyward behind them.

He'd only met up with Trader again for a few hours, and already he tasted the familiar flavors of blood and fire.

Chapter Five

A warmer, moist wind blew in across the land from the distant, fog-shrouded side of Puget Sound.

It was very late afternoon as the four friends stood and looked out across old Seattle. Behind them the horses were cropping eagerly on a patch of cleared grass. They'd made remarkably good time along the narrow, twisting highway, not seeing another living soul until about an hour back, when they passed three separate wags of travelers.

"Where's the fucking funeral?" shouted the driver of the first vehicle, a beat-up truck of dubious parentage and unguessable pedigree. None of the four friends bothered to answer, ignoring the bellowed laughter.

The second wag was horse-drawn, loaded high with rusting scrap iron. Two brothers sat side by side on the driver's seat, looking like they couldn't have mustered the intelligence of a fence post between them.

"Hey, White Hair!" one of them yelled at Trader. "Where's the fucking funeral?"

Their merriment followed the hearse and its outriders for the next quarter mile.

J.B. was still holding the reins to the team as they breasted a rise and saw a converted camper lurching slowly toward them, blue smoke belching from the dangling exhaust.

"If they ask where the funeral is, then I swear to the nuke gods that I'll blow their fucking heads clear off of their bodies!" Trader had already unslung the Armalite.

"Easy," Ryan cautioned. "No point in chilling for such a small reason, Trader."

"I decide what I think is a good reason for chilling, Ryan Cawdor, and you can do the same. Just don't try to tell me what to do. All right?"

Ryan didn't answer, but he wondered briefly about the merit of putting a 9 mm round through his old leader's head.

The wag came closer, edging to the right side of the highway, one of its front wheels wobbling so much it looked as if it were holding on with only spit and a prayer.

The cab was partly covered with a torn sheet of dark green canvas, which was flapping loose in the rising westerly. An old woman was hunched up in the cab, glaring out through the starred shield at the oncoming procession.

"Howdy!" she screeched, heaving on a welded lever at her side that seemed to be some kind of auxiliary brake. The camper slewed sideways, partly blocking the blacktop. J.B. reined in the team, bringing the hearse to a halt.

It had all the classic makings of a trap, with steep banks on both sides of the road.

Ryan had his blaster out faster than immediately, as did the other three. Trader leveled his Armalite at the crone, who threw up her hands in alarm.

"No!" she shrieked.

Ryan glanced around them, seeing instantly that the lie of the terrain might have indicated an ambush. But the land itself was bare of any bushes or scrub, totally lacking cover.

"Hold it, Trader," he called. "Looks safe."

The older man swiveled in his saddle, eyes raking back. "You reckon?" he rasped.

"Yeah. I reckon. Look for yourself. Not a blade of grass to hide a flea's ass."

"Don't mean harm, friends. Want me to climb down?"

"Who you got inside?" Trader asked, gesturing with his blaster for her to switch off the rattling engine and get down out of the cab.

"Nobody, mister. Just me, these days."

"You got any kin in these parts?" Abe asked, fighting hard to try to control his own mount, the big Colt Python waving around in the air.

"Used to have." She clambered down, carefully closing the door on the driver's side of the cab, which seemed to be held in place by baling twine.

Ryan noticed that her right arm ended in a stump just above the elbow. And her face was hideously scarred, the skin puckered and folded.

"Like what you see, mister?" she said, staring at him. "Looks like you don't relish star-gazin' at yourself in the mirror no more than I do."

"What happened?" he asked.

"You want to know in just one word, outlander? That one word is fucking mutie stickie scalies."

"Four words," J.B. said from the high seat of the gleaming hearse.

"Scalies in the ruins," Ryan prompted. "You mentioned scalies and stickies. Which?"

"Bugs is bugs."

"Which?" Trader insisted.

"Was going to offer blow jobs all around if you'd let an honest woman get on her way." She leered at Trader. "But I doubt you got more than a soft little shrimp tucked away inside your breeches, outlander."

"You want to be dead, slut?"

She shrugged her shoulders. "Tell you the truth, couldn't care less. Lost my husband and three little ones back there." She jerked her left thumb toward the distant township.

Ryan heeled his horse a little closer to her. "I asked you once. This is the second time. The last time. You talking about stickies?"

"Sure. But muties is muties, mister." She leered at him through a mouthful of broken teeth. "Sure you wouldn't care for me to go down on you, mister. Figure you pack a bigger load than your old father there."

She nodded toward Trader, who turned away, ignoring her cackling laugh.

"He isn't my... isn't really my father. The stickies, they this side of the ville?"

"All sides. Place is rotting from the inside out. There's a couple of small, vicious hot spots. Mostly way off to the north. Beyond Lynwood. And the place is riddled with the karpies." She used her teeth to roll up the ragged sleeve on her left arm, revealing the recognizable purplish patches of what had once been called Kaposi's sarcoma, the familiar badges of impending death from one of the most deadly diseases in all of Deathlands.

"I reckon we should turn back right now," J.B. said from the box on the hearse.

"No." Trader didn't even glance toward the Armorer. "We agreed to go in. Take a look. Just a couple days is all. That's what we'll do."

The old woman watched the exchange. "Least you got the right sort of wag for that place of death. Right pretty chill rig it is, too."

J.B. lowered the reins into his lap, looking at Ryan. "What do you figure?"

"Why ask him?" Trader snapped.

Ryan stared at his old leader, locked eye to eye with him. "Not the time or place," he said. "But you have to know that the wheel's turned. Things are different. Different rules. Time was you said to us to jump, and we just asked you how high. That's long down the pike, Trader."

"Is it? Is it?"

"Yeah."

Ryan turned to the old woman. "Get your wag started again and move on. Thanks for your help."

"Welcome, outlander. If I was a mite closer to my grave, I'd hitch a ride with you." She paused with one foot on the step up into the cab of the camper. "One thing."

"What?"

"There's things that move at night in Seattle ville. Things like nothin' I heard of or seen. Things that don't seem to take to the sunlight."

"Hey, what kind of things?" Abe shouted, his face showing his alarm at her warning.

But he was too late. She was behind the wheel, the ignition grating over, the engine finally kicking tiredly into clattering life.

She waved a hand to them and engaged something between first and second gear. The wag kicked up a shower of muddy slush as it lurched forward again, its sliding rear end narrowly missing the near side leader on the hearse.

One of the pack animals reared and whinnied in fright, but Trader moved his mount in close and fisted it on the side of the head, quieting it.

The backfiring engine echoed off down the hill, heading in a roughly southeasterly direction.

For several seconds nobody spoke.

Finally it was J.B. who broke the uncomfortable silence. "What Ryan said was right, Trader."

"What did he say? Don't remember."

Ryan flicked a tumbled lock of hair from his face. "You can remember real fine when you want to. The bottom line is that you aren't in charge of a hundred men and women and two big war wags anymore."

J.B. interrupted him. "Fact is that you aren't in charge of anything, anymore, Trader."

"Just what the fuck does that mean?"

"What I said. All of us are equal."

Trader snorted, genuinely amused. "Mebbe. Mebbe not. But some of us are more fucking equal than others."

THEY HAD PICKED their way around the outskirts. Breasting yet another ridge in the winding highway, they finally found themselves within four or five miles of the rotted heart of the old city.

"Best we don't take the wag in," J.B. said. "I could stay with it and the rest of the animals. Rest of you go into the ville on foot."

"I'll stay, if you like." Abe blinked nervously as his sudden outburst brought everyone's attention on him. "Be happy to stay. Not that interested in ruins."

"Not all that long to dark," Ryan said.

"Camp out here and go in at first light," the Armorer suggested.

"We'll go right—" Trader stopped, shaking his head. "Shit up a pole!" He made a great effort to change the sour tone of his voice. "If we went in now, leaving Abe and the livestock, we could pick a good safe house for the black hours. Then, come dawn, we'd be where we want to be."

Ryan nodded. "Makes good sense, Trader."

"Glad you agree with something I say." The note of bitterness rang loud and clear.

"Cut the crap." Ryan swung off the back of the bay mare. "Self-pity is for stupes, Trader. You know damned well that there haven't ever been many things you said that I didn't agree with. You know that."

"Sure." He climbed slowly off his horse, straightened his back and sighed. He patted the steaming animal on the side of the neck. "Got out of the way of riding." Trader sniffed. "I know what you and J.B. are telling me. Yesterday's man."

"That isn't it."

"Oh, yeah, Ryan? It surely is. Just remember that one day you'll get old."

THE HEARSE STOOD in the lee of what could've once been a garage. It only had two walls and one roof, so it was hard to tell. But it gave cover from anyone passing along the blacktop two hundred yards down the hillside. There was even a primitive corral for the horses.

Low cloud had closed in with the evening, settling all around their campsite. Abe had lighted a small fire to warm up one of the cans of soup, knowing that the smoke wouldn't be visible. He'd unpacked some of the provisions from the hearse and was settled in for a snug wait.

"Two days from now," Ryan said. "Sundown, two days on. If we aren't back by the dawn of the third day, then something's gone badly wrong."

"I'll come looking," Abe promised, wiping beads of fog from his mustache.

"Okay. But if we're late, there'll be a good reason.
So step eggshell-light, Abe."

The gunner nodded. "Sure, Ryan."

"Come on," Trader said. "Never do after sunset
what you could've done before."

J.B. patted Abe on the shoulder. "Don't take any
wooden jack."

TRADER SET A GOOD PACE, striding into the shadowy
suburbs of Seattle, past the abandoned wasteland of
Renton Municipal Airport. He had the familiar Armalite slung over a bony shoulder. Ryan had left the
Steyr SSG-70 with the wag, contenting himself with
the SIG-Sauer. J.B. had placed the Uzi inside a layer
of waterproof cloth in the hearse. He carried the
deadly Smith & Wesson M-4000 scattergun, with
its full load of eight of the 12-gauge Remington
fléchettes.

The light was fading, the coppery ball of the sun
vanishing over the dull mirror of Puget Sound.

Not much time remained for them to find somewhere secure for the fast-approaching night.

Chapter Six

The friends traveled past a quiet row of suburban houses that showed the familiar ravages of a hundred postdark years, years that had brimmed over with unbelievable extremes of weather—winters of a hundred below and summers of a hundred and twenty above. A fine layer of gritty ash lay in the corners of some of the gardens, revealing that the region around the ville had lain beneath the falling detritus of a major eruption in the Cascades sometime in the past few years.

They had seen nobody else as they picked their way along the deserted streets, coming down off the ruins of an elevated section of a highway.

"Best not to get too far in," Ryan said.

Trader nodded. "Always a sight easier getting out when you haven't gone too far in."

It was beginning to drizzle a little, misting over the lenses of J.B.'s spectacles and making safe progress difficult for him. And dangerous.

The silent avenue had once been lined with elegant trees, but they had long vanished, all chopped down to rotting stumps for fuel by the ragged and starving during the bleak horrors of the long winters.

The three men spread out without a word being said, adopting the usual skirmish line, Trader ahead on the left side of the footpath, with Ryan just a little behind him, on the opposite flank of the road. J.B. was last, on the left, about fifty yards farther back, keeping in the deeper pools of shadow, guarding their rear.

Ryan wasn't surprised to find most of the buildings in pretty good shape. Most had lost windows, some of them roofs, and a few had collapsed altogether. But at least ten percent seemed solid and secure.

It had been something that had amazed Mildred and, to a lesser extent, Doc, when they'd first appeared in Deathlands—the fact that there were still tens of thousands of houses, scattered all across the continent, untouched and unentered since the faster-than-sound missiles raged from the empty skies and civilization died.

"How come refugees from the worst-affected areas didn't raid them and take them over?" That had been Mildred's puzzled question.

Ryan knew the answer to that. His father's father had been alive as the endless cold war finally turned white-hot. The deaths in the first forty-eight hours of the war that ended all wars were incalculable.

Millions, without the least possibility of a doubt.

Tens of millions for certain.

Hundreds of millions?

Probably.

The Russkies had used neutron bombs and missiles, which cleansed away all life, but left everything standing. The idea behind that had been that the winners could then march in and inherit a land instantly fit for heroes. It was a good plan, but with one overriding weakness—there were no heroes and no winners, just cities turned to boneyards.

There weren't enough refugees after the first six weeks of ninety-eight percent rad sickness to be able to loot more than a fraction of the homes still standing across what was already Deathlands.

And this southeastern suburb of Seattle was no exception.

TRADER PUSHED OPEN a rusted gate, taking care to lift it in both hands when the fragile hinges gave way. He laid the gate in the coarse grass of what had been the front lawn. Only the posts remained of the original chain-link fence that would have demarked each neighbor's neat territory.

He waited on the porch, eyes scanning the deserted street, covering Ryan and then J.B. as they came along to join him. Trader pointed to Ryan with the Armalite, gesturing for him to go around the back.

His combat boots grated in the volcanic grit, but he had that indefinable feeling of safety. No prickling at his nape, no dark shapes that skulked into the bushes ahead of him. But he still made sure and kept his index finger snugly on the trigger of his blaster.

The house that Trader had selected seemed to be totally untouched, either by man or nature. There was even a cord of firewood cut and stacked under the tattered remains of a canvas cover along the side passage. A dog kennel, with a pile of dark bones, was visible inside.

Ryan came to the back door and waited.

The dark wall of clouds that had lowered earlier across the hills had been blown away by a fresh breeze from the deep bosom of the ocean, revealing a chunk of silver moon, bright enough to give a good light.

Enough light for him to read the painted iron sign: Wipe Your Feet Or Mom Wipes You.

The breeze stirred the branches of a huge eucalyptus, making Ryan spin. The topped remnants of a pergola lay near the bay hedge to the right of the house. He stretched out his fingers and touched the damp handle of the inner door. The outer screen door had been gone for decades.

Ryan took a slow breath, held it and released, then did it again. He put his weight against the handle and felt it turn, slowly and reluctantly.

He tasted a smell that was as familiar to him as his own sweat, a smell that he'd encountered in every corner and crevice of Deathlands.

Ryan entered the kitchen and hesitated, getting his bearings, wondering just where in the abandoned house he was going to find the corpses.

He heard the thin sound of breaking glass, followed by the creak of the front door opening.

"Ryan?"

"Nobody, Trader. Nobody living."

A SUPPLY OF CANDLES filled one of the drawers in the kitchen. Most of them were plain household candles, with a scattering of scented ones, cherry, melon, blueberry and cinnamon. Ryan pressed them to his face, trying to catch the elusive flavor of predark days.

Most of the curtains had rotted, but J.B. went around and closed the shutters that overlooked the street, keeping them safe from chance passersby.

Candles were set up on shelves and tables, and they filled the first floor with their golden, flickering, shifting light. Their burning seemed to swallow up a part of the other smell that Ryan had noticed as soon as he'd entered the kitchen, the smell that both J.B. and Trader had also noticed as soon as they were in the front hall.

It was likely that nobody had entered the deserted house for nearly a hundred years. All of its doors and double-glazed windows remained closed tight.

The scent of decay had gradually infiltrated every inch of the old building, so that even the walls seemed to be contaminated by it.

"Not down here," Ryan said, catching the unspoken question in Trader's eyes.

There were five.

J.B. found the first of them, in a small room to the right at the top of the dusty stairs. It had obviously been the bedroom of a little child. The wallpaper portrayed a superhero that none of them recognized, the design echoed on the comforter that covered the bed.

"Little girl," Trader observed.

That was about all they could guess, basing it on the long blond hair that was spread out like a tracery shell across the smudged pillow.

The next room along the corridor had been for the two sons of the family. From the height and the approximate build of the mummified corpses, one had been around ten or eleven, the other probably in his early teens.

"No wounds," Ryan commented. "Fireblast! This kind of tragedy always brings me down."

"We'll find their parents in the big bedroom at the back of the house," Trader stated.

He was right.

Even after the passage of so many empty years, it was still easy to reconstruct the last hours.

The father lay on his back on one side of the double bed, wearing stained pyjamas. It looked like his wife had been overtaken by some sort of pain or distress close to the end, and had tried to make it over to the neat bathroom across the corridor.

She lay doubled up on the carpet, nightdress rucked around her waist, knees drawn to her chin, one hand reaching out toward her husband, on the bed.

"Went wrong at the last," Trader said quietly, stooping to pull the fragile material over the dark bones of the thighs and the pathetic patch of curling pubic hair.

"Sleepers," J.B. said, picking up one of the two empty pill bottles on the trim cabinet at the side of the bed, along with a wristwatch and a pair of glasses.

And the note.

"THERE'S NEARLY ALWAYS a note, isn't there?" Trader said, peering at the two sheets of paper as he sat in the living room.

"Like they know that there won't be anyone along to read it, but they still feel a need to communicate why they did what they did," J.B. replied.

Ryan put another log on the fire, and he reached out to Trader. "Mind if I read it?"

"Course not. Writing's faded and it gets worse. Read it out loud to us."

"Sure." Ryan sat on the sofa. "Starts off 'To anyone passing by.' Guess that's us. 'My name is James Williamson, My wife's name is Henrietta. Our boys are Stewart and Jim Junior. Our daughter is—' that's crossed out '—was Darlene. Lived here in Seattle most all our lives.' "

The logs crackled and spat, burning fast, filling the cold, dead house with warmth and brightness.

"'We were lucky. Were we? Went camping when the missiles came in January, up in the Cascades. Kids didn't want to come. Maybe, the way things have panned out, they were right. Roads blocked with stalled cars. No gas. Fires everywhere and the sky just smoke from sea to shining sea. Darkness at the edge of noon, like someone once said. All the time, dark. But we made it home after about ten days. Darlene was ill by then. Asthma from the smoke and fumes. All of us felt sick and coughing all the time. Mustn't go off at a tangent. Gave the children their pills an hour ago. Watched to see it was going well. All deep asleep. Henrietta and I followed a few minutes ago. Think I can just feel them starting to work some.'"

"Remember that suicide letter we found up in Ohio?" Trader asked.

"Oh, you mean that real long one," J.B. replied. "Filled three notebooks, didn't it?"

Trader laughed. "Yeah. Joke was, but the time he finished writing it, the guy decided that he wasn't going to chill himself after all."

"Want me to go on with this one?" Ryan asked. "Near the end of the first page."

"Sure," Trader said.

"'I'd read enough in papers and on TV to know about radiation sickness. But after the sky got dark with missiles from the Russkies, then... But if anyone reads this a few months into the future, you'll know all about the war to end all wars, won't you? Henrietta got it first. Bleeding gums. Then Jim Junior got the same. Coughing. Played up his asthma as well. Fingernails started to drop out and...' Can't read the next bit. Crossed out. Then he goes on about how they hadn't seen the sun for weeks. Black all the time. He repeats about bleeding gums. Hair falling out. Sores around the mouth."

"The usual," Trader said.

Ryan tilted the paper toward the fire, struggling to read the increasingly uneven scrawl.

"Chunk about arguments with his wife. What should they do? The drugs are working and he's losing it. 'Since Jim died two or three days ago, we knew the end was closest and closer to them.' Not making proper sense. 'Darlene took the sleepers and lay on H's lap like a princess from a fairy tale. Slipped asleep and we kissed her and put her to bed. Stewart didn't want and we had to...' Can't read the next bit, either.''

J.B. shook his head. ''Far as I'm concerned, you don't need to read any more, Ryan.''

''Right at the end now. Looks like the poor bastard could hardly hold the pen.''

Trader stood. ''Got to take a leak,'' he said. ''Back in a minute.''

'' 'Told her I loved her. Thanked her good days and days. Head feels like tumbling slurry of... Lay together. I'm ahead. Behind. H is restless. Sick noises. Don't think write more of any...''' Ryan looked at the Armorer. ''That's it. Ends there.''

''Yeah.'' J.B. sighed. ''Yeah.''

Chapter Seven

They had all agreed there was no point in placing a guard on watch during the night.

The mere fact of the house standing empty and untouched for so many years was a clear enough sign of how deserted these outer suburbs were.

"Closer in we get, the more risk there'll be," Trader said. "Keep a good watch out for those night people the old slut said she saw."

"What do you reckon?" J.B. asked, carefully checking the action on his scattergun.

"Ghouls. Some sort of ghouls. Kind used to feed on flesh. Muties. Something like that," Trader said vaguely.

Ryan laughed. "Facts like those at your fingertips and you can't lose."

IT WAS A DULL, overcast day, with no sign of the sun lurking above the low clouds. The wind was westerly, bringing the bitter taste of salt. It was a little warmer than it had been, but the darker sky out over the ocean promised rain before the morning was done.

They had been walking for only a few minutes, still sticking to their skirmish line, when J.B., out at point, stopped and held up a hand.

"What?" Trader called, moving back into the shadows of a fallen wall.

"Check your rad counters."

Ryan glanced down at the tiny button in his lapel, seeing that it had changed color, going from the safety of green, through yellow into deep orange, verging on crimson.

"Hot spot," the Armorer called. "I can see some nuke damage ahead of us."

Ryan moved up from the rear, looking in front of them, where the street went down a slope. The houses there showed increasing damage, roofs missing, all the windows stove in by the shock waves of the missiles. And the area was devoid of trees or shrubs.

"Crater?" Trader asked.

"Yeah. Filled with water." J.B. wiped his glasses on his sleeve, cleaning off the fine drizzle that had just started to fall.

"Best cut around it. North or south?" Trader looked at the other two.

"North," Ryan suggested.

"Why?"

"You can see where the main ruins are, jutting down there, where the land gets more narrow."

Trader nodded. "Makes some sense. I'll go out front now."

THE DETOUR OF THE AREA of ancient but still lethal radiation took most of the morning. There was the familiar ripple effect on the streets, where solid stone had melted and turned to frozen, corrugated taffy.

Whole blocks of the pleasant frame houses had fallen away like paper, many of those nearer to the impact zone of ground zero completely vaporized.

"Not surprised to find nobody around," Ryan said, checking his rad counter again. "It's still up in the high yellow zone, and we're a good mile past the crater."

The rain had eased away again, and there was the hope of the clouds breaking during the afternoon.

Trader had stopped to relieve himself again, going along a narrow alley by the side of a ruined church.

"Never met a man piss so much as Trader does now," J. B. commented. "Never used to. Did he?"

"Comes with age." Ryan rubbed his hands together. "Come to all of us."

"If we live long enough."

"Trader's lived long enough. What was that?"

There had been a muffled yell, sounding only a couple of hundred yards away from them, farther in, toward the center of the ville.

The noise wasn't repeated.

Trader came running, doing up his pants with his left hand, the Armalite gripped in his right, almost like a prosthetic extension of himself.

"Hear that?"

Ryan nodded. "Man shouting. That direction." He pointed with his SIG-Sauer.

"We'll go take a look."

"Trader."

"What?" The man turned to face his one-eyed companion. "What's eating you now, Ryan?"

"Why are we going in?"

"Look see."

"Why?"

"Never knew you ask that kind of question, Ryan." The older man was confused. "I don't get it. Honest, I don't. There's a problem here?"

"When we rode with you, Trader, and you said for us to follow you, we knew there was always a reason. Jack. Trade. Blasters. Save someone. Save ourselves. Pay a debt. Collect a debt. Always a reason."

"Sure." Trader nodded and ran a hand across the top of his cropped, grizzled hair.

"So, why are we going into the middle of a ruined, rad-blasted ville?"

"See what there is to see. Hear what there is to hear. Come on, Ryan, sure you aren't losing your nerve for a little adventure? By oak and ash! Wouldn't have ever thought that of you. Not in the old days."

Ryan looked away for a moment, trying to control the unexpected burst of violent anger that came grinning up out of the back of his mind. Without his being aware of it, he was suddenly on the edge of a flaring rage. The scar across his face began to throb like a fiery heart.

"Drop it." J.B. had stepped quietly in between the two men, the M-4000 12-gauge threatening neither of them, threatening both of them.

"No problem." Ryan holstered the blaster, passingly wondering at how tight his index finger had been on the trigger. "No problem at all."

Trader seemed momentarily out of his depth. "I'll be hung, quartered and dried for the crows. It never used to be like this, back then."

"Back then was a different world, Trader. Different rules. Different strokes."

Trader didn't reply for a moment, looking once at the sky. "Might get some sun later. Be good. Let's go in a tad closer, shall we?"

THEY PASSED THE RUINS of Boeing Field Airport, and there was still no sign of life.

There had only been one sign of death.

A body lying crumpled in a leaf-choked gutter, its throat cut in a great bloodless gash. The busy predators had been at the naked male corpse, and there wasn't much left of the face or the exposed extremities.

"Where did all the blood go?" J.B. asked, staring down at the remains. "Nothing on the highway. Not a sign. Wound like that it must have come spurting out like the fountain of life."

Ryan knelt. "Rain wouldn't have washed it away, would it? Still have been staining on the concrete."

"Unless the stupe was chilled someplace else and dumped here," Trader stated.

Ryan straightened. "Well...yeah, never thought of that. Could be."

"Could be," J. B. agreed, looking embarrassed that he hadn't thought of such an obvious explanation.

"Young men nowadays." Their former leader grinned, delighted at how he'd scored over them. "Plenty of gall but no sand. No imagination."

He strode off northward, ever closer to the long-stilled heart of the metropolis.

"MERCER ISLAND," Trader said, pointing to their right. "See where there used to be a big bridge over to it. Main interstate east ran over it."

"Seals." Ryan had spotted the silky movements of the gray hunters, moving through the dark waters of Lake Washington. "That part of the sea?"

"Figure so. Don't know if it always was. I know there was some triple-bad quake damage not far off the north of the ville. Cific got through in places."

The open vistas of the suburbs were gone.

The three companions constantly had to detour around the crumbled wreckage of towering buildings, picking their way with the greatest of caution, never knowing when a block of stone might tip them into a blind abyss. A lichen-covered shambles of jagged, powdery rock, with the rusting remains of the supporting substructure emerged here and there, like the bloodied spears of giant adversaries.

"Light's going," Ryan observed.

"Not time for that." J.B. Dix checked his chron. "Dark night! Where did the time all go? Doesn't seem all that long since we left Abe, yesterday."

"Covered some miles." Trader was showing signs of tiredness, his breathing harsh and ragged. Twice he'd been doubled over with a coughing fit. The second time Ryan was almost certain that he'd seen a spray of scarlet on the older man's breath.

"Best look for somewhere to hole up." Ryan had been uncomfortable for the last half hour, the hairs at the back of his neck warning him that they were being shadowed. Twice he'd casually stopped and glanced around, once pretending his bootlace had worked loose.

But he hadn't seen anything.

"You reckon there's..." Trader began. "Been feeling for a good few minutes now that..."

"Me too," J.B. agreed. "Like an itch you can't quite get at to scratch."

"Seen nothing." Trader looked slowly around, scanning the mountains of rubble.

"One of the first things you taught us was that when you couldn't see the Apaches, it probably meant they were about to attack you, Trader."

There came that familiar barking laugh, like a wolf in a thicket. "Glad you remember something I taught you, Ryan."

THE SUN SEEMED to fall out of the western sky like a boulder off a high cliff. The clouds had finally slipped away, leaving long shadows that stretched up and over the ruins of Seattle. Now they were gone.

Only the few buildings that still remained with more than a half-dozen floors were lighted, a bright golden glow on the dappled walls that faded quickly, the final light of the sinking sun moving upward.

Once it was gone, the darkness became like a potent living force, flowing all around Ryan, J.B. and the Trader like a soft black velvet.

"Need someplace," Trader said.

"Left it late." J.B. had the shotgun at his hip, head turning slowly from side to side, as if he could already see an enemy approaching them.

"Some kind of mall ahead there," Ryan said. "Thought I saw an entrance before the sun moved away."

"Underground?" Trader shook his head, his face a pale blur in the deepening gloom. "Can't say I ever cared much for burrowing underground."

"Me neither." Ryan heard the faintest quiver in the Armorer's voice, and remembered that his oldest friend suffered from claustrophobia.

"We don't have a lot of choice. Seems that this part of the ville is just wasted. No houses. No stores. Nothing much for shelter."

"Sleep out?" Trader offered.

"In the heart of a ruined ville? Come on," Ryan said. "We all know better than that."

THERE WAS some white-painted graffiti, just inside the entrance. "This is a place of God's carelessness," it read.

None of them commented on it.

They also saw what might have been a street-gang symbol. Ryan had seen similiar daubs in the heart of old Newyork—skulls or squares or circles of one color or another. This was an inverted cross, in red.

"Think this was an underground shopping mall?" Trader asked, hesitating at the opening, constantly turning to peer back over a shoulder.

"Looks like it." J.B. sniffed. "Smells like it's been used as a public outhouse for the last hundred years."

"Best go in and find us a corner before it gets to be full dark." Ryan led the way into the noisome chasm, picking his way among the rubble.

Though Ryan's night sight wasn't anywhere as good as Jak Lauren's, it was still adequate to see in the darkening gloom, inside the mall.

The place had been completely stripped. Not a shard of glass or splinter of wood remained. The shelves and signs had gone from all of the individual retail units, and there were no doors or windows, just the bare concrete boxes, looking like the unoccupied stalls in a gigantic stable.

"You still got that feeling, Ryan?"

"Yeah. You, Trader?"

"Strong. I might've been out of the way of firefights for a while, but you don't forget that feeling."

J.B. nodded, the fading light glinting off his glasses. "Shame we haven't got Krysty here. She could 'feel' if there was any real threat around."

Trader sniffed and spat. "Don't need a redhead mutie bitch to tell us that."

Ryan already had the SIG-Sauer unholstered, and he half turned toward the older man, aware of that same dangerous flush of bitter anger.

Controlling it.

"We can always walk right out. Head south and east and we'll be back with Abe around dawn. Is that what you two would like, huh?"

Neither J.B. nor Trader answered him.

Ryan carried on. "Then we find a nice quiet stone box and set our backs to the wall and wait out the night. That the general idea, is it?"

"For fuck's sake, Ryan..." Trader began the sentence with anger riding high and strong in his voice, then allowed it to trail away into the moist dripping stillness around them. "Let's get settled."

"Sure. Sure."

IT WOULD HAVE BEEN unthinkable to spend the night in such a place, at the heart of a huge nuked ville, without taking every precaution.

Ryan picked out a corner unit, to one side of the mall, where nobody could come at them from the back without being spotted. He offered to take first watch. J.B. picked second and Trader agreed that he'd be on guard through the last part of the night, toward first light.

They all nibbled at some of the beef jerky that they'd taken from the ranch outside Seattle, drank some water. Then the Armorer and Trader lay down, each wrapped in a single blanket, to pass the night.

Ryan sat close to the entrance, where he could look both ways out across the atrium space. His blaster was in his hand, and he leaned his back against the cold wall. J.B. had folded his glasses and tucked them safely in a pocket, lying down and falling almost instantly into a quiet sleep. His scattergun was close beside him.

Trader was less peaceful.

He had twitched and snored as he started to doze off, then began to make a peculiar clicking sound, a noise that surprised Ryan by its shrill, piercing quality, and he nudged the old man with his foot to partly wake him. Trader had simply moaned and muttered, then rolled over onto his other side, still snoring, but not so loudly.

Ryan listened to the oppressive stillness that gathered all around him. He'd read enough horror comix and books, as well as occasionally watching flickering bits of ragged vids, to know that abandoned shopping malls were a favorite resort of monsters and ghouls.

The mouth of the mall acted as an echo chamber for the far-off sounds of the night. Ryan heard screams and barking and snuffling, but nothing seemed to enter the catacomb. Water dripped across the far side of the building, and he once heard what might have been a large frog or a lizard, splashing through one of the dark stagnant pools that lay between the pillars.

It was tempting to get up and stretch his legs, perhaps walk around the cavernous mall for a little while.

But to do that would make himself a vulnerable target if there was anyone watching for him.

He became aware of a thin, fluting sound, like someone playing a tinny, repetitive dirge, the music floating in and around him. Trader seemed aware of it, stirring in his sleep, then becoming quiet again.

Ryan listened to the tune, finding that it was peaceful and restful, lulling him away from any thoughts of potential risks within the deserted mall.

It was very odd that the reedy music had seemed to be so far away, drifting in from somewhere over the western slopes of the distant Cascades, carrying the first flavor of ice and snow. But now it was closer.

A warm, sensual sound enveloped Ryan in its beauty, taking away the threat of imminent danger from the creatures of the night beyond the mall.

It took him back to his early childhood, before violence and hatred had marked him for its own, in the gentle, blue-misted Shens, when life had been secure and he had known brief periods of true happiness.

All of that came to him borne on the feathered wings of the swelling music.

He ran barefoot over cropped turf beneath a golden summer sun, the scent of clover fields filling his nostrils.

Ryan was smiling in the pitchy blackness.

He slowly lifted his right hand and brushed it softly over his face, skirting the patch that covered the weeping empty socket of his left eye.

Now the flute was playing much more quietly, a dreamy, rhythmic beat, holding steady, bringing its own true vision of warmth and security.

It felt so good that Ryan closed his eye for a moment, allowing his breathing to gradually slow, keeping the soft tempo of the music.

Now it was playing very, very close to him, inside his own mind, filling his head, washing away all of the other thoughts and worries.

Ryan slept.

Unaware that they had company in the mall.

Chapter Eight

"By the Three Kennedys!"

"What now, Doc?" Jak had been less than keen on the idea of Doc going off on his own for a few days, on some sort of mysterious expedition, where he would apparently do some sketching and scribble a few lines of verse. And try to come to terms with his own innermost thoughts.

"What we used to call 'getting our shit together,' Doc," had been Mildred's offering. "Us Woodstock guys and gals with flowers in our hair."

"Sticks and stones could, and probably would, do fearsome damage to these old bones, Dr. Wyeth. But your mocking words will harm me. Not."

The previous evening, after the old man had gone early to his bed, the other four companions had sat around the big dining table and discussed his request to have some time alone in the backcountry.

Dean's voice had been loudest against the idea.

"Get himself chilled before he's been gone for a half hour," he predicted.

Jak had also been opposed. "Why? Why, Doc? Just that. What's point? We know Doc. Doc knows Doc. We know danger. Ryan comes back finds Doc chilled. Bad news."

Krysty had a sudden bleak vision that almost stopped her heart. The repetition of the word "Doc," by the teenager, had the monotonous sound of a nail being hammered into an oak coffin. Or the sonorous, slow ticking of a long-case clock, set against the wall of a chapel of rest.

"Ryan," she whispered.

"What is it?" Mildred had seen the way that Krysty's face had gone sheet-white, her green eyes standing out like burning emeralds, her sentient hair suddenly curling in on itself.

But the moment had passed.

Mildred had been very ambiguous about Doc's idea to journey off alone. Part-joking, she'd suggested that if anything happened to the old goat then they could all enjoy a more peaceful life.

"But seriously... This could be just a part of the endless process of coming to terms with grief and bereavement for him. My deep suspicion is that a part of Doc Tanner will always be locked firmly away, back in the nineteenth century, with his wife and his children. I know it's not easy to lose loved ones like that."

For a split second the black woman glimpsed a charred log, still smoldering, shaped like a man, smell the stench of roasted flesh above the sickly scent of the magnolias on the southern breeze. Her beloved father had been murdered by men who hid behind white hoods.

Krysty had been the only one who had positively pressed for Doc to be given their blessing for his planned expedition into the New Mexico canyons.

"Despite his pose of being a blundering old fool—"

"Some pose!" Mildred exclaimed.

"Despite that, we all know that Doc's a cunning and resourceful man. With great courage. None of us would doubt that." She looked around the table. "Would we? No? No."

"But there's all sorts of danger out there," Dean protested. "Why don't I go with him?"

"No." Jak was insistent. "If goes out there, then goes alone. Agree with Krysty. Doc no fool."

"Dad wouldn't let him go."

Krysty shook a finger at the eleven-year-old. "Don't you dare try that one on with us, young man! Don't ever try and blackmail us by saying what Ryan Cawdor would or wouldn't have done. Understand me?"

"Sorry."

The conversation lasted another hour or more, but by then everyone in the room knew that Doc would definitely be going. All they were discussing was simply what he would need to take with him to try to maximize his chances of survival out in that most hostile land.

"BY THE THREE KENNEDYS!"

It was early morning. Doc had been checking the cinches on Judas, and the mule had rolled a baleful eye at him and made a determined effort to take a hunk out of the old man's skinny rump.

"You sure about taking that animal, Doc?" Mildred asked, allowing her concern to show through.

"Judas and I intend to sink or swim together, my dear Dr. Wyeth."

"I can see the sinking easily enough, Doc," Krysty said. "Just that I don't get quite such a clear picture of the two of you swimming."

"Let me do the worrying, dear madam."

Jak squinted out of the shadows of the porch, toward the low smudge of mountains where Doc was headed. "Look like thunderheads," he said.

"The wind may blow and crack its cheeks, Master Lauren, and we shall give neither jot nor tittle for it. For we are bound for the far places."

"Come back safe, Doc," Krysty said.

"Of course." The morning breeze ruffled his mane of silver hair. The sword stick was jammed down the side of the saddle, along with the two packs of provisions. Jak had pressed Doc to take along a rifle for hunting, but he'd been firmly refused. "I have my Le Mat for close combat work. Anything beyond fifteen feet is, I fear, also beyond my eyesight."

"You remember everything that we've all told you about safe camping, Doc?" Krysty folded her arms across her breasts, feeling a sudden chill.

"But of course. Near sweet water. Endeavor to keep rocks to my back. Beware of the Hun in the sun. Don't allow the bastards to grind you down. Never eat at a restaurant called Mom's Place. Look for the spoor of malign creatures. Sleep with the blaster under my pillow. Though I don't have a pillow with me on my odyssey. Don't draw to an inside straight. Never lend money to a Republican. The first cut is the deepest.

Never borrow money from a Democrat. Talk is cheap, but the price of action is colossal. Keep your dreams as clean as silver."

Mildred held up her hand. "Enough, Doc!"

"Main thing is take care," Jak told him.

They watched him go.

"Man on a skew-backed mule." Mildred laughed. "Look at the way his bony legs stick out both sides of Judas. Nearly scrape the ground. All he needs is a stovepipe hat and he'd be the spitting double of Lincoln."

"Who's Lincoln?" Dean asked.

"IF ONLY MAN COULD TURN back the clock, Judas," Doc said, as the memory of Emily and his lost family filled his mind. "The thought that tortures me most, in the dark hours of the night when death is closest, is that the white-coats turned the clock forward for me, but they lacked the skill to return me home again to see my love once more."

Doc was talking about the trawling experiment that had ripped him away from his young and lovely wife and two beautiful children, that had torn him from comfort and security to the nightmare of Deathlands, where death waited gibbering in a thousand nightmare forms.

"I may choose not to return to my friends," he said, hardly noticing that the mule was moving slower and slower, taking advantage of his lack of concentration.

Now that he'd said it out loud, Doc was slightly shocked at the idea.

Yet, it had been something growing inside his mind for many months.

It was often difficult to recall his life in the distant past. Emily was clear in his memory, and Rachel and little Jolyon. But so much else had vanished into a blurred patchwork of confusion.

Friends were particularly hard to remember.

But he thought that he had never had friends of the caliber of Ryan, Krysty, John Barrymore Dix, Mildred Wyeth, Jak Lauren and young Dean.

"Greater love hath no man but that he will lay down his life for a friend," he said.

Yet he had found that he was increasingly yearning for solitude.

A time to himself.

A time to try to shake out the cobwebs that gathered in the west wing of his addled mind.

"A time to reap and a time to sow. A time to think and a time to dream."

A gila monster dragged itself slowly across the dusty trail, some fifty paces in front of the mule, but Judas took no notice of it. A little closer and the mule might easily have been tempted to charge at the reptilian intruder and trample it to pulp under its sharp hooves.

They were up into the lower slopes of the foothills that surrounded the basin where the ranch lay, climbing through sagebrush and mesquite, past the weathered mesas. There were only a few wisps of high cloud, off to the north. The thunderheads with their threat of stormy weather had vanished.

Doc found that his mood was intensely change-
able, veering between exultation at the beauty of the
day and despair at his own predicament.

"Not mad," he whispered, making the mule prick
up its ears again. "Let me not be mad."

The afternoon drifted by.

Jak had given Doc careful instructions on the best
and safest places for camping, pressing home the
warning that he'd seen the tracks of a big cat, not far
from the corral where they kept their own horses.

"Mutie fucker, Doc. Cougar that size could take
head off in one bite."

But he had also pointed out that Judas wasn't likely
to allow any large predator to creep in too close without giving some sort of warning.

"Such as breaking its tether and running away like
goose shit off a shovel, Doc, leaving you out there."
Mildred had been amused at the picture.

Doc was aiming for a box canyon for his first night's
camping. There was a trail from its mouth that would
then lead him higher, into the total desolation of the
mountains, opening up limitless options for the rest of
his journey. However long it might eventually be.

THE CANYON WAS ALIGNED east-west, so that the setting sun flooded through in the last hour before dusk,
heightening the vivid reds and oranges of the sheer
walls, throwing the cracks and fissures into deeper relief.

There was a shadowed pool at the end, just as the
albino teenager had described it, surrounded by some

scrub willows and feathery tamarisks. Doc walked around it, trying to see if there were any tracks that might give him cause for concern. But it hadn't rained for several days, and he found it impossible to guess how old some of the spoor was.

"Deer," he said. "That is less than difficult for an old frontiersman like myself. Doc Tanner. Last of the moccasins. A man whose eyes focus only on the far, misty horizons. Known to the Native Americans by his Apache name of Trail Breaker." He laughed, his voice echoing back from the rocks around. "Talking to oneself is supposed to be the first sign of incipient insanity, is it not? Well, I care not for that. There is nothing so satisfying as having a conversation with someone who is your perfect intellectual equal."

There was a set of tracks to and from the edge of the water that he thought might have been wolves. Or coyotes. And another set that he squatted and stared at for several seconds, wishing that he had Ryan or Jak with him to help him out.

"Far too big for a feral cat," he mused. "Not a bear? Though a big grizzly might... No, I confess myself totally defeated by this one."

THE FIRE BLAZED brightly—at the sixth attempt.

Doc had his pan of water bubbling merrily, with a small stew of meat and vegetables that Krysty had prepared for him to take and cook.

Judas was securely tethered to a tree within easy reach of the water and ample grazing.

The flames gave enough light for Doc to be able to read the slim volume of verse that he'd brought with him. He browsed through some of his old favorites, by Herrick and Marvell, some Frost and even a little Emily Dickinson.

Finding that his eyelids were drooping, Doc carefully tucked the book back into his pack, unrolled his quilted sleeping bag by the fire and climbed in, dutifully checking that his Le Mat was ready at hand.

The flames died down to a ruby glow and Doc fell asleep, content with his first day.

Less than a hundred yards away, upwind, a pair of unblinking golden eyes watched.

Waited.

Chapter Nine

Ryan was stretched out on the softest feather mattress, beneath a rich coverlet of silken brocade, relaxing into that delicious state that lay partway between a warm languor and the waiting delights of deep, satisfying sleep.

A fire blazed in the hearth, the scented logs filling the bedchamber with their perfume.

He could hear music, very faintly, brushing at the furthest edge of his consciousness. Perhaps it was coming from an adjacent room.

It was a flute, picking out and repeating a delicate, ghostly, haunting theme.

A tiny part of Ryan's mind was aware that someone was close to him.

"Krysty?" he breathed silently.

A hand was at his collar, touching him on the side of his throat, moving away the curling black hair. He felt gentle pressure on the carotid artery.

"Krysty?"

It was like a lightning bolt, exploding from a clear summer sky.

Ryan felt as if he'd been trapped far, far beneath the waters of some gigantic lake, deep within a sucking gruel that gripped his entire body.

The pleasant sound of the flute was suddenly discordant, a grating, morbid noise that seemed to strip the layers from his bones and pick at the sensitive marrow.

He blinked open his eye.

It took all of his fighting instincts, honed to a razored edge over the years, to work out precisely what was happening, where he was.

The underground mall in Seattle had been as dark as pitch when he'd fallen asleep.

Fallen asleep while on watch!

Now there was a dim light, coming from a number of shielded lanterns, all around him. And someone loomed over him, breath hot on the side of his neck.

Ryan managed to move his head a little, seeing a face close to his. The creature's face was as white as the winter moon, with eyes that glinted red in the filtered glow of the lamps. Its flattened nose had wide nostrils, and its mouth was half-open in an expression halfway between a smile and a kiss.

And its canine teeth, sharpened to needle points, were almost touching the skin of Ryan's exposed throat.

He threw arms and legs out wide, yelling as loudly as he could, thrusting the nocturnal apparition away from him, knowing in that single beat of the heart since waking that he and the others were as close to death as they could possibly be.

Then there was no time for any kind of thought.

He was aware of a hissing snarl of frustrated rage from the creature he'd repelled, the foul stink of rotting meat from its breath. There was a confusion of shouting from the other muties that had gathered in the catacombs around them.

Something struck him a painful blow on the left shoulder before he could even get up to his feet, sending him tumbling back against the damp concrete wall. Ryan had been reaching for the butt of the SIG-Sauer, but it was now out of reach.

He didn't hesitate for a single splinter of frozen time. His right hand dropped to the hilt of the panga, drawing it in a smooth whisper of steel.

Someone grabbed at him, jagged nails catching at the material of his coat, hindering him as he fought to stand. But he used the point of the blade, shortening the stroke. He thrust in the general direction of his closest adversary, feeling the familiar, satisfying jar of the panga slicing through flesh then grinding against bone.

There was a scream of shock and pain, and the grasping hands let go of him. Ryan snatched the breathing space and pulled himself upright, steadying for a brief moment against the wall at his side.

His sight was quickly acclimating to the dimness, aware of a dozen or more of the bloodsucking ghouls, many of them holding lanterns.

Behind him and to his left, J.B. and Trader were both on their feet, having been shielded by Ryan from the first and worst of the onslaught. The older man had his Armalite ready in his hands, while the Armorer had just picked up the murderous Smith & Wesson scattergun.

A body writhed at Ryan's feet. It was a tall man, wrapped in a black cloak to mask himself in the darkness. His hands were pressed to his belly where he'd been stabbed, and he cried out in a long, toneless shriek.

Two more of the ghouls headed directly for Ryan, both holding short-hafted axes. Both had the same deathly white faces, the same sharpened teeth as the first of the attackers, and both were hissing at Ryan, their noxious breath almost making him gag in revulsion.

He swung at the first, parrying the lunge of the hatchet, sparks bursting from the clash of blades. But the second was sidling to the left, trying to aim a cutting blow at his legs. Ryan heard the familiar crack of the Armalite, much louder in the confined space, and the mutie went spinning backward, dropping the ax to the wet stone floor.

The creatures of the night were more determined than most muties, not put off by the resistance of their intended prey, all surging forward in a wave of horror.

Ryan feinted toward the ghoul's stomach, making the thing drop its guard. Then he cut high at the pallid face. The panga barely caressed the mutie's cheek, but opened a shallow gash from forehead to chin. Blood flowed in a curtain, dark in the gloom, and the thing yelped.

And came again at Ryan.

The one-eyed warrior readied himself, when he saw horror upon horror. Another of the monstrous creatures slunk out of the shadows in a curious scuttling, sideways run. But instead of attacking the norm, it leaped upon its wounded brother. A long, lizardlike tongue darted from between the white, parted lips and lapped at the spilling blood, sucking it down with every evidence of macabre pleasure. Its head lifted for a moment from the feast, showing the carmined mouth, the protruding eyes wide with its unholy desire. Then it plunged its teeth deep into the wounded mutie's throat, meeting with an audible crunching sound.

Ryan used the stolen moment of safety to sheathe his blood-slick panga and stoop for the blaster, leveling it at the nearest lamp and firing. He saw the lantern fall, the burning oil spilling across the uneven floor with a shimmering blue light, like St. Elmo's fire.

He heard the thunderous boom of the M-4000, and saw one of the ghouls disintegrate under the hideous power of the tiny dartlike fléchettes.

The brief pause in the action gave Ryan time to check out the numbers of the opposition. Six more of the muties held lights, and four or five others, two of whom appeared, possibly, to be female.

None of them had any weapons, beyond the assortment of knives and hatchets, but the overwhelming firepower of the three norms didn't seem to worry them. Ryan wondered whether the ghouls had any real awareness of facing death. Perhaps they had become used to their victims falling into their hands without any fight. He remembered the sound of that bastard evil flute and the effect it had on him.

The Armalite barked three more times, putting down a trio of the whey-faced creatures, including one of the women. J.B. also fired three more of the 12-gauge rounds, each containing twenty of the inch-long needle darts.

Ryan took his time, leveling the 9 mm blaster and picking his targets.

"Fish in a fucking barrel, partners!" Trader yelled, his voice thick with the excitement of the chilling field.

Less than thirty seconds had passed since Ryan had jerked himself out of the bloodsuckers' trap.

Less than thirty seconds and they were all down and done for. All but one.

The other female, who'd picked up a fallen lantern, was backing slowly away from them, mewing like a kitten with a wounded paw.

Ryan drew a bead on her with the SIG-Sauer, at a distance of less than twenty feet, tightened his finger on the trigger and heard the explosion.

But it was Trader's Armalite, fired from behind him, that blew the mutie's face apart.

"Ace on the line!" the older man crowed, holding the rifle high above his head in an atavistic gesture of triumph, his lean, wolfish body illuminated by the burning oil that was spilled all over the floor.

Ryan thought ruefully how like old times life had become, standing knee-deep among dead muties, blood hot on his hands, splattered in his face, holding a warm gun, while Trader whooped his victory.

J.B. went silently to the three wounded creatures of the night and, kneeling, carefully slit their throats from ear to ear. He wiped the blade on one of their sable cloaks, straightening, moving back to avoid the eerie flames of the oil.

"That's it," he said.

Ryan nodded. "Be a good idea to get the fuck away from this place."

Trader was busily reloading the trusty old Armalite, levering in a handful of fresh 9 mm rounds from one of his pockets. "Guess I'll drink to that," he said, panting from the effort of the chilling.

Ryan stood still and listened, but the outburst of anarchistic violence didn't seem to have reached the ears of any of the other inhabitants of the desolate ruined ville. Or, if any had heard it, they chose to mind their own business.

Trader had walked to look down at the woman he'd shot last. The bullet had taken away most of the upper part of her face, including the nose. But he was fascinated by her gaping mouth. "Think they file their teeth to get them pointed?" He laughed. "Who gives a shit?" In falling, the skirt of the female mutie had ridden up over her waist, showing her muscular thighs and the dark patch of pubic hair. Trader touched the corpse with the end of the Armalite's muzzle, and laughed again. "Either of you ever get the clap from a dead mutie?"

IT WAS STILL FULL DARK as the three men emerged from the tomb into the fresh air.

Stars twinkled brightly above them, and there was enough moon for them to be able to pick their way safely through the rubble-strewn avenues of the ville.

Trader had abandoned his plans for going farther into the old heart of Seattle, leading the way back toward the east and south, where Abe was waiting for them with the hearse and the horses. But nothing had actually been said about changing their purpose. Ryan was more than happy to get out of the sinister ruins, but part of him knew he shouldn't have let Trader make the decision for all of them.

THEY WERE HALFWAY out into the suburbs, with the first ethereal hint of the false dawn at their backs.

"Being watched again," said Ryan, who was out at point position.

Trader stopped, close to a tall yew hedge on the right of the street. His head swung around, and he checked both sides. J.B. was at the back, and he too looked behind them.

They closed up the skirmish line so that they could talk quietly.

"You sure, Ryan?"

"Sure, Trader. Not a feeling. Saw a skinny young guy, carrying what looked like an M-16. He cut across the garden of a house about six down on this side. Just caught a glimpse of him moving fast and low."

"Ambush?" J.B. tugged his fedora down. "Better get moving. There's enough cover around here for a whole bunch of killers to hide up."

"Take a side turning and try and get around who-
ever it is waiting for us." Trader sniffed the dawn air.
"Smell a fire someplace close."

The bullet missed him by less than a yard, slashing
into a thick holly bush. They all spun toward the hollow echo of the shot, seeing the tiny cloud of powder
smoke drifting from around the corner of the wrecked
house, less than a hundred yards behind them.

For an almost fatal moment, Ryan hesitated.
Countless years of combat reflexes nearly destroyed
him as he looked toward Trader for a command. He
realized in that single heartbeat that his former leader
had been taken totally by surprise and was simply
standing on the sidewalk, staring back, the Armalite
unlifted, as if he were waiting for further shots.

"This way!" Ryan yelled, shattering the spell,
breaking through the hedge into the front garden of
the nearest house, followed by J.B. and Trader. A fu-
sillade of gunfire came at them from in front as well
as behind, one of the bullets breaking a window at the
front of the building, passing close enough to Ryan for
him to feel the hot, angry buzz.

Moments later they were all inside, as a cascade of
lead tore into the wooden walls, splintering glass and
ricocheting off doors.

"Safe," Trader said, having thrown himself flat on
the floor.

Ryan shook his head. "For a while."

Chapter Ten

The second day passed slowly for Abe. The campsite
was well hidden from the nearest highway, with water
and good grass for the horses. Every now and again
the little gunner would patrol around the imaginary
perimeter, but he didn't see a single living soul.

In the distance he could make out the dark satanic
ruins of old Seattle, with the smoke from a number of
cooking fires rising slowly into the still air.

To move the tardy clock along, Abe spent some time
with rags, cleaning and polishing the hearse. He
washed mud off the elegant wheels, bringing the
paintwork to a mirrored perfection, buffing up all the
glass until he could see his own lugubrious, mus-
tached face reflected in it.

That took him into the afternoon of the second day
since his three companions had left.

He sat back, leaning against one of the wheels,
munching on a sandwich of bread and cheese, with a
tasty apple to follow for dessert.

Abe had been looking forward to the moment of the
reunion between Trader, Ryan and J.B. ever since he
first tracked down their old chief. But, as he sat there,
eyes closed, relishing the warm sunlight, he was only

too aware in his heart that something had gone radically wrong.

He'd had the dream of the four of them, all for one and one for all, having adventures together, just like they used to in the great days of the all-powerful war wags. They'd chill a few stickies and rescue some beautiful—and painfully grateful—gaudy sluts, then sit around the fire in the evening, while the women cooked up a storm, retelling the old stories of battles fought and won and friends gone before.

But it wasn't like that.

Abe wasn't the most sensitive man in Deathlands, but he was painfully conscious of the edge that now lay between Trader and Ryan. And it hadn't proved too difficult to work out just why that was.

There was a common saying that you were a baron today and worm-food tomorrow. Trader himself used to say that a war wag could have only one driver. Now their little group of four had two separate and distinct leaders. That was both a worry and a disappointment.

With that somewhat melancholy thought, Abe drifted off into sleep.

THE WHINNYING OF ONE of the packhorses woke Abe with a start, and he fumbled in near panic for the butt of his stainless-steel Colt Python. He stood, half-asleep, and nearly fell over.

The horse whickered again, stamping its hooves, head tossing. Abe moved cautiously toward it, the heavy gun cocked in his fist, eyes raking the land around for any danger.

All he could see was a tiny, bright-eyed rodent, with a long twitching tail, scampering away toward its burrow, in the line of sight of the horse. The moment the dusky brown mouse disappeared, the pack animal quietened, carrying on grazing as though nothing had happened.

"Stupe bastard," Abe muttered, holstering the .357 blaster again.

As he turned back toward the hearse, it struck him how long his shadow was, elongated like some spidery giant. Abe lifted a leg, waving his arms, grinning at the capering response from the shadow.

"Gettin' dark already," he said.

One of the team of four matched blacks for the hearse turned at his voice, ears going back. Abe walked over and patted it, feeling the silk and velvet skin soft against his hand.

"Good old fellow, aren't you?" He looked westward, beyond Puget Sound, where the sun was hulldown on the horizon. "Said they'd be back by dusk. No sign of them yet. Knowing Ryan, Trader and J.B., I'd be surprised if they weren't on the button. Still, I'll go riding to the rescue if they haven't shown by dawn. Probably having a fine old time in a drinker, with sluts draped all over them. Forgotten about poor old Abe with the animals. Lucky bastards!"

"NEAR DARK," Ryan called from his lookout position at the top of the stairs.

The first-floor front of the abandoned house was covered by Trader, occasionally creeping to one or another of the windows, checking on the besiegers. He snapped off a shot now and then from the Armalite to keep them at a distance.

J.B. was moving on hands and knees between the kitchen and what had probably been a dining room, keeping his eyes open across the overgrown vegetable garden and small orchard at the rear of the building.

There were upward of twenty men in the undergrowth. Or there had been at one point. They'd made the mistake of trying to rush the defenders and had paid a heavy toll for their stupidity. Six corpses lay sprawled around the house, one of them having made it onto the front porch, his hand reaching out as though he'd been stricken while trying to deliver an important message to the inhabitants.

"Be tough at night," the Armorer called. "Not much chance of holding them off. Creepy-crawl in and fire the place. Go like a tinderbox. Chill us when we have to get out."

"Why the fuck are they all so eager to try and chill our asses?" Trader's angry voice floated up the broken staircase toward Ryan.

"Started because we were outlanders," he replied. "Now they know the kind of blasters we've got, they're ready to pay a high blood price for them."

"Already paid big."

"Plenty more in that kind of ville gang. Life gets to be triple cheap when it's so short." Ryan ducked as a bullet came through a window at the back, showering more broken glass on the floor, bringing down a chunk of the ceiling as it buried itself above his head.

"We going after them?" J.B. asked, moving briefly into the hall to be able to talk more quietly to the other two.

Trader answered first. "Have to. Like you said. Night'll bring them like flies to honey."

"We told Abe we'd be back by now." Ryan lay flat on his stomach, looking down into the shadowed hallway. "Said he'd come looking, if we weren't with him by the next dawn, at the latest."

"Will he come?" Trader asked doubtfully.

"He came looking for you," Ryan replied.

THE SHOOTING HAD virtually stopped. Ryan and the others had agreed that the gang outside had almost certainly run very low on ammo. Once it was full night, they wouldn't need blasters to get the outlanders from the house.

Ryan had crept down to join the others on the first floor. They kept up a constant patrol around the building, catfooting from room to room, watching for the earliest warning of any sneak attack on them.

There was still the last residue of light, filtered from the western sky.

Something moved above their heads; the faintest skittering sound, making Trader swing toward the stairs, knuckles white on the Armalite.

"Rat," J.B. said.

"I knew that."

"Soon be time for us to make a move." Ryan glanced out of one of the broken windows to the side. "I figure they'll be so pissed at us that they'll want revenge and come running for it. Want it right up front."

"One of us could stay behind. Fire and move." Trader turned, questioningly. "Make the shitheads think we're still here. Other two go out and coldcock them from behind."

"No." Ryan shook his head. "They know the ground. Might be two or three dozen, scattered around us. We blunder around and they'll soon hear there's only one blaster firing. That way we all get to be dead, Trader."

"Guess you're right at that. So, all out together, fast and hard."

"Yeah. Best is we cut through that side window. The bushes are closest there. We can charge them, J.B. at the front with the scattergun. Don't stop."

"Unless one of us goes down. We never leave a wounded man behind, Ryan, you know that."

There was a stillness, broken by a piercing whistle from somewhere out in the darkness.

Ryan spoke quickly, urgently. "This isn't war wag days, Trader. Just three of us. Anyone goes down he's on his own. No argument. The way it is. We'll meet up when we can. Passed an old water tower, good mile east of here. Near the top of a real steep hill. Remember it?"

J.B. nodded, his glasses catching the last drop of half-light in the hallway.

"Trader?"

"Sure. Good luck."

"Right. Meet up there. Here we go."

Ryan ducked his head, folding his arms over his face, the SIG-Sauer in his fist, and ran directly at the window.

As he burst through it, there was a cataclysmic explosion and a dazzling burst of bright purple light that flooded the land for miles around.

Ryan rolled and came up on his feet, part of his brain numbed by the blast, deciding that one of their attackers must have been hoarding an implode gren.

But the more logical part of his mind told him that a massive chem storm had crept up silently from over the ocean, waiting over the center of the ville, with impeccable timing to release its nuke-born venom.

There was another flash of lightning, the thunder following on top of the brilliance, the air filling with the familiar sour taint of ozone.

It wasn't a moment for thinking.

It was a time for running and killing.

In between the first and second flashes of chem lightning, Ryan heard the puny crack of a smoothbore musket, but he had no idea where the ball had flown.

He headed straight for the bushes, seeing a figure a few feet to his right. Ryan stood and got off a shot, feeling the blaster buck in his hand. The figure vanished as though it had been smeared from sight. Someone else, holding a long-bladed knife, raced toward Ryan. A second round from the SIG-Sauer punched the man to the ground, his face a mask of silver-black blood. The one-eyed warrior slipped, a trailing branch catching at his ankle, then he was up and cutting right, vaulting another hedge, landing on someone, clubbing with the barrel of the automatic, twenty-five and a half ounces pulping the cheek and splitting the eye socket. Trader was at the corner of his vision, swinging the Armalite by the barrel, like Davy Crockett on the crumbling, shot-blasted stone walls of the fortress of the Alamo. There was no sign of J.B. anywhere.

More lightning flashed, followed by a scream from someplace. Ryan shot a young boy, Dean's age, no older, who sprang up out of the ground in front of him. He heard the boom of the Smith & Wesson from the left and saw a stout old-timer, gray hair pasted to his skull, fall back, both hands clutching the gaping hole in his guts where the fléchettes had ripped the life from him. Someone went down behind Ryan, Trader? The old man got up again, lips torn back off his white teeth, looking crazed as he ran. A grove of tall willows. Was water nearby? Ryan dodged between the smooth silvery trunks, something splintering a hole in one of them, hip-level. More thunder, violet lightning, rain, torrential, a stream ahead of him that the one-eyed man tried to leap in a single bound but failed, combat boots slipping in fresh mud, landing knee-deep and wading out to the other bank.

Farther, the noise falling behind him.

The storm behind him.

Running, breath like a fire in his lungs, heart pounding, legs weary.

Escaped.

Alone.

THE WATER TOWER WAS deserted when Ryan reached it, struggling up the steep hill, the highway streaming like a river with the aftermath of the great storm that was now rumbling harmlessly away to the south.

Every few steps he turned around to see if anyone was coming after him.

Friend or foe.

But there was nobody, the blank street lined with eyeless houses, the moon breaking through and casting a baleful gleam over everything. Over the deserted suburb.

The door had been propped shut with a rusting girder, and Ryan had to set his shoulder to it, levering it open with a grinding crash. The inside smelled of urine, the moon darted through the holes in the crumbling brickwork, higher up. Ryan had the SIG-Sauer ready, but he could see immediately that the place was empty.

All he had to do now was wait.

Chapter Eleven

J.B. arrived less than fifteen minutes later, limping slightly after twisting an ankle breaking through the grove of willows.

"Crazy sons of bitches," he said, joining Ryan in the old water tower. "Dark night! Ankle's painful."

"Not a break?"

"No." J.B. sat on the floor and cautiously moved his foot backward and forth. "Bit of a sprain." He took off his glasses and tried to clean them, shaking his head in disgust. "Damned chem storm soaked me through."

"Helped us, though."

"Yeah. Guess it did."

"Trader?"

The Armorer stood, flexing his ankle. "Saw him ahead of me, close by you."

"I saw him as well. Looked to me like the old man was having the time of his life."

"Mebbe the last time of his life. I lost sight of him near that stream."

Ryan went and peered outside into the still night. "Nothing stirring."

J.B. joined him. "Then we wait."

"WHAT DO YOU MAKE IT?"

Ryan angled his chron toward the faint beams of moonlight that still filtered into the ruined tower. "Little after three. Eight minutes past."

"How long we wait for him?"

"Dawn, I reckon. That street gang was so jolt-crazed that they might decide to come after us again at first light. Wouldn't want to hang around any longer than that."

"Think Trader'll make it here?"

Ryan steepled his fingers, resting his chin on them. "Who knows, J.B., who knows? Years ago we'd both have backed Trader to run naked through an army of stickies and come out the other end without a scratch."

"Not now, Ryan."

"No. Not now. Sure the old man's still tough. Look at Abe's stories about him. Taking out all of that posse in the night to rescue him."

"If we wait for dawn, do you think Abe might come looking for us?"

Ryan hadn't really thought that one through. "Guess he might. Could be we go before dawn."

THE LITTLE GUNNER WAS a few miles away from them, dozing in the back of the glass-lined hearse. When he'd seen the raging chem storm moving across the center of the ville, he'd abandoned plans to sleep outside.

The heart of the storm hadn't come that close, but the noise and light had spooked the animals. He'd gotten up twice to check that they were still secure, tightening the line between the trees and taking the extra precaution of putting hobbles on the horses' forelegs.

There had been a few dashes of rain, streaking the polished glass, but there was little of the fury that Abe had watched over Seattle.

"Hope those three get good and wet," he'd muttered, grinning, to himself. "Teach them to leave me on my own."

But now he was awake again, getting out of the back of the hearse to relieve himself. He unbuttoned and stared across country toward the ville, turning as one of the horses moved restlessly. Abe realized that he could actually see the line of horses, though they were still faint and indistinct.

"Shit a brick!" he exclaimed. "Close to dawn already, and they ain't back."

He finished urinating and did up his pants, whistling softly through his teeth. "Ryan said if dawn came on the third day... Looks like being me to the rescue again." But not even Abe was convinced by his own tone of voice.

"HOW MUCH LONGER, Ryan?"

The one-eyed man was just outside the broken door to the big tower, head on one side, straining to listen. "Sure I heard dogs, far off. Wonder if the gang's still out there, mebbe hunting Trader. Could be he's wounded."

"Wouldn't want to be the one bent down to cut his throat," J.B. commented. "Even a dying Trader would bite your face off and spit it in the dirt."

Ryan turned back. "Just a touch of light from the east. If we're going to Abe, then we should move on." He paused. "What was that?"

"What?"

Both of them stood together, with blasters ready, staring into the blackness that lurked down the steep hill from their hiding place.

"Someone coming."

J.B. was so close that their shoulders brushed. "Walking crook."

The sound of a limping man's footfalls reached them, as did the noise of labored breathing.

"Trader?"

"Soon know."

The voice was high and strained, but instantly recognizable. "Yo, inside! Anyone there?"

"Yeah. Both here, Trader. Need a hand?"

"Need a couple of fresh legs, Ryan. Mebbe a new set of lungs. And I admit, between you and me, that the old dick isn't quite as good as it used to be."

They went toward the voice, each putting an arm around Trader, helping him into the shelter. Ryan felt a passing shock at how frail the old man seemed, more like a bundle of dried branches held together with whipcord.

"Got a knife in the ribs, but it went shallow and long. Nothing serious touched. Bled some. Burns like fire. Another of the stupes missed me point-blank with a Kentucky musket. Flash blinded me, and the fuck-head broke the butt across my left thigh. Near broke my leg. And I fell in a bastard ditch and swallowed five gallons of gnat piss.''

"Apart from that, Mrs. Lincoln, what did you think of the play?" Ryan said, using one of Doc's favorite jokes.

But Trader didn't laugh, preoccupied with his own wounds and exhaustion.

"Go outside, J.B., and see if I was followed. I heard dogs. Reckon they might be trailing me. Hope to pick us all up at once.''

The Armorer eased himself through the gap in the shattered door. Ryan knelt by Trader.

"You got your blaster?''

"Course. Nearly right out of ammo for it. Your SIG-Sauer fires 9 mm rounds, don't it, Ryan? Pass me some spares.''

"Yeah. I got a full mag and about half a dozen more. Won't last long.''

"J.B.'s got a few rounds for the M-4000. Not the best of blasters to use in a siege situation.''

"No nines?''

Ryan shook his head. "Plenty up with Abe.''

"Then we best get back to the camp.''

"Could be that Abe's on his way.''

J.B had come back inside the tower, overhearing the last part of the conversation. "Hope so," he said. "Because we got some company coming.''

ABE WAS in a ferocious temper.

Back at the farmhouse there had been four of them

to handle the harnessing of the quartet of jet-black mares for the hearse. Even then it had proved difficult and complex. Now, alone, he was finding that trying to cope with four horses was close to impossible.

"Stand still, you bastard!" he screamed, spittle flying from his open mouth. The animals reacted against the blind anger in his voice, stamping nervously, backing away from the traces, one of them getting hooves tangled in the trailing harness, kicking out so hard it nearly broke one of the shafts.

"For the sake of bleeding Christ, keep still," he moaned, almost in tears at his own helplessness.

The light was gathering with every wasted second, and he could see no hope of getting the rig ready for at least an hour. Abe shut his eyes and attempted the technique for calming himself that Krysty had tried to teach him, slowing his breathing and counting backward from twenty, trying to clear his mind and focus on a white-painted wall.

Gradually he felt self-control seeping back.

TRADER OFTEN SAID that life came down to two choices—run or fight. With his injuries, running anywhere away from the water tower was out of the question, and the deteriorating ammo situation was making the prospect of a successful defensive fight of the ruined building seem increasingly remote.

Thirty or forty of the ragged hunters spilled from the southeastern flank of the devastated ville, pursuing the trio of outlanders with the powerful weapons. There was also a pack of eight or nine lean mongrels, baying their eager hatred to be set free to harry their enemy.

"Should have brought the Uzi," J.B. said, watching the approach of the posse from an upper window.

"And the Steyr rifle," Ryan agreed. "Anything to hold them off."

Trader sat on the floor, holding the gash in his ribs. They'd bandaged it with strips of rag, but he'd lost a significant amount of blood and it was obviously hurting him. The twisted ankle had become stiffer and more painful, so that he could hardly hobble.

He looked up at his two colleagues. "Man weeps over spilled milk gets blinded by the tears," he said.

"Empty words," Ryan snapped. "No time for it. We can't hold them off for long, even if you have all the bullets for the Armalite. Unless they're triple stupe, they'll hear the noise and know we're down to one blaster."

"Give them a shock for a while, with the scattergun, if they break in," the Armorer suggested.

"Still means too many."

"Easy." Trader spoke quietly, not looking at either of them. "Easy."

"How's that? Make it quick. We don't have a lot of time before we need to slow them down."

"Sure, Ryan. Anything you say." Trader paused. "You and J.B. grease it. Take the scattergun and your SIG-Sauer with some emergency rounds. I stay here with the Armalite and the rest of the ammo. Give you my word I'll slow them some. Give you good time to break clear away."

"Fireblast!" Ryan closed his eye, utterly disgusted at the situation.

"No," J.B. said. "Don't know what Ryan thinks, but I'm telling you that's my answer."

"Only way, brothers." Trader pulled himself upright, limping heavily toward the doorway. "No time to argue."

Ryan spit in the oily dirt on the floor. "Tempting, Trader. But I didn't travel halfway across Deathlands to meet up with you again, just so I could leave you behind while I turn and run."

"Always had a soft, weak streak, Ryan." Trader laughed. "And you, too, J.B. Soft. Little-girly soft, both of you."

"Shut up and start using that Armalite," Ryan growled. "And make them count."

ABE EVENTUALLY SUCCEEDED in hitching three of the team into the traces, but the fourth mare steadfastly refused to cooperate with him, prancing and rearing away, snatching the reins from his hands.

"I swear to God that I'll put a bastard bullet through your skull if you don't stand still." He waved the gleaming blaster at the horse. "And I'll drive the death rig with just the other three. Or hitch up one of the pack animals. You fucking hear me?"

He was so angry that he inadvertently fired the Colt Python, the Magnum round kicking up a furrow of mud and water in front of the recalcitrant horse, which promptly stopped being stubborn and stood, trembling, while Abe finally backed it into the traces.

By the time they were ready to go, the sun was well up, and Abe had the sinking feeling in his guts that his clumsy attempt at a rescue mission might be too late.

ONE OF THE DOGS, a lean and ferocious brindled mastiff, had been so blood-crazed that it had kicked and struggled to reach Ryan's hand on the hilt of the panga, even though that action drove the eighteen-inch steel blade deeper and deeper into its chest and lungs.

The animal had eventually died in a welter of choked blood that fountained over Ryan's fingers. It joined six of its brothers and sisters, which the one-eyed man had chilled as they came at him, howling and tearing, through the gap in the doorway.

At least five of the men in the gang lay sprawled and still in the opalescent light of early morning. The survivors had spread out across the hill, working their way closer to the tower, moving more slowly and cautiously after Trader had made good use of the last rounds of 9 mm ammunition.

Moving more slowly, but still moving.

The attackers were also short of ammunition, only firing occasionally, their bullets chipping stone splinters from the thick walls.

"Getting to be close," Ryan said. "Best wait now and stop shooting. That way we can at least be sure that every round buys us a corpse when they come in at us."

J.B. suddenly scrambled down to join them. "Time's come now. They're gathering for the big charge, about a hundred and fifty yards down the hill. Behind a tall hedge'll give them cover. This is it."

Trader sniffed. "I knew that little... What's his name? Would be too late."

"Abe," Ryan said. "His name's Abe."

Chapter Twelve

"Once you've lived with love, then you cannot truly ever live again without it."

Doc was pleased with the aphorism.

He was snug inside the sleeping bag, lying on his back, knees drawn up slightly into something like the fetal position. He'd had a vivid dream that faded even as he slithered back toward waking. He'd been on a railway train with Emily and the children, making a transfer to another platform for another destination. But he'd left a carryall and gone back to retrieve it. By the time he'd chased across the rambling station after his family, it was already aboard the next train.

It had been grotesquely full, with people hanging out of doors, squeezed through open windows. It was out of the question for Doc to board the packed coaches nearest him. There was a whistle and the train began to move off, shuddering with the load. He heard Emily calling out to him, though he couldn't see her face in the crowd.

"Don't worry, my dearest," he shouted confidently. "Wait for me and I shall be along shortly. Wait for me."

Then he was awakened by something.

"What?"

The night was still, with a breeze that seemed to spill over the end of the box canyon, out and along to the open plateau beyond. The fire was quite dead, the moonlight gleaming on the pile of soft white ashes.

Judas was lying down, asleep, still tethered securely to the tree by the pool.

Doc's nostrils twitched. In his Victorian youth he'd often smoked, either small black cigarillos or a meerschaum pipe that he believed made him look grave and mature. Since being dragged into Deathlands he'd totally abandoned the foul weed and had found his sense of smell and taste had both improved by quantum leaps and bounds.

There was the tang of sagebrush; the faint scent of the fire; the indescribable odor of water and wet earth; his own sweat; the film of oil that coated the action of the big Le Mat, lying by his side.

"Something else?" he whispered.

The scent was allusive, bringing back a memory of something from his distant past.

Doc lay still, brow furrowed, allowing his dozing mind to free-associate as it sought the reference for the slightly acrid smell.

A trip out with the family? A dull, damp afternoon in a large city. Perhaps it had been on one of their visits to Manhattan. But where had he smelled that odd, acidic scent? Little Rachel hadn't liked it. He was sure of that.

"Nasty, Papa." Her little face screwed up with distaste as she peered in through the bars.

"Bars," Doc breathed.

A cage?

The zoo!

"The lion house," he mouthed, feeling his heart leap into his throat with the sudden fear.

For several erratic, jerky beats of the heart, Doc found himself utterly unable to move a muscle. He lay there, staring fixedly at the sky, his breathing fast and shallow, aware that the scent was stronger.

And closer.

Control eased back into his body, and he started to turn his head to the left, infinitely slowly.

The cougar was crouched on its haunches, belly down in the dry dirt, less than twenty feet away from Doc, its golden eyes gleaming directly into his, fixed on him with an unearthly, blankly unemotional stare.

For a few moments Doc found that he'd forgotten how to swallow and breathe. His mouth was sandpaper dry, his tongue feeling eight sizes too large for his mouth. He knew that there was nobody within twenty miles who could come to his rescue. Even so, shouting for help was a physical impossibility.

He tried to judge how big the predator was, but his mind refused to cope with the question. Over the years Doc had seen other pumas, but they'd all been somewhere between six and ten feet in length.

This monster was closer to twenty-five feet, looking from the wedges of muscle across shoulders and back to weigh around half a ton.

The feathery tip of its long tail moved back and forth, just brushing the sand, the noise no louder than the breathing of a sleeping baby.

There was enough light for Doc to be able to see the tremors that ran across the powerful corded muscles, giving warning that the mutie animal was literally trembling on the edge of staging its attack.

Out of the corner of his eye, Doc could see that Judas wasn't going to save him this time. The mule was still locked away in deepest sleep.

Eternities passed.

Doc had cramps in his legs from the desperate struggle not to move or do anything that might finally trigger the cougar's murderous assault. As long as he was completely still, there was the one-in-a-thousand chance that the creature might lose interest and simply go away.

One in a million, said the tiny, scared voice inside Doc's head.

Now he could hear the cougar's rhythmic breathing, overlaying a faint sound of purring, like a distant buzz saw. Doc looked at the creature, finding that the animal's great yellow eyes were widening, seeming to draw him into their amber depths. It suddenly came to him that the cougar was deliberately hypnotizing him, like a snake with a petrified rabbit.

"I think not," he whispered, finding that some of the dryness had gone from his mouth.

The noise of his voice registered with the crouched beast. Its sharp ears flattened along its skull, and the purring ceased. But the twitching of the muscles along the back and thighs redoubled, and the cat's great jaws opened a little wider, enabling Doc to make out the gleam of moonlight on needle-sharp ivory.

Doc tried to remember everything he'd ever read about attacks by big cats. Often they brought up the powerful hind legs to disembowl their prey. Or they would use their front paws to slap at the victim, their claws ripping away chunks of flesh like a butcher's cleaver. But a cougar of this size could easily take a full-grown man's skull into its mouth and crunch it like ripe apple. Doc shivered.

"It is not death itself that I fear," he murmured, "but the manner of my passing."

The cougar growled softly, deep in its throat, at his words. And Judas stirred in its sleep. Doc lay between the two animals, and he hadn't a scintilla of doubt that the cougar would take him first. The noise of his slaughter would rouse Judas, but the mule would be equally helpless against a predator of that size.

"Sorry, Judas," Doc said.

He actually managed to smile at the thought that his famous last words would be addressed to a vile-tempered mule and wouldn't be heard by human ears, to lie forever, unrecorded in the endless dirt.

The cougar opened its jaws wide and Doc winced, closing his eyes in anticipation of the charge. There was the foul stench of the carnivore's breath, but no movement.

The cramp was insufferable and Doc could no longer stop himself moving. He wriggled to one side of his sleeping bag, groaning with the relief that the change of position brought him. Lying partly on his side, he found that his right arm was freed from the confines of the heavy bag.

"By the Three Kennedys!" The cougar watched curiously as the old man wormed his hand into the dirt at his side, until it encountered the cold weight of the Le Mat.

For the first time since he'd been tugged from sleep, Doc glimpsed the feeble candle-glow of hope. If he could bring up the blaster, cock it, aim it and fire . . .

Even a gigantic mutie cougar could bite broken teeth against the .63-caliber shotgun round.

He risked another sideways glance.

The predator responded by changing its own position, moving into a menacing crouch, the hind quarters rising in the air, the back legs braced to pounce. The tail was still moving, more and more slowly.

Stopping.

Doc's brother, Cyril Tanner, had once owned a small tabby kitten, which had ended its days crushed under the wheels of a brewer's wagon. Doc had often watched it hunting sparrows, or readying itself to leap on a trailed length of cotton in Cyril's trim apartment. He noted the way that its scrawny tail would move slower and slower, until, just a second before the attack, it would stop.

With the fluid ease of the professional shootist, Doc sat up, leveling the Le Mat and squeezing the trigger. The mutie cougar was actually in midspring at the moment that the blaster fired, its jaws open, front paws stretching out toward its helpless victim.

Doc had a splinter of a second of frozen horror to realize that he had missed. The great weight of the cougar landed on top of him, kicking and growling, one flailing hind paw knocking the Le Mat spinning from his hand.

There wasn't even time for a snatched prayer.

The old man's brain was enveloped in a vast shroud of black velvet that sucked him into its darkness.

DOC'S FIRST SENSATION was one of impending sickness. Overcome by nausea, before he was even properly awake again, he rolled onto his hands and knees, kicked away the entangling sleeping bag and puked, splattering into the dirt. His heaving stomach brought up the remnants of his supper, floating in a sea of yellow bile. The taste of his own vomit made him retch and moan again, mouth open, eyes squeezed shut.

It was a good twenty seconds before Doc remembered what had happened before he'd slipped into unconsciousness, the roaring leap of the monstrous cougar and the explosion of the blaster still ringing in his ears.

Now he was aware of noises, raging around him: splashing water, growling, the shrill whinny of a mule that he recognized as Judas. He wiped his mouth with the back of his hand and looked toward the pool.

Judas was standing, back pressed against the tree, the tethering rope as taut as an iron bar. The mule's head was back, eyes rolling white in the moonlight, facing the mutie predator that was moving at the edge of the dark pool that lay under the shadows at the head of the box canyon.

The cougar was still very much alive, snarling, standing hock-deep in the water, its gigantic head turning from side to side, seeming to be watching both the mule and the recovering man.

Doc looked around for his blaster, but he recalled it being knocked from his hand and it had disappeared into the bushes around his campsite.

The sword stick was still at his side, and he reached for it and stood, feeling his legs shaking as though he were suffering from typhoid.

The steel slid from its ebony sheath, and Doc had a brief moment of confidence. Then he looked down at the slender strip of metal, across at the half ton of ferocity a few yards away from him. His confidence ebbed away.

"*Morituri te . . .* Now what the devil was it that the gladiators used to say as they faced their ghastly ending in the sand and blood of the Roman arena? I fear that this encounter has turned my brain to a puddled gruel." Doc sighed. "*Salutamus?* Was that the word? It was a deep regret of my parents that I had small Latin and less Greek."

He walked cautiously toward the pacing cougar, peering at it, where it lurked in the dark shadows of the pool, seeing, for the first time, that the trusty Le Mat hadn't missed its target after all.

The thing was badly wounded.

What he'd initially thought were probably just streaked patterns of black mud on its golden pelt were slobbered patches of blood.

The 18-gauge shell from the gold-engraved commemorative blaster had struck the cougar between chest and head, the pellets starring out in a devastating pattern. Some had driven into the muscles across the upper ribs, some lacerating the mutie animal's throat. But the bulk of them had ripped directly into the giant cat's jaws.

The lower part of its mouth had been destroyed, leaving its tongue to flop obscenely onto its bloodied chest. One paw had also been hit and dangled from the shoulder, more blood dripping softly into the pool.

Despite its horrific injuries, the cougar was a country mile from being dead. It kept up a low snarling, limping back and forth in the shallows, its eyes watching both the tethered mule and the unsteady figure of the man.

"What now?" Doc said, advancing slowly, the sword blade ahead of him.

The mutie cat threw back its head and gave out a dreadful, strangled, choking roar of rage and pain. A spray of misty blood pattered in the water. It pushed Judas into a state of total panic, the mule jerking at the rope again and again, then starting to saw at the cord with its uneven teeth.

"It's all right, Judas, my dear old friend," Doc said, amazed at how shaky his voice had become.

The cougar decided the course of action, trying to leap at him, its shattered paw letting it down so that it toppled helplessly over into the water in a great welter of silvery spray. It emerged, shaking its massive head, picking its way through the mud toward the waiting man.

Doc swallowed hard and stood his ground. He straightened his right arm, tensing the wrist, and sighted along the slender blade of the rapier like a matador facing the moment of truth. He centered the point between the creature's shoulders, watching it carefully as it plodded toward him.

"Yes," he breathed.

The Le Mat had taken a lethal toll, sapping the cougar's energy, stealing away something of its heart for the kill. But it still made a try for Doc, rearing onto its hind legs, swinging its good paw at him, the unsheathed claws missing the old man by a whisper as he swayed back.

It dropped down again onto three legs, head lowered for a moment, giving Doc the single opportunity that he knew he would have to take.

The point entered precisely where he'd aimed it, and Doc leaned on the hilt with all his weight and strength, feeling it slide through muscle, nicking the spinal cord, passing on into the mutie animal's lungs.

To the heart.

It dropped like a sack of meat, eyes glazing, voiding a string of slimy, stinking fecal matter as it died.

Sensing the death, Judas stopped his thrashing panic, suddenly standing quite still, looking over its sweat-smeared shoulder toward Doc, who had withdrawn the sword from the dead cougar, kneeling to clean it in the dry sand, a little way off from the corpse.

"Well, now, upon my soul, but that was what writers might call a rather rude awakening, might they not, Judas? I would fling myself upon your neck and weep copiously as we comforted each other...were it not for the fact that I imagine you would snatch the opportunity to bite off my ear, you rascal, you." He walked back to his sleeping bag, sitting down rather more suddenly than he'd intended when his legs ceased to function.

"Shock. Clinical shock. Interesting phenomenon. Should have a mug of hot sweet coffee, but I fear I don't possess such a brew. Perhaps I'll sit awhile and rest and recover. After that, Judas, come the dawn, and my hands have stopped their recalcitrant trembling, we shall once again be up and on our way. With a fine adventure under our belts."

Then, somewhat to his surprise and shame, the closeness of his brush with a hideous death caught up with the old man, and he began to weep.

Chapter Thirteen

Abe went around a bend in the narrow, winding highway, carefully steering the team past a substantial pothole, knowing that the delicate wheels of the hearse wouldn't stand up to any serious jolting.

Once he'd gotten them hitched, they hadn't made bad progress. But the sun was already well up, glinting off the distant expanse of the sea, beyond the ruins of the ville. Abe had reined the horses in at the top of a steep hill, levering on the clumsy brake, appreciating for the first time just how vast Seattle had been. Then he realized the utter hopelessness of his lonely quest, the impossibility of trying to locate three men among the endless, barren wilderness of fallen stone and iron.

"Man who doesn't try, doesn't get," he said aloud to himself, unconsciously parroting one of Trader's base sayings. Abe released the brake, clicked his tongue and drove the hearse onward. He had seen that the road went down into one more dip, then breasted a shallow rise, close by what had seemed like the ruins of a predark water tower. From then on in it had looked all downhill.

THE ATTACKERS HAD MADE the mistake of sending in their surviving dogs before risking their own lives against the lethal trio of outlanders.

As the slavering, howling brutes hurled themselves into the gap between the broken door and the dusty stone, it was child's play for Ryan to neatly butcher each and every one with his panga.

Trader stared at the pile of steaming carcasses. "Now they'll come at us. Nothing for them to wait for."

Ryan wiped the blood-slick blade and stuck it, point-first, in the dirt by his feet. "Might as well keep it handy," he said. "Waste of time sheathing it."

J.B. had taken off his glasses, giving them a final wipe and polish. He carefully adjusted his fedora, then rubbed at the stubble on his pale face. "Would've liked to have a decent shave before . . . before we go."

Trader reached out suddenly and pulled both men to him, hugging them with a fierce grip. "Couldn't have chosen better company for this," he said, his voice nearly breaking with emotion. "Not even if I'd planned it."

Ryan nodded. "Thing is, Trader, if you *had* planned it, then it would have turned out better than this."

All three of them laughed, stopping as they heard howling from the hunting posse, a little farther down the hillside.

"Here they come, friends," J.B. said, levering a round under the hammer of the scattergun.

"Take some of the bastards with us." Ryan stood foursquare and waited, holding the SIG-Sauer loosely by his side.

After the initial yelling, to build up its own courage, the gang advanced in silence, more slowly, none of them keen to be the first at the tower.

In that menacing stillness, it was J.B. who first heard the noise.

"There's horses coming."

Ryan moved to the gap, keeping out of any line of fire, listening. "Yeah. I can hear harness jingling. Wheels rattling on the blacktop."

"Abe?" Trader gave a whoop of delight. "Well, that runty little son of a bitch came through."

"Best get out there to give him some cover." The Armorer squinted around the broken door. "Friends down the hill've heard it. But they can't see him yet. The rig's behind us, still in dead ground."

Now the sound of the hearse was much louder, Abe whooping at the leaders, cracking his whip, lashing at the backs of the team with the reins.

Ryan was first out, J.B. giving Trader a supporting hand into the open.

He heard a cry of anger, and a musket boomed, but the ball flew high and wide of them, striking chips of stone from the top of the old tower.

Once he was around the corner, Ryan saw the hearse, speeding toward them, like some creation out of a horror vid—the black horses, with their hooves striking fire from the pavement, the polished glass hearse gleaming in the morning sunlight. Abe saw him and stood on the box, flourishing the long whip, the swaying of the rig nearly throwing him off.

Ryan waved a hand to him, turning and firing two careful rounds from the automatic at the rushing mob, seeing the pair of men at the head both go down, rolling into the gutter in a tangle of arms and legs.

"Nice," Trader said dryly, as he hobbled past Ryan, taking cover with the Armorer behind the flank of the building. "I'll have a piece of the action with this—" he held up the Armalite "—before we get out of this place."

Abe was wrestling with the galloping, foaming horses. For a dreadful moment it looked to Ryan like the little gunner had completely lost control and was going to simply gallop past them, ending up in the middle of the posse.

But Abe pulled it off, slowing the team and starting to swing them around in a wide circle in the graveled drive of the water tower.

"Good man, Abe!" Trader shouted.

"Company down the hill," Ryan called, running to open the rear door. "Trader's taken a hit. Soon as we have him aboard, light out for the country."

A high-velocity rifle bullet whined off the blacktop, less than a yard from the rear wheels of the rig, the noise making one of the horses buck and rear.

Abe stayed up on the box, fighting for control. He looked over his shoulder, watching as the Armorer unlatched the rear door of the hearse and, helped by Ryan, heaved Trader inside.

"Leave it open," the old man yelled. "I can slow the fuckheads down from here."

"Whip 'em up, Abe!" Ryan shouted, standing for a few moments in the classic pistol-shootist's stance, arm extended, looking down the barrel of the SIG-Sauer. He fired several carefully spaced rounds at the advancing mob, putting down at least three men, sending the others scattering to find cover among the bushes and trees.

J.B. climbed quickly onto the box alongside Abe, hanging on the side rail, waiting for Ryan to join them.

The little gunner was poised, whip in hand, watching as the one-eyed man swung onto the foot plate. He didn't try to climb up alongside J.B. and Abe, knowing that he would only have impeded the driving of the team.

"Now."

The whip cracked, ringing out into the bright morning like a dueling pistol. The horses whinnied and began to move, hooves slipping. Abe bellowed at them, lashing them unmercifully to get the hearse on the road.

Ryan faced the rear, blaster in his hand, ready to open fire on any of their pursuers who were stupid enough to appear. Through the gleaming glass he could see that Trader had settled himself comfortably into a prone shooting position, Armalite at his shoulder.

From somewhere, J.B. had found a handful of pebbles and he was flinging them at the team, driving the animals to greater efforts.

The rifle barked, the noise muffled by the walls of the hearse and the sound of the horses working their way up to a full gallop.

Ryan was hanging on by his left hand, the toes of his boots only a scant inch or two from the rolling wheel. The first hesitant members of the pursuing mob appeared, and he put a couple of rounds in among them.

"They're giving up!" J.B. called, able to see better from the extra height of the seat.

"Don't flog them to death, Abe," Ryan yelled. "Don't want them blown in half a mile."

Trader fired once more, but the bucking of the wag over the uneven ribbon of highway made further shooting pointless. The first of the raggle-taggle posse had gathered by the old water tower, their jeering and cursing made feeble by the rising breeze. Then a turn in the blacktop took them out of sight.

Abe eased back, tugging on the reins to slow the team from a full gallop.

Trader whooped triumphantly from inside the hearse. "Done good, Abe, my man!"

"Want to come up on the box, Ryan?" J.B. asked. "Tight squeeze."

"No. I'm fine here. Thanks, Abe. Razor of the man in the black cloak was coming a tad close to our throats back there. You done good."

"Sure thing," the little gunner replied, grinning with pleased embarrassment. "Took me a long while to hitch up the horses, or I'd have been here quicker."

They were approaching an avenue of ancient yews, the dark green foliage thick and lush, some of the main branches spreading out over the road.

The attack came without warning.

Three men, all slim and wiry, dropped from the overhanging trees, two of them landing on the backs of the lead horses, the third aiming for Abe on the box. All held long-bladed knives.

Facing backward, muffled inside the body of the wag, Trader had no idea at all that they were suddenly under threat.

The first Ryan knew was when he heard the deep roar of J.B.'s Smith & Wesson 12-gauge and saw the flicker of movement out of the corner of his right eye.

The combat reflexes of the Armorer were so unbelievably fast that he actually shot the assailant while the man was still in midair, the twenty miniature darts hitting home in the lower belly, tearing the attacker's stomach and groin apart. The impact was so violent that the mortally wounded man was thrown back and to the side. He bounced off the neck of the near-side horse and rolled into the muddy ditch at the side of the highway, loops of greasy intestine spilling from the gaping gash.

Abe had both hands filled with the reins and could do nothing to dislodge the pair of attackers who were trying to saw through the harness and free the leaders from the traces.

Ryan managed to turn himself, fighting for balance against the pitching and swaying of the wag, seeing immediately that they faced a serious problem.

J.B. had been able to chill the first attacker without any trouble. But the other two were over twenty feet away from him, leaning close against the horses they were trying to steal. The scattergun's choke meant that the fléchettes would star out very quickly. At short range they were terminally lethal. If J.B. tried to shoot the two young men with the M-4000, he would inevitably cause terrible wounds to the animals.

"Take them, Ryan," he called.

It was a crucial moment.

If they lost the leaders, then it would no longer be possible to use the hearse for shelter and transport. They had no spare wag-trained horses, and the others wouldn't work in the team. The two remaining matched blacks couldn't pull the heavy rig any distance on their own.

Ryan hung out over the road, gripping the rail with his left hand, knowing that one slip would send him under the wheels of the hearse. Even with the SIG-Sauer, his problem was similar to J.B.'s. A miss would likely chill the animal. It could go down between the shafts and tip the hearse, still moving at a fast canter, over in a tangle of dead horses and splintered wood and glass.

"Keep 'em straight, Abe!"

Worried about shooting too low, Ryan fired the first bullet well over the head of the skinny man, adjusting his aim and putting the full-metal jacket round through the left shoulder. It drilled apart the scapula, angled down and smashed three ribs before exiting in a welter of blood and bone through the lungs.

The man screamed and dropped the knife. He slumped between the leaders, screaming once more as he was pounded by the horses, then pulped into end-less silence under the wheels of the hearse.

The leap made by the rig as it ran over the dying man nearly threw Ryan off.

Warned by the demise of his colleague, the last of the horse thieves had slipped farther down, out of range, hanging around the neck of the animal, still trying to use his knife to cut it free from the traces.

"Mine," Ryan shouted. He holstered the blaster and drew the panga, gripping it between his teeth, the steel cold and bitter on his tongue.

He steadied himself for a moment in front of the box, both feet on the bucking center shaft. The ground rushed by below him at what seemed a murderous rate, and he was deafened by the pounding of the hooves on the road.

"Don't let him take you with him, Ryan," J.B. called.

The sweat of the animals was rank in Ryan's nos-trils as he dived forward, fighting for balance, steady-ing himself on the backs of the rear pair of horses. He saw his adversary, crouched in front of him, a wiz-ened face like a monkey leering back, the knife blade waved menacingly in his direction.

Abe was still tugging on the reins, but the team was, if anything, going ever faster, thrown into a blind panic by the shooting and the smell of human blood that had sprayed over their flanks.

"Come on, outlander!" the figure raged. "Come on, get gizzard sliced."

Ryan could see that he'd almost succeeded in cutting the lead horse free. Another few seconds and the last of the traces would have been hacked through.

In any knife fight, the relative positions of the combatants were often crucially important. Hunched over between the animals, the little man had the distinct advantage. Ryan had to come at him, with no protection, facing the threat of the lethal upward cut at his stomach.

He stayed where he was, staring at his opponent, trying to work out the best way of attacking him.

"Come on, you bastard." Seeing Ryan hesitating, the small man took the opportunity to reach down to start cutting through the last inch or so of soft leather, to free the horse.

It wasn't much of a chance, but Ryan realized that it was the best he was likely to get.

He flung himself forward, the eighteen-inch blade adding to his longer reach. The wildwooder attempted to parry it, the sharp steel opening up a bone-deep gash in his left arm. It deflected the lunge from his throat, the point entering the side of his face, just below the right eye.

Ryan felt the jarring shock run up his arm as the blade grated against the flat plane of the cheekbone, then slipped upward into the wet softness of the eye socket. The man screamed once, shrill and thin.

Before the steel could be withdrawn for another, positively fatal stroke, Ryan had to duck quickly away from a savage upward thrust, nearly losing his grip on the blood-slick hilt of the heavy panga.

"You fuckin'..." his opponent grunted, a river of watery crimson flowing from the blinded eye.

Ryan jerked the blade free, slashing sideways at the man's throat, but it was again blocked by the desperate use of the forearm.

Totally panicked, the all-black team was raging along like the wind, hooves pounding, heads thrown back, eyes rolling white in scarlet sockets. Ryan was vaguely aware of angry yelling from J.B. and Abe, but they were a thousand miles away in some alternate universe.

Despite his hideous wound, the crouched figure hadn't given up. Trapped at the end of the shafts, with nowhere to go, he elected to try it all on a single, desperate throw. He punched with his left hand at Ryan's knife, jabbing with his own shorter blade as he dived toward his assailant.

Ryan had been expecting it and parried the clumsy charge easily, thrusting the panga home under the guarding ribs, feeling the tip catch the notch between two of the spinal vertebrae. Twisting his wrist with all of his power, he drove the eighteen inches of cold steel into the man's body, twisting it a second time as he withdrew it, knowing without any doubt that he'd won. The man was dying, his life hemorrhaging away through the long slit in his stomach.

But it wasn't over.

As he started to topple from the rig, the one good eye already starting to cloud over, the slender man grabbed at the sleeve of Ryan's coat.

He'd been in the act of backing away, already starting to sheathe his own bloodied blade, his concentration wandering, thinking how he'd be able to get back to the relative safety of the driver's box.

His balance had been precarious as the hearse bounced and jolted, fishtailing around a steep curve, the rear wheel on the near side spinning in singing space.

Now, with the mortally wounded man gripping his coat like a drowning man snatching at a spar, Ryan knew with a sick certainty that he was going over and off.

Using every ounce of his strength and agility, he managed to throw himself forward, knocking away the clinging fingers, reaching out for the back of the galloping leader, feeling slick, powerful flesh pounding under him.

The attacker slipped off, body draped across the wag hitch for a few thundering steps, then slipping away and vanishing under the hooves and wheels.

But Ryan knew he was safe.

For five or six seconds.

Until the sliced strips of leather finally parted under the strain of the galloping horse.

The powerful animal broke away from the rest of the team, carrying Ryan Cawdor, helpless, with it.

Chapter Fourteen

Mildred was stewing up some apples, helped by Dean. Krysty was sitting in the swing seat out on the porch, watching the morning shadows of the house shorten as the sun rose steadily behind her.

Jak had gone out to finish the milking, walking back toward her, slightly bowlegged from the weight of the two brimming buckets. His stark white hair blazed like a distress flare, tumbling over his shoulders.

"How do you think he's getting on?" asked the young boy in the kitchen, putting the big iron spoon to his lips, wincing at its heat. He blew hard to cool it so that he could taste the sweetened fruit.

"Who?" Krysty asked, as if she didn't know.

"Dad."

"Thought you might've meant Doc."

"Or John," Mildred interrupted. "And stop licking that spoon, Dean."

"Tastes good."

"Not the point. You can spread germs that way."

The boy looked at her, the spoon frozen halfway to his mouth. "What's germs, Mildred?"

"Germs are . . ." She laughed. "Never mind."

Krysty stood. "And the answer is that we think that they're all all right. All right?"

Dean grinned, lifting his left hand to push back an errant curl of black hair from over his blue eyes, sending a frisson through Krysty at the strong similarity between the boy and his father.

Jak had put the buckets of fresh milk on the back porch and he came into the kitchen, stretching. "Apples smell good," he commented.

"No sign of life?" Krysty asked.

"Nothing."

Mildred was washing her hands in the sink. "No sign of the old goat, either?"

The albino smiled. "Doc's fine. Got Judas to keep eye on him. Think needs time alone."

"We all do," Mildred agreed, drying her hands on a faded linen cloth. "But I guess Doc needs it more than most. Loss like he suffered comes hard."

Jak turned to stare at the black woman, his ruby eyes drilling into her face. "I know that."

"Shit, I'm sorry, Jak. Me and my big mouth. Least Doc's had some time to get over it. Still only weeks, really, since Christina and baby Jenny were..."

"'Murdered' is word," he said, turning away, his voice as cold as cemetery stone.

AFTER THE NOON MEAL, Jak went out back to repair a broken hinge on one of the barn doors. Dean did the washing-up, then drifted after the older boy.

The sky was clear of clouds. As he looked up, Dean spotted the familiar purple-silver streak of yet another piece of predark nuke space junk burning its way back through the atmosphere.

Though his back was turned, Jak seemed to sense the skyburst and looked up at it, shading his eyes, saying nothing.

"Want a hand?"

"Sure, Dean. Mebbe even two hands."

The eleven-year-old carefully unholstered his Browning Hi-Power and placed the heavy 9 mm automatic on a chopping block.

"Blaster's too much blaster for you," Jak said.

"You greasing my wheels? You know I can use it well enough, don't you?"

"Man doesn't need hammer kill gnat."

"But you need a tool big enough to do the job, Jak. Dad says a small blaster can be worse than no blaster at all. What do you say, huh?"

The teenager shook his head at the younger boy's burst of enthusiasm. "Wouldn't often argue Ryan. Knows most about most. More any man knew."

Dean nodded. "So you admit a good blaster's important, then, do you?"

"Sure. Times is. Times isn't."

"When isn't it?" Dean asked, rolling up his sleeves and looking at the weather-scarred wood of the big doors.

"When need quiet."

"Quiet?"

"Get wedge under door. Take weight. Hold steady while remove broke hinge."

For a couple of minutes they were both fully occupied in wrestling with the stubborn door, fighting as it tried to twist and topple over sideways and rip all three of the rusting iron hinges from the frame.

Dean soon found that his dark-blue work shirt was soaked with sweat. But he was never one to give up as long as he had breath left in his body. Eventually they had the cross-framed door propped up in the right position for Jak to carry out the necessary repair work on it.

"Take five," the teenager said.

Dean slumped down, feeling the muscles like strips of fire across his shoulders and chest. His fingers were sore, and he had two broken nails and a cluster of splinters that he would have to ask Mildred to remove for him later.

"Done good," Jak said, making the boy flush with pride. Other than his father, Jak Lauren was the closest thing to a hero that Dean knew.

"Thanks. You were talking about blasters not being good all the time."

"Sure. No good when need quiet."

"Obvious. That when you use your knives?"

"Yeah."

Despite the heat of the afternoon, Jak was still wearing his usual jacket, the one made from leather and canvas, with tiny strips of razored steel sewn into it. He sat and leaned against the wall of the outbuilding, closing his eyes, looking totally relaxed. Dean stared at him, seeing the three scars that seamed across Jak's face. An ancient cicatrix sliced jaggedly across the left cheek, tugging the corner of the mouth up into something that might be mistaken for a smile. The other two scars, one along the jaw and the other close to the mouth, had been caused by a run-in with cuddlies.

"Don't like being watched, kid," he said suddenly, eyes blinking open.

"Don't like being called 'kid,' Jak." He waited a moment to make sure that the teenager wasn't seriously angry with him. "Show me your knives?"

"Which ones?"

"Throwing knives."

"No."

"Please, Jak?"

"Point is knives are hid. Well hid. Show you and one day you tell someone else and I'm chilled."

Dean was shocked. "I'd never betray you, Jak. I'd never betray anyone."

The albino shook his mane of pure white hair. "Not so, kid. Sorry. Not so, Dean."

"It is so!"

"Everyone has breaking point."

"Not me. I'd rather die than betray anyone, Jak. You can't be serious, man."

"Nothing more serious, Dean."

"I'd chill myself, if it came down to that."

"Sure would. Me too. Not always real possible. Seen good men—and good women—break down and cry. Give up daughters, sons, mothers, fathers, brothers, sisters. Couldn't take it."

Dean coughed. "You say so, Jak. Krysty reckons you can sort of take yourself out of the pain, where they can't touch you with it. You heard her say that?"

"Yeah. Believe her. Don't know could do it. Not when triple evil comes calling."

While the sun shone down and the cooling breeze blew across the New Mexico wilderness, Jak Lauren told the boy about a time of betrayal.

IT HAD BEEN when Jak was only eight years old and a member of his father's gang, fighting against the dreadful oppression of Baron Tourment in the swamps of Louisiana.

It had been high summer and one of the baron's sec patrols had caught a senior lieutenant of the gang, a man in his middle thirties, with intimate knowledge of all the secret routes through the treacherous bayou country, as well as knowledge of numbers, camps, weapons and plans.

"Name was Al Brooks. Lost two fingers to gator and two more to gaudy slut in Tallahassee. Tough son of bitch. His son, Ike, was good friend."

Tourment had Brooks held prisoner in a cell on a small island, close to his base. The man was naked, and chained hand, foot and neck. He had no way of moving at all.

Jak's father had sent him in at night, the pale-skinned child smeared with stinking mud and gator shit. He slid through the dark waters like a moccasin snake, waiting for an hour, as still as a log, watching for his moment. He scampered to the hut and used his preternatural agility to worm his way onto the roof. Then he burrowed patiently through the overlapped leaves until he was perched on a supporting beam, able to see and hear everything without being seen or heard.

"Guard all time. Got Armalite. Like they say Trader carries. Couldn't do anything help Al."

All the ghostly little boy could do was sit and observe while Brooks was tortured by Tourment's henchmen. The baron himself had told his prisoner that he would only bother to come and see him when he'd been softened up, ready to spill his guts and betray the others.

"Took turns. Torture's fuck-tiring to do. Hour and need rest from it."

Dean asked him how long he'd stayed hidden.

"Dark to day. Day to dark. Lose sense time."

Jak explained how the best torture was subtle. Anyone could break arms or knock out teeth. But that was crude and clumsy and often resulted in the accidental and premature chilling of your victim.

"Break spirit and you break body. Bit at time. Repeat it again and again, so he knows won't ever stop. Until talks."

Al Brooks had reached the point.

Each of his remaining fingers and toes had been slowly and delicately broken; each knuckle had been crushed. Most of the major joints had been dislocated, including elbows, shoulders, knees and hips.

The litany of horror had gone on and on.

"And women had worked on cock and balls and—"

At that point Dean, his own face almost as pale as the whispering narrator of the horror story, had held up a hand.

"I get the picture. Yeah, I see."

Jak had nodded, unsmiling. "Al was ready talk to Baron Tourment."

"So? What did you do?"

"We should be finishing door."

"Come on, Jak. Please?"

"Waited until guard went out to take leak. Dropped down. Al saw me. Think recognized me. Tried to speak."

"What did he say?"

The albino sniffed and shook his head. "Can't tell. Never listened. Cut throat quick and hard. Guard heard death rattle. Came back. Saw little eight-year-old kid. Slowed reactions. Cut his throat too."

Dean clapped his hands together, whooping delightedly. "Hot pipe! That showed the bastards!"

Jak was on his feet with a startling speed, his hand lifted as though he were about to slap the boy. Dean shrank, his right hand going for the turquoise hilt of his knife. But Jak let his arm drop down.

"Dean, you got good sense for young boy," he said very quietly. "But you gotta learn lesson that chilling and torture aren't . . . fun."

The boy stood, looking around, eager to change the subject and ease his own embarrassment. "Can't you just show me your throwing knives, Jak? Please?"

"Right." The teenager looked, pointing to a circular blemish on the feather-edge timber wall of the barn. It was about the size of a man's palm, roughly thirty feet from where Jak was standing. "See that, Dean?"

"Sure."

"Watch it."

The boy kept one eye on the slightly built teenager, seeing how he stood in a half crouch, looking both tense and relaxed at the same time. Both hands dangled loose at his sides, fingers flexing, as if he were practicing to play a complex piano concerto.

"Give word, Dean."

"Ready and *go!*"

The albino seemed to slide into a bizarre, shifting dance, spinning at least twice, maybe three times. He dropped into a deeper crouch and straightened to his full height of five feet four inches. His hands were a blur of movement.

Dean heard a number of small, hard thudding sounds, but they came so close on top of one another that he couldn't hope to count them.

He turned to look at the blemish on the barn wall. "Holy shit!"

Six short knives quivered in the wood, every one within that tiny area.

"I would have bet you couldn't get them all in there, Jak."

Catfooted, graceful, the teenager walked toward the barn to retrieve his weapons. "Would've lost."

Chapter Fifteen

At the best of times and on the best of horses, Ryan would never have considered himself to be one of the world's great riders.

Sprawled half on and half off a powerful runaway carriage horse, hanging on to its mane to save himself from taking a terrible fall, Ryan was totally out of control.

The animal was going at a full gallop, the severed harness and reins trailing dangerously in the mud and dirt. Every single pounding step sent an agonizing jolt through Ryan's stomach and groin, making him feel desperately sick.

His legs hung down, so that the toes of his trailing combat boots were only inches from the highway. The vibration made it impossible to even see where they were going.

There was a real temptation to just give up and let go, open his cramped fingers and release the coarse hair of the black mane, slide off the side of the charging horse and take his chance on making a safe landing.

A tiny part of his mind was intrigued by the fact that he wouldn't have hesitated to try to save himself by throwing himself off the side of a wag traveling at an equivalent speed. But there was something about the raw animal power of the horse and its pounding contact with the highway that made the prospect much more frightening.

Trader's voice shouted inside his brain. "Man don't try, don't get."

The horses' skin was slippery with sweat, and Ryan's groping left hand was losing contact. Making an enormous effort, he kicked out with both feet, simultaneously heaving with his right hand on the flying mane.

He was so successful that it nearly turned into a lethal disaster.

Ryan's desperate effort heaved him up onto the animal's broad back—and nearly straight off, head-first, the other side.

With a struggle he got his legs astride, head leaning forward on the horse's neck, both arms grasping it. The first sensation was of his balls being jellied by the uneven stride, but he managed to acclimate to that, rising and falling with the horse, rather than against it.

"Fireblast!"

Now Ryan had a transient, fragile sensation of security. Not total safety, but at least some measure of control over his own destiny.

He tried shouting at the animal to slow it, but there was no response. Ryan risked a glance behind him, nearly losing his balance, and saw no sign of the hearse or of his friends. The carriage horse was still thundering along at a full gallop, heading in a vaguely southeasterly direction, out and away from the heart of the ville.

The houses were more scattered, gardens bigger, the trees and bushes thicker. Not far off, to the left, Ryan glimpsed water, shining beyond the lush grass of a wide meadow. Some rotted tables might once have been at the heart of a picturesque area for picnics.

The sight gave him hope.

Not letting go of the mane with his right hand, he stretched up and grabbed hold of the animal's pricked left ear with his own left hand. The powerful head jerked away, but he persisted, digging in his nails, pulling at it, making the horse whinny in angry, pained protest.

But it had some effect.

They veered a little toward the left, still staying on the road, but edging toward a screen of sagebrush that guarded the flank of the pasture.

Ryan tugged harder, feeling blood trickle over the velvety softness of the animal's ear, over his own clenched fingers, down his arm.

Unable to shake him off, the horse had to follow, cutting to its left, vaulting the sagebrush as though it weren't there. The noise of its hooves was instantly softened by the damp grass that brushed by, fetlock-high. Clouds of tiny insects, with iridescent wings, rose about them.

The horse was slowing from the full, flat-out gallop, but still going too fast for Ryan to want to risk throwing himself off his precarious perch.

The water was getting closer.

It was a large pool, roughly semicircular, fringed with tall reeds, looking to Ryan's blurred vision to be about one hundred paces across. There was no way to judge how deep the water might be, or what kind of dangerous mutie creatures might dwell below the mirrored surface.

"Slow down, you bastard," he grunted, hanging on desperately as the black horse tried to shy away from the tearing pain in its left ear.

Ryan banged his nose on the animal's neck as it jerked away, bringing tears to his eye, and a trickle of crimson running down his chin.

Now the lake was very close.

As the horse reached the fringe of the water, it kicked up a rainbow spray. Ryan knew that this was going to be about as good a chance as he'd get.

"Yeah!" he shouted, letting go of the mane and the lacerated ear and bailing out.

He experienced a moment of flight, then the air became water. Ryan swallowed a huge mouthful of the large pool, nearly choking as he rolled, helplessly, over and over.

Light and dark and light again.

The fear of drowning receded as he kicked and struggled, finding that the lake was less than four feet deep. He stood, sucking in great breaths, seeing that the panicked horse had also been stopped by the water, standing belly-deep, less than twenty yards from him. It was trembling as though it had an ague, head drooping, sweat caked across its chest, a worm of blood inching down from the damaged ear.

Ryan waded out into the sweet grass and sat down to wait for the others to arrive.

"THINK WE'RE FAR ENOUGH from that howling posse?" Abe asked as he leaned forward to throw another couple of branches onto the fire.

J.B. had fieldstripped his scattergun and was carefully wiping it dry and clean with a cotton rag. "Must've covered eight or nine miles since we lost them. We're way outside the ville now."

Ryan nodded. He'd taken off most of his wet clothing, hanging them on an elaborate framework of sticks by the fire, while he kept himself warm in the afternoon sunshine, bustling around with a blanket across his shoulders, replacing the cut harness. "Agreed," he said.

Trader was stirring some herbs that he'd gathered into a thick greenish ooze in a pot on the hot ashes at the edge of the flames. He was making himself a poultice that he swore Silver Light Feet, a Native American shaman, had shown him how to prepare, which would take away any risk of infection from the long, shallow knife wound across his ribs.

"Reckon we shouldn't stay camped here for the night. If the sickheads really want us, they could be here in less than three hours."

"They've had enough," J.B. said.

"We thought that about the posse that nearly chilled me," Abe insisted. "They kept coming after us and then kept on coming some more."

They were all silent for several long seconds, each man preoccupied with trying to work out the degree of risk that they faced.

Ryan spoke first. "True, Abe." He turned to Trader. "You were the one who taught me never to underestimate how triple stupe a vengeance gang can be."

The older man nodded. "I did, didn't I, Ryan? Damn right that I did. Well, we better get a move on, hadn't we?"

SINCE THERE WAS NO SIGN that the mob from Seattle had any form of transport, there was no great hurry. They allowed the team to draw the hearse on at a steady pace, with the packhorses tied behind. The friends took turns to drive the rig into the surrounding hills, with Trader stretched out at ease in the back, recovering from his injuries.

The weather had turned much more mild, with a gentle breeze from the southeast caressing their faces.

They stopped only once before evening for everyone to relieve himself, J.B. stopping the hearse at the crest of a steepish hill to give the team a break.

Trader's wounds had stiffened during the ride, and he had to be helped down. He cursed as he stumbled and nearly fell, hanging on to Abe's arm.

"Bitching bastard!" He spit in the dirt. "I'll be hung, quartered and dried for the crows! There's times I wished I'd died before I got to be old."

He steadied himself against the smooth trunk of an elegant silver birch while he urinated.

There was the roofless remains of a brick shelter near where they'd stopped, and Ryan wandered over to take a look, finding faded graffiti on one wall that had been protected from the harsh prevailing winds.

Two different hands had written it. The first in crimson had been sprayed on. "We shall drive a tunnel of hope through the mountain of despair" was followed by the initials MLK.

Underneath in white, less elegantly daubed, was "The mountain of despair fucking fell in on our tunnel."

"HOW FAR DO YOU RECKON we are from the ville?" Abe asked, lying on his back by the fire, arms crossed under his head, staring at the star-spangled banner of the sky.

"Twenty miles," Ryan replied.

"Nearer twenty-five." J.B. polished his glasses, angling them to the flames to check for smears.

Trader was changing the dressing on the knife wound, peering down at it. "Look healthy to you, Ryan?" he asked.

"Too early to be sure. Can't see any redness spreading away from it. How's it feel? You must've had enough cuts in your life to be able to figure if it's healing."

"Yeah. Times it feels bad. Times it feels worse. When you get past the big five-oh, Ryan, you discover everything takes a lot longer than it used to."

Abe laughed. "I found that happened when I passed the big three-oh, Trader." He sat up. "Takes me all night to do what I used to do all night."

"Nice one, Cohn."

Abe looked at Trader. "Not Cohn."

"I know you're not! You're Abe, aren't you? What do you mean saying I called you Cohn? He was one of the navigators. And communications. Think I don't know that?"

Nobody spoke.

Ryan reached out and helped himself to another hunk of bread, spreading it with the sweet orange preserve that they'd liberated from the ranch.

Trader was smiling again, seeming to have instantly forgotten his sudden fit of red anger. "Meant to ask you boys something."

"What?" Ryan wiped crumbs from his stubbled chin.

"You heard any word of a gang come into Deathlands from some other place?"

"Russkies?" J.B. asked. "Over the narrows up by Alaska? Had a run in with them once."

"No, not the fuckin' Russkies!"

"Who?"

"Chinese or Japanese. Nobody seems to know for sure. But they're yellow as gold, with slitty eyes. Heard word of them every now and again, when I was traveling way up north."

"Orientals?" Ryan queried. "I come across them a lot. Specially out the West Coast, inland from what used to be California, and around some of the ruins of the big villes, east.''

Trader shook his head, massaging his bruised leg with both hands, bending and flexing the knee. ''They got a name. Word like 'Sam an' I.' Real weird name.''

''Samurai?'' J. B. said. ''Was that the name you heard, Trader?''

The smile broadened. ''That was it! By God, J.B., but you got brains where other people just have hard white bone. That was it. Samurai.''

''I heard the word.'' Ryan finished eating. ''What are they, J.B.?''

''Warrior cult from Japan. Not from China, I think. Kind of dedicated traveling sec men. Used swords. Sort of a bit like priests, as well.''

''You mean, there's a gang of these guys around Deathlands, Trader?'' Abe asked.

''What I heard. Never met anyone actually seen them. Someone's brother knows a gaudy slut in some pesthole who heard a traveler say he saw a dying man who'd had a run with them. But you keep hearing the same sort of story. My belief is that you don't get steam without hot water.''

''You believe this, Trader?'' Ryan looked across the fire at his former chief.

''I reckon that you can live a long while by ignoring rumors and stories like this one. Then, just when you thought you'd made it across the river, one of them rumors jumps up, alive and grinning, and tears out your throat. Know what I mean?''

Ryan nodded. ''Yeah. Know what you mean.''

"Thing is, I heard first of them far up north. Then each time there was a story of these Samurais, they were getting farther south. Organized like a regular little army, someone told me."

"From what I read about them, it would only take a few to run a ville. Incredible discipline." J.B. whistled between his teeth. "Sure would like to see them."

"If they exist," Ryan added.

"Sure. If they exist."

THERE WAS NO DISCUSSION about whether they'd need to post a guard during the night.

Ryan took the last watch, through the small hours of the night, into the dawn. He sat by the dying embers of the fire, shrouded in a thick blanket, looking across the land, where pockets of white mist filled the hollows.

Now that he and J.B. had found Trader, and the old man had fulfilled his wish to visit the ruins of the ville, there was nothing to prevent them from setting out for home again.

Ryan felt a lifting of his spirits at the thought of seeing Krysty, Dean and the others again.

Chapter Sixteen

They lost the hearse four days later.

It wasn't a dramatic accident, no rumbling fall of packed mud and snow, no ambush by screaming wildwooders, no forest fire with the flames leaping like napalm grens from tree to exploding tree, no flash flood.

Ryan was at the reins, at the head of the party, as they made their way cautiously along a badly rutted side road, south of Mount Rainier, not all that far from the ville of Yakima. Abe and J.B. rode saddle horses, leading the pack animals. Trader's leg and knife wound were both much improved, but he had taken a liking to riding in style inside the glass-walled wag, lying back on blankets, watching the world move serenely by him.

It was early morning, a little after eight o'clock by Ryan's wrist chron. There had been a sharp frost overnight, which left a layer of gray ice coating the puddles and rutted pools along the trail.

Most of them were only a couple of inches deep, but Ryan had still been very carefully, easing the team along.

There was a sudden cracking of ice, and a far louder cracking of wood. The hearse lurched to the right, nearly throwing Ryan from the box. Trader yelled out in dismay, sliding sideways, nearly crashing through the polished glass.

The team reared and kicked, unable to move on, while Ryan hauled at the reins, trying to calm the leaders. He looked over his shoulder to see that the rear right wheel had grated down into a far deeper pothole than any of the others.

And had simply disintegrated.

The metal rim had immediately buckled, and the delicate painted spokes had proved unequal to the pressure. They snapped one by one, the whole wheel crumbling into the frozen mud, dropping that corner of the rig, the distorted suspension springs protesting noisily.

"NO CHANCE," J.B. said, once a degree of order had been established from the chaos.

The team had been unhitched and tethered in a nearby grove of larches, along with the pack and saddle animals. Trader had been helped out of the back of the toppled rig, rubbing his elbow where he'd taken a nasty blow.

Ryan shook his head sorrowfully. "Yeah. No way we can repair that."

"Mean losing some of the provisions," Trader said. "Pack animals are already carrying good loads."

J.B. disagreed with him. "Not like when we left that place, Trader. We've eaten a fair bit since then, as well as using some of the ammo."

Abe nodded. "True. I reckon we can strap blankets and stuff on the saddle horses."

"Why not use the four blacks? Shame to let good horses go to waste." Trader fingered his Armalite. "Least we can do is butcher a couple of them."

"We got meat." Ryan looked at the matched team. "Fine animals. Be a shame to slaughter them just like that. I reckon we could use them to barter for more food." He was proved right the next afternoon.

They had seen a side trail, with a notice warning strangers that it was the Springham Ranch. "You got business then come ahead, but if you don't then you best keep out. Ignore this and you don't even get buried."

"Friendly," Abe commented.

"Businesslike," Trader said.

TRADER WAS RIGHT.

They passed two sec gates, each time being looked over by hard-eyed, unsmiling men who wanted to know what they wanted at the spread. The guards waved them through when they were satisfied, muttering into short-range walkies the news of the four strangers' arrival.

Before they got to the main house, which was built like a miniature fortress with an encircling moat and gun towers, half a dozen more cowboys halted them.

"You want to deal them blacks?" asked the ramrod, a tall man in a poncho, smoking a narrow cigar.

"Sure. For provisions," Trader replied. "Like to know who I'm talking to."

"Name doesn't matter. Deal with me, you deal with the Springham place. All you need to know, old-timer."

Ryan felt the sudden tension and wished he was on his feet rather than high in a saddle. If Trader had one of his red rages, then there would be a lot of blood spilled.

"Shame that your ma and pa never bothered to teach you any manners and respect," Trader said, the Armalite balanced easily on his lap.

"Who the fuck do you think you are, old man, talking to me like that with two guns to your one?" He laughed. "You sure got some nerve."

"I'm called Trader. This is Ryan Cawdor, J.B. Dix and the little guy's Abe."

"Trader's long dead." But the note of confidence was gone. Ryan could see the other six hands shuffling and glancing at one another. "Died up near the South Fork of the Brazos."

Trader sniffed. "I don't have the time to talk to the performing bear. I got four good wag horses to deal. You want to do it, then let's get on. If you don't, then move out of my way, kid."

"You really Trader?"

"One way to find out and..." He stopped, swallowing, controlling himself with a visible effort. "We got off on the wrong foot here. We carry on and there'll be some widows and orphans by sundown. Can we trade?"

"Yeah, sure," the cowboy replied quickly. "Sure."

It didn't take long.

Everyone involved knew the quality of the four black horses, and there was little attempt to haggle.

At one point Ryan noticed a short, stout man with gray hair walk out onto a balcony at the front of the house and study the proceedings through a pair of binoculars, the sun glinting off the lenses.

"That Springham?" he asked.

The ramrod looked around. "Sure is. Grandson of old man Springham."

"Bart the name of the grandfather?" Trader asked.

"Yeah. Founded this spread. Comanche got him, hunting south. Must be thirty years ago now. What's left of him got brought back and buried in the family mausoleum out back by the stream. You knew him?"

"I knew him."

THE SUN WAS SINKING behind the hills as they finally got off the Springham land, with an extra packhorse in tow and enough smoked and cured meat to keep them going for at least the next three weeks.

Trader reined in his gelding and looked back, his face splitting into a broad grin.

"What's so funny?" J.B. asked.

"Close call."

"When he called you old-timer, you mean?" Abe queried. "Thought you were going to lead off and blow him clean out of his boots."

"Not that."

Ryan made a guess. "The little guy watching us from the balcony of the house?"

"Gettin' warm, pard."

"His grandfather. One called Bart."

Trader's grin grew even broader. "Gettin' positively hot, Ryan."

"You said you knew him." J.B. was beginning to get the story. "How come?"

Trader punched his right fist into his left hand, loud enough to make all the horses prick their ears.

"Old story, John Dix."

"Wasn't Comanche, was it, Trader?" Ryan felt his shirt sticking to his back with sweat and eased his shoulders. "Wasn't any fireblasted Comanche at all."

"Hell, I knew the name was familiar. But thirty years ago, Ryan."

"You knew they thought it was Indians that did for this Bart Springham?"

"Sure, sure." He hesitated. "Well, didn't really sort of *know* it."

"You could've gotten us all chilled there, Trader." J.B. removed his fedora and banged dust off it, then replaced it. "Dark night! All of us."

"Slipped my memory. Common sort of name. Think I can remember every single man, woman...or child I ever sent over the black river? Bart Springham. Yeah. Little feed off the Pecos. Had three men with him. Kids, tell the truth. I always figured he had a taste for young boys. I came to his camp. Fed me. Had a beautiful Winchester repeater."

"Which you went and stole." Ryan couldn't believe it. "I heard that story a dozen times from you, Trader. Two of the boys were jerking off, they spotted you sneaking out the camp with the blaster."

"Right. Used the rifle. Five bullets to waste all four of them. Damned lovely gun, that Winchester. Silver inlay and engraved."

"I remember that good old story, too, from the war wag times." Abe laughed. "You lost the blaster in a buffalo run the very next day, didn't you?"

Trader held up a hand like he was sitting in a court of law. "As God is my witness, Abe, I cannot tell you a lie. Just the way it was."

"And that was Bart Springham you murdered, Trader?" Ryan felt his own anger building. "Then because of your memory like a torn fishing net you let us ride straight into the mouth of hell. Brilliant."

"Nothing happened, Ryan." There was a hint of an apology in Trader's voice.

J.B. heeled his horse forward. "More luck than judgment, wasn't it, Trader?"

Nobody spoke for the next quarter hour.

Two NIGHTS LATER, in a desolate area, it seemed safe enough to camp without putting out a watch. The horses had been skittish all day, and there was no doubt in anyone's mind that they would give instant warning of anything or anybody approaching.

They were at the bottom of a sheer-sided canyon, having picked their way down a steep trail that doubled back on itself like a brain-dead rattler. The river was fast-flowing for most of its visible length, but the track came to it at a place where there was a stretch of shallows, making fording easy.

The banks were wide enough at that point to drive a wag along them, though it looked through the distant pillar of spray as though they quickly narrowed downstream. There were scrub willows, and a grove of slender aspens, nearby.

As evening closed down and the light faded, the animals became even more restless.

"Could be a cougar around," Trader suggested.

"Or just the noise of the river." Ryan had checked a little way around their campsite but found no tracks of any predator. No tracks of any kind.

Just as they were dropping off to sleep they all heard the rumble of a rockfall, somewhere farther up the canyon. But it wasn't repeated and they all slept well.

RYAN HAD BEEN DREAMING. There had been some sort of ancient temple, hewn from the living sandstone, with immense humanoid figures around its periphery that towered so high into the sky it made your neck hurt trying to look up at them.

Priests in feathered headdresses carried short axes of black stone. Some of the men wore ornately carved masks of birds and lizards, with golden beaks and teeth.

Twenty-eight columns stood around the site. Though he didn't know how he knew it, Ryan knew that they all had mystic and astrological alignment and significance. The mysterious name Aldebaran came to him.

There was a noise like a huge drum beating, its resonance so deep that it moved the marrow of his bones.

And shouting. Screaming. Women screaming, high and shrill, the sound barely human.

More like horses.

"Horses," he whispered, turning in his sleep.

"Horses," Ryan repeated, his eye flicking open.

The moon was close to being full, hanging over the canyon, throwing everything into brilliant silver light and razored black shadows.

He tried to sit up, seeing that the line of horses was totally freaked, rearing and kicking one another, eyes rolling, froth dribbling from their bared teeth.

But Ryan couldn't even sit up, fighting against the ground that was trembling, waves of movement shaking him. A deafening noise thundered below the earth.

"Quake!" he shouted, his voice feeble, barely audible, even to himself, above the limitless power and wrath of nature.

The air began to fill with dust and spray, and Ryan was chillingly aware that the whole of the huge canyon was folding in around them.

It felt like the end of the world.

Chapter Seventeen

The morning after the run-in with the giant mutie cougar, Doc was in excellent spirits.

He had left the place of death before breaking his fast, leading Judas out of the canyon, onto a narrow trail that Jak had told him about, one that would take him higher, into a region of clear streams and still lakes.

The trail was lined with piñon pines, their heavy scent filling the air as the sun rose to warm them. Twice he passed extensive alpine meadows, covered with an assortment of delicate wildflowers. Among them were carpets of the so-called Deathlands daisy, with its fragile green stem and corona of white petals surrounding the golden heart.

As Doc munched on an apple, washed down with a drink of crystal clear water from a spring nearby, he was able to lie back on the cushioning grass and relax.

Judas was tied securely to a lightning-blasted juniper a few paces away, munching contentedly.

"If there is such a place on this blighted Earth that might still seem to be the Garden of Eden, then this must come close," Doc said.

He stretched out his thin legs, wincing at the creaking from his knees, looking at the cracked patina of dusty polish on his high boots.

"I swear that my dear wife would not have tolerated such sartorial sloppiness. If it had been possible, Emily would have insisted that the sun wiped its feet before entering our front parlor."

He lobbed the core of the apple to Judas, who totally ignored it, then closed his eyes and thought back to the all-too-brief time of happiness. He remembered their fifth wedding anniversary, their last wedding anniversary before the white-coats from the future trawled him away forever.

Jolyon had awakened them from his bassinet in the corner of their bedroom, insistent that it was past time for him to receive some sustenance.

His mewling cries woke his sister, Rachel, who had graduated to sleeping in her own little bed in the anteroom beyond the open door. She had climbed out in her nightdress, eyes blinking, rubbing at them with her pudgy fists.

"Ith thomething wrong, Mama?" she asked, in her sweet lisping voice.

Emily had thrown back the coverlet, with its simple Amish design, allowing the child access to their bed.

"This seventeenth day of the month of June, in the year of Our Lord 1896, is most special to us, my chickadee," she said. "For it was on this day, five years since, that your papa and I pledged our troths to each other."

Rachel had wanted to know what that meant, and Emily Tanner, cradling baby Jolyon to her breast, had tried to explain to her the significance of the marital vows.

"It means that Papa and I will love each other, and try to do what each other wants. And it doesn't matter whether we are in good health or whether we shall sometimes become a tiny bit poorly. For as long as we both shall live."

"Won't you and Papa live forever?" Doc remembered how the scarlet ribbons in Rachel's hair had bobbed and bounced as she'd asked that question. It was as clear in his memory as though it had only happened yesterday.

Emily had laughed and squeezed his hand, kissing him gently on the cheek. "Of course, my sweet angel," she replied. "Papa and I intend to live forever."

"Forever," he whispered to himself. "My own words, a thousand times."

He sat up abruptly, sniffing, wiping away a tear that had trickled down his cheek.

"Mustn't give way to this," he said fiercely, his angry voice making Judas turn his head toward him.

Doc stared, unseeing, across the beautiful land.

The memories crowded in, day and night, sleeping and waking. Yet life in Deathlands with Ryan and the others tended to be somewhat hectic, not giving time for any serious, considered thoughts about what he should do.

The old man sighed. "Dearest Emily," he said quietly.

IT WAS such a heavenly morning that Doc decided to forgo the dubious delight of splitting his groin apart on Judas's serrated spine.

He chose to walk, leading the mule by its bridle, picking his way along the pebbled trail.

Judas had mixed feelings about this change of role. At first the animal had seemed pleased with its burden-free day. Then, with its own singular perverseness, the mule decided that Doc was treating it badly, slighting it.

First it nipped at his hand, snagging its long, yellowed teeth on the sleeve of the faded frock coat. Doc virtually ignored the attack, brushing at the mule as though it were an importunate mosquito.

"Pray desist," he said mildly.

But the mule was insistent in its own malevolent way. It waited for a slightly downhill section of the trail to make a four-footed jump forward, taking Doc by surprise. Its attack was actually too successful, and it overshot its target. The intention had been to nibble a slice out of the back of Doc's right thigh, but Judas banged its muzzle into the old man's skinny buttocks, quite missing its bite.

"Whoreson bastard! By the Three Kennedys, but it's time for another lesson, you ditch-spawned drab!"

He looked around and spotted a fallen ponderosa pine a few yards off the trail, tugging at the bridle and pulling the stubborn animal after him. He looped the reins around a broken branch to hold the mule still.

"Judas by name and Judas by nature. You damnably traitorous brute. Trying to take a pound of my poor flesh rather than your thirty pieces of silver. If there was a convenient tree, I would happily string you up like your treacherous namesake. Since there isn't..."

He reached down and drew out his blaster, flourishing it at the mule.

"See this? It is one of only five hundred ever made. Etched, gilded and polished with gold. The General Stuart commemorative Le Mat pistol. Jeb Stuart. Let me search my memory for a moment. Jeb. John Ewell Brown Stuart. Good. The little cells of my memory still function in part. Now, Judas, I propose to beat you harshly about the head with this fine example of American workmanship. It weighs in at around three and a half pounds and might drive a small measure of sense into that vexatious skull of yours."

He hefted the gun by its double-barrel, bracing himself to begin the punishment.

"Touch that poor defenceless animal and I'll give you a whipping, you bad-tempered old bastard!"

The voice was female and very angry, coming from among a tumbled mound of sandstone boulders a little way behind Doc. He hesitated, not striking the mule, and not lowering the blaster, either.

"The animal merits chastisement, madam," he said, his eyes straining to see where the woman was lurking.

"Chastise it and see what you get."

"I am not a man to be swayed from his purpose by an empty threat."

"Empty. How do you like these apples, mister?" The words were followed by the crack of a small-caliber pistol, the bullet hitting the trail a yard from Doc's feet and making Judas jump even more than he did.

He lowered his own pistol, but didn't holster it, having spotted the puff of powder smoke from the left-hand edge of the rocks.

"I have no wish to open fire upon a defenceless woman, madam," he called.

"But you're happy to beat the shit out of a poor donkey. *And* I don't take too kindly to that 'defenceless' crap."

"Firstly it is not a donkey. Secondly it is not poor. It is the most vicious animal ever placed on this planet by a malevolent deity to plague us human beings. Thirdly I apologize for the 'defenceless' slur."

"You sure speak strange, mister. You from the east?"

Doc hesitated. "I would say that I am from the east, madam, but also from the north and south and west."

"You sound like Johnny fuckin' Appleseed." There was laughter in the voice.

"Bad language in the mouth of a woman is like unto a worm within the fruit."

"Sorry, I'm sure. If I come out, do you promise not to blow me in half with that pretty cannon you got there?"

"Of course. Are you alone, madam?"

There was a long pause, the voice sounding suddenly less aggressive to Doc, far more vulnerable. "Sometimes I am. Then again, sometimes I'm not."

"What sort of time is it right now, if I may make so bold as to ask?"

"Right now it's sort of alone time."

"Then might I offer you a drink, fresh from Adam's own brewery. And a little fruit, perhaps?"

"Might take you up on that, mister."

"Come ahead, madam." Doc had learned enough from his time with Ryan Cawdor to keep the Le Mat free of the holster, ready in his right hand. He coughed, letting the sound cover the faint click as he cocked the hammer over the shotgun round.

Judas neighed, trying to turn his head to look at the figure that had finally appeared from behind the jumble of frost-riven boulders.

She was around average height—Doc guessed somewhere close to five foot six—lightly built, with the sun catching the glint of silver threads among the gold of her shoulder-length hair. She wore a divided skirt over riding boots, a white blouse that had seen better days and a dark blue jacket. A necklace of rough-cut turquoise was around her slender neck.

Her complexion was tanned by the New Mexico weather, her teeth showing white in a small smile. Doc noticed that she walked a little unsteadily, as though her feet were blistered, or she was fatigued. He also spotted that she was holding an automatic pistol in her right hand.

She stopped twenty paces away. "Best we introduce ourselves. Then we can mebbe both tuck our blasters away."

"By all means. My name is Theophilus Tanner. My friends call me 'Doc.' And you are..."

"Susan Smith. Out of Hildenville. One-hoss burg in the middle of the plains. You'd not have heard of it, Mr. Tanner."

"Doc. Please call me Doc."

"Surely. And you must call me Sukie, if we are to be friends, Doc."

"Pleasure." He bowed, his silver hair tumbling forward to frame his face. "And as a token of the friendship to come, I shall holster this ponderous gun of mine."

"I'll do the same. You sure talk funny, Doc. Kind of old-fashioned."

"A fair comment. Now come sit with me and let us pass some time with a loaf of bread and a jug of... of water."

"And this will be paradise enough, Doc."

"You are familiar with the Rubaiyat of Omar Khayyam, Sukie!" he exclaimed, delighted.

"That stuff about moving fingers writing and moving on? Sure. My father had a copy he used to read out loud most nights." She swayed and put a hand to her face. "Sorry, but..."

"My dear lady." Doc sprang forward to her assistance. "Allow me to offer you my arm."

"Been walking some ways since..."

GET 4 BOOKS

FREE

Here's a chance to get four free Gold Eagle® novels from the Gold Eagle Reader Service™ —— so you can see for yourself that we're like no ordinary book club!

We'll send you four free books ... but you never have to buy anything or remain a member any longer than you choose.

Find out for yourself why thousands of readers enjoy receiving books by mail from the Gold Eagle Reader Service. They like the convenience of home delivery . . . they like getting the best new novels before they're available in bookstores . . . and they love our discount prices!

Try us and see! Return this card promptly. We'll send your free books under the terms explained on the back. We hope you'll want to remain with the Reader Service — but the choice is always yours!

Yes! Please send me my 4 free Gold Eagle novels, as explained above and on back of card.

Name _____

Address _____ Apt. _____

City _____ State _____ Zip _____

164 CIM AQYW (U-DL-11/94)

THE GOLD EAGLE READER SERVICE™: HERE'S HOW IT WORKS

Accepting free books places you under no obligation to buy anything. You may keep the books and gift and return the shipping statement marked ''cancel.'' If you do not cancel, about a month later we will send you four additional novels, and bill you just $14.80 –that's a saving of over 12% off the cover price of all four books! And there's no extra charge for shipping! You may cancel at any time, but if you choose to continue, then every other month we'll send you four more books, which you may either purchase at the discount price…or return at our expense and cancel your subscription.

FREE MYSTERY GIFT

We will be happy to send you a free bonus gift along with your free books! To request it, please check here and mail this reply card promptly!

Thank you!

BUSINESS REPLY CARD

FIRST CLASS MAIL   PERMIT NO. 717   BUFFALO, NY

POSTAGE WILL BE PAID BY ADDRESSEE

GOLD EAGLE READER SERVICE
3010 WALDEN AVE
PO BOX 1867
BUFFALO NY 14240-9952

NO POSTAGE
NECESSARY
IF MAILED
IN THE
UNITED STATES

Before Doc could reach her, Sukie Smith fell to the dirt, her head striking the sandy earth with a sickening thud. Her skirt rode up as she fell, revealing her naked thighs. And her jacket dropped open, showing Doc the great stain of fresh, bright blood across her chest.

Chapter Eighteen

There weren't many people in all of Deathlands better than Ryan Cawdor when it came to trying to cope with a sudden, horrific emergency.

But the monstrous earthquake that struck at their camp near the river at the bottom of the steep-sided canyon was so devastating that all his combat reflexes were useless. The natural laws of time and space seemed to dissolve around him.

For a moment it occurred to him that the scrambled-brain feeling wasn't unlike making a mat-trans jump while still remaining conscious.

It was total disorientation.

He could do nothing but close his eye and curl up and try to make his body limp.

And wait it out.

The quake probably lasted less than sixty seconds from the first paralyzing jolt of the deep-buried seismic plates to the time that the dust began to settle.

But the earth was still quivering and rolling as Ryan finally succeeded in getting to his feet, fighting for balance, rubbing dirt from his good eye. He looked around for the others, the heaving and pitching beneath his feet reminding him of being on a ship in the middle of the ocean.

"Fireblast!" he breathed, wincing at the deafening noise that surrounded him.

Ryan was suddenly aware of water around his feet, rising quickly to midcalf. The place where he stood had been at the center of their camp and had been a dozen feet above the level of the nameless river.

He could just make out the noise of the horses, screaming in their terror. One of them had gone down, its hind legs crushed beneath a great slice of raw rock that had fallen from the cliffs above them. At first there was no sigh of Trader, J.B. or Abe.

Then he glimpsed Trader, Armalite slung over his shoulder, staggering toward him, his face gray with dust, eyes staring from a mask of shock.

"Can't see others!" he shouted to Ryan.

The water was still rising inexorably, helping to settle the whirling cloud of dirt. Three of the horses—two of the pack animals and one of the saddle mares—breasting the river, battling back toward the northern bank, heads held high above the foaming current.

"Goin' to lose them!" Ryan yelled, grabbing Trader by the arm and pointing to the escaping animals.

A little way upriver, J.B. swung onto the bare back of another of the saddle broncs, a hat jammed on his head, despite the madness of the monster quake. Ryan watched as he urged his horse into the water, obviously bent on pursuing the fleeing animals.

A dead horse floated by, a raw stump of muscle and bone where its head should have been.

The noise level was easing, and the swaying and rippling of the ground was also becoming less.

"There's what's his name!" Trader bellowed, pointing with the muzzle of his blaster.

"Abe?"

"Yeah. Think so. Someone in the river. Trying for the other side."

Ryan narrowed his eye, but he wasn't sure that he saw anything. There might have been someone, or something, at the farthest point of what had been a shallow ford, near the far bank. Then a bunch of debris surged into view, with uprooted trees in its teeth, passing the figure. When it had cleared, Ryan was no longer able to make out anyone in the water.

"Gone!" Trader called. "Horses look to be dead or gone across. We best follow."

It was a good idea, but Ryan had serious doubts that it was still practical.

He retreated even farther up the bank toward the unclimbable rock face, now less than six feet behind them, watching in the moonlight as the river grew higher and faster, its course twisted by the quake.

More broken branches of trees were carried swiftly by, with a large white bird, like a heron, dangling dead among them. Clouds were drifting across the face of the moon, darkening the canyon, making it impossible to see anything that might be happening on the far, northern bank.

"We're in trouble, Trader," Ryan said.

"Always a way out. Over, under, around or through." He grinned at Ryan as he trotted out what was probably the best known of his many sayings.

"Looks like under to me."

The quake had faded now, the noise replaced by the roaring of the swollen river. It had reached their ankles, and they were backed up against the cliff wall with nowhere else to go. The solid bank where they'd spent the night was being washed away, cutting their footing.

Ryan had managed to grab the Steyr, and he adjusted the strap across his shoulders.

"Going swimming, Trader," he shouted.

"Could do with a bath. Meant to have a dip in the river this morning, anyway."

There was another trembling shock, which brought a shower of small pebbles and earth down on top of the two men as they cowered in the lee of the cliff.

"Look," Trader shouted, pointing upstream. "Coming on down the pike for us."

It was another uprooted tree, a big willow, most of its smaller, feathery branches stripped away by the tumbling waters and the grinding rocks.

"Too far out," Ryan yelled.

"Can't wait for anything better." Trader didn't bother to see if Ryan was following him, throwing himself into the muddied river and striking out on a diagonal course that he hoped would bring him up against the tree.

"Fireblast!" Although already soaked, Ryan still got a shock from the surprisingly cold water. The Steyr SSG-70 banged painfully on the back of his neck as he half dived, half fell into the foaming torrent.

The waves were rolling and breaking all around Ryan, making it dangerously difficult to see where he was going or to calculate just what he needed to do to try to make contact with the racing length of timber. Rising and falling, he blinked water from his eye, glimpsing Trader only a few feet ahead of him, and the jagged branches of the willow, less than twenty yards away, moving fast toward him.

Ryan kicked out desperately, knowing that it would likely prove fatal to miss the tree. With nothing to bear him up, he would have little chance of surviving the maelstrom of rapids that he knew waited a little farther down the canyon.

Something brushed against his right arm, and he grabbed at it. But it was only a short, brittle branch off another tree, not even large enough to support a starved rat. Ryan pushed it away and gave it one last, long-bursting effort.

His elbow was jolted and he snatched upward, finding the solid smoothness of the tree. But it was slipping inexorably past him, going faster than he was. Despite all of his attempts, Ryan knew with chilling certainty that he wasn't going to make it.

Then he felt roughness, with long fronds, as thick as a man's finger. It was the root end of the willow's trunk. Despite the weight of water in his clothes, Ryan managed to heave himself up, pausing to draw breath and look around him.

He spotted Trader immediately, face as white as parchment in the stark moonlight.

He had managed to lock an arm around the stump of one of the broken side branches, hanging on helplessly, dragged along, unable to pull himself up onto the main trunk. His mouth opened as he saw Ryan appear above and behind him, but the roar of the river drowned his words.

There was a brief second of recognition in Ryan's memory, seeing the flickering, scratched remnants of a predark video about men hunting a huge white whale. The captain had been dragged under, caught in a web of harpoons and ropes, tugged through the ocean by the rampaging beast.

For a moment Ryan looked ahead, seeing the vast walls of sandstone towering high above them. They were going unbelievably fast, racing through the solid water. About a quarter mile farther down, the canyon angled sharply to the right. There was a great wall of mist from what had to be a major stretch of rapids. If Trader was to be saved, Ryan had to haul him aboard the willow before they reached that bend.

The only factor in his favor was that the big tree was remarkably stable, showing no sign of pitching or rolling.

He began to work his way forward, half-astride the willow, shuffling toward Trader.

The rifle had slipped and he stopped for a moment to adjust it, pushing it around across his back again. The sound of the river was growing louder and louder, like the screaming of a banshee, deafening him. He closed his eye for a moment, fighting for control. The noise was so loud that it seemed to be sucking all the sense from his brain with its thunderous pounding.

He was less than six feet from Trader.

Four feet.

Ryan risked a final glance up and ahead. To his horror he realized that their speed was increasing and they were already entering the crown of the bend. The view in front of them was almost obscured by the curtain of water thrown up by the stretch of jagged boulders that broke up the river's flow.

He threw himself flat, his right hand reaching for Trader, who clutched at it with his left hand, the right still gripping the precarious hold on the stump of the broken branch.

There was only going to be the one chance. Once they were plummeted into the raging passage of broken water immediately ahead of them, Trader's chances of survival would drop from five percent to nil.

The deathly strength of the old man's grip took Ryan by surprise. And nearly brought disaster. His own fingers were cold and numb, and when Trader clamped onto his hand, Ryan nearly let go. But he managed to sustain his balance on the tree, leaning back and hauling upward.

The moment Trader let go of the tree was the most hazardous. Thrown back and downward with his full weight tripled by the powerful drag of the river, Ryan was nearly thrown on top of him.

For a frozen splinter of racing time, it seemed that they hung balanced together, like a classical piece of statuary, motionless in the midst of the whirling inferno of rock and water.

It was muscle-crackingly difficult. Ryan faced forward on the tree trunk, but the full impact of Trader was pulling backward, behind him.

"Move, you bastard!" Ryan yelled, knowing that his old leader couldn't possibly hear him.

There was a final convulsive struggle, and Trader was up, using the same matted root section that had helped Ryan to clamber onto the willow.

But there was no time for rejoicing.

They were into the maelstrom.

The surface of the trunk had occasional blemishes of burrs and stumps of branches, giving just enough of a handhold to avoid being pitched off at the first spine-wrenching drop.

Ryan couldn't worry about Trader, hoping that he would be clinging on behind him. If he wasn't then he was dead.

And nobody worried about a dead man.

There was noise and a turmoil of water and blinding, freezing spray.

The trunk was tossed around like the flotsam it was, actually revolving in its own length, so that Ryan had the illusion that they were traveling backward through the tomblike walls of the endless canyon.

Once they seemed to fall vertically for thirty or fifty feet, plunging deep below the river into a bottomless pit of black, icy water. The breath froze in Ryan's lungs, and the strap of the Steyr wrapped itself round his neck like the tentacles of some subterranean kraken.

They rolled over through three hundred and sixty degrees, and Ryan was so disorientated that he wasn't even sure whether he was still holding on to the uprooted willow.

Finally the trunk emerged from the deeps, like a sub-to-air missile, exploding into the silvered blackness, then crashing down again, spinning in a succession of swirling saw-edged pools and shallows.

There was a brief moment of stasis, a beguiling, treacherous few seconds of stillness.

Even the noise of the river seemed quieted and Ryan risked a quick glance behind him, relieved to see the drowned-rat figure of Trader still clinging on, the Armalite still strung across his shoulders.

"How's it..." Ryan began.

It was like being slammed into from behind by a three-hundred-pound pesthole bouncer.

The gentle pool where the willow had rested for a dozen beats of the heart vanished, and they rattled down another series of savage, jolting steps, each of them threatening Ryan's precarious hold on the slick, wet wood.

Nothing mattered anymore, just to lie flat, the river surging up over his head and shoulders, knowing that at some point all of the suffering would cease.

Either in death or in safety.

IT ENDED—one way or another, everything always did—winding up in a final series of racing rapids, the teeth of the rocks tearing long strips off the bottom of the willow trunk, making Ryan's and Trader's fragile hold even more dangerous.

And then they were through.

Ryan had kept his eye closed for what seemed hours, knowing that there was no point in seeing what was coming. Not when you didn't have an iota of control over it.

Now he blinked his pale blue eye open once more, sensing a change in both the pace and movement of the river, a new gentler calm.

"Trader?" he said, coughing and spitting up a mouthful of the cold, sand-filled water.

"Fuck."

"Trader. You okay back there?"

They were in a wider, shallow section of the canyon. The walls were still fifteen hundred feet high above them, but the gorge itself was less constricting, the actual river nearly fifty feet across, meandering through willow-lined shallows.

Ryan glanced behind them, seeing the towering column of spray hanging in the moonlit air, showing the white water that they'd run through and survived.

Immediately at his back, Trader was still lying flat on his stomach, arms and legs spread, as if he were riding the coils of some monstrous sea beast.

Ryan tried again. "Hey, Trader! We made it."

"Who gives a flying fuck? I don't have an unbroken bone in my body, Ryan. Half my guts are stuck in my throat, and the other half's hangin' out my ass."

"Sit up and look around."

They were moving at a little more than walking pace now, the shore unrolling past them. Ryan looked farther down the canyon, then rubbed at his eye again, trying to make sure what he'd seen. It seemed like the walls were closing in again. Out of the corner of his eye he thought for a moment that he'd spotted a ruined building, perched on the edge of the chasm far above. But he wasn't certain of it.

The certainty was that he could see more of the dread spray less than a quarter mile ahead, and it seemed, already, that the uprooted willow, setting markedly lower in the river than before, was starting to move faster again.

"Fireblast!"

The concern in Ryan's voice at last made Trader sit up and take notice. It took less than five seconds for him to realize the danger of their situation.

"We're fucked," he said quietly.

Chapter Nineteen

"Never much cared for swimming," Trader panted as he lay flat on his back in the soft sand.

"Nor me."

The first glow of the true dawn was already beginning to show itself above the top of the cliffs to the east. The river had continued to rise for half an hour or more after they reached land, but now seemed to have leveled off.

There had also been several aftershocks of diminishing strength, the last of them more than a half hour back. A number of fallen trees had been carried past them, toward the sheer rapids they could hear a quarter mile or so to the south. Another dead horse and several drowned deer drifted by on the swelling current.

The swim to safety had been a desperate struggle.

If the river had been moving any faster, Ryan very much doubted whether he'd have been able to get Trader to the muddy shallows. The old man was exhausted by the terrible buffeting that he'd received going through the turbulent stretches of white water and could hardly muster the energy to kick out with his arms and legs.

In the end it had been Ryan, weighted down by his boots, rifle and soaked clothing, who'd taken his old leader around the shoulders, supporting him beneath the chin, dragging him with agonizing slowness toward the gentler-moving edges of the wide river.

Even when they could both stand, he had been forced to half lift and half pull Trader through the shallows, up the sloping shelf of soft damp sand, to collapse among the willows that lined the banks.

"HATE FUCKING SWIMMING, Ryan."

"You told me."

"Love fucking. Hate swimming."

Ryan laughed. "Don't we all, Trader? Don't we all?"

The top dozen feet of the western cliffs were tinted with the gentle opalescent light of the full dawn. Far above them the sky was a blur of thin, high cloud, with the promise of some fine weather to come.

Ryan stood and stretched. "Shouldn't take too long to get ourselves dry."

"No. Best check the blasters."

That statement brought the urgent memory of the missing J.B. and Abe.

The men looked at each other, stricken by the thought that their oldest friend was gone.

"Crossed the river at the ford. Went after the spooked animals," Trader said.

"Sure. And Abe went after him."

"River rose."

"Trapped them."

"Be cutting out the horses. Get them corraled and gentle them."

Ryan nodded, brushing sand from his hair and picking grit from both ears. "That'll be it, Trader. Probably having to go all the way along the rim on the north side. Eventually they'll find a trail down and we can meet."

"How far?"

"What?"

Trader also stood, limping heavily on his bruised leg. "Stiffened," he explained. "Wondered how far we might've been carried down the gorge."

"No real idea. Might have been only as little as four or five miles."

"Bullshit! Fifty miles if it was a fucking inch, Ryan. You lost some of your skills being away from me."

Ryan sniffed, taking his time before answering Trader. "Might be twenty miles. No more. Still a double-long way for them to go. Lot farther overland. Wouldn't be able to do much moving until after dawn."

"Might be a full day before they see us. Reckon we should get us out of here."

"Right. North rim?"

"More like east by the sun." He peered up into the brightness, shading his eyes. "That some kind of building up there? See where I mean?"

"Saw it before. Can't make it properly against the rising sun. But it looks too big to be a house. Mebbe a church or something like that."

Trader looked around. "Well, a man never got to sit and rest himself in the shade of a tall oak tree until he planted the bastard acorn."

"How's the knife wound?"

"It's about as welcome as a poxed-up gaudy slut at a Quaker christening."

"Worse than it was?"

His grimace might have indicated pain or humor. "Little of this. Little of that. On the scales, I'd say better. Cold water's often good for an open wound."

Ryan had been looking more carefully at the river below them, trying to make out any sign of a trail that could offer them a way out of the canyon. But the red rock walls were still drowned in deep shadow.

"Only way is to keep moving. Get in closer to the cliffs and take anything going."

"Long as it doesn't mean too much free climbing, Ryan. I hate fucking climbing."

"Funny. But I hate climbing and like fucking."

They were both laughing as they set off together, moving in what was a roughly southerly direction.

IT HAD BEEN thirty minutes of hard slogging over soft, tiring sand before they found anything.

There was a rectangular steel sign, corroded and weathered by a hundred years of climatic extremes. Its iron supports had rusted away, but it leaned against the trunk of an ancient juniper. The paint was long gone, but the blind-embossed lettering could still be felt and read.

"Overlook Trail. Three and one-quarter miles. Twelve hundred feet elevation. Average trail time three hours. Warning. Carry sufficient water."

Trader laughed harshly as Ryan finished reading the notice. "Nearly drank enough water to float me clear onto the last train west."

With the loss of the pack animals, they had lost all of their provisions—meat, fruit, fuel and water, as well as most of their spare ammo. But both men, from long force of habit, carried a couple of spare clips for their blasters in their pockets.

"Best drink our fill while we're down here." Ryan went to the edge of the river and glanced cautiously around him before kneeling and cupping his hands into the icy water, drinking long, slow and deep.

Trader joined him. "Tastes better when you have a choice about how much you take." He wiped his mouth on his sleeve. "Over three miles and over a thousand feet. Really fucking looking forward to this, Ryan."

IT HAD PROBABLY BEEN a popular hiking trail, back in the lost, innocent predark days when, if it could be believed, people used to walk up and down mountains for their own pleasure. Ryan had seen enough references to this absurd practice but he still found it hard to credit.

The century of summers and winters had taken a severe toll of the yard-wide track. Rains, sun and snows had furrowed and ridged it, while trees and bushes had fallen across it. And dozens of quakes, including the big one on the previous night, had totally shattered several long sections, washing dirt down the side of the cliff.

It became obvious very early in the climb that it was going to take a whole lot longer for Ryan and Trader than the three hours suggested by the old notice.

"Only about one step in ten's left of the trail," Trader complained. "Look. We've climbed around a hundred feet and I'm clapped out already."

Ryan was beginning to appreciate the warning about taking sufficient water with them, apart from the fact that neither of them now had a canteen.

The sun was soaring, flooding the bright walls of the canyon with its fiery light.

And its ferocious, scorching heat.

Trapped within the sandstone cliffs, the lower part of the gorge swiftly became an oven.

By the time they were only one-quarter of the way up, it was Ryan, by far the younger man, who was suffering most.

"Take five," he panted, sitting down and leaning against the rough bark of a bristle-cone pine. His breath was coming in rasping bursts, and he could feel his heart pounding in his chest like a trip-hammer.

A band of iced steel tightened around his forehead, and his eye felt as though a stickie were pushing at it from inside his skull.

"Problem?" Trader said, leaning on the Armalite, glancing at the heights above them. "Still a long way to go."

"I know. I can fucking well see that for myself!"

Trader grinned maliciously. "Finding it hard to keep up with the old man?"

"Think I'm dehydrated. Felt a touch feverish for a couple of days."

Trader's smile vanished. "Sorry for greasin' your wheels, Ryan. Anything I can do?"

"No. I'll sit a spell."

But when he tried to carry on, he found his knees were turning to jelly after three or four minutes, and his sight was blurring. The pain in his chest was worse, and it crossed Ryan's mind that he might be having a heart attack.

But that was a profoundly worrying thought that he chose to keep to himself.

"Want me to go ahead, or stay with you? Could be I might find some water or some help on top. Then I could come back for you, Ryan."

"Just let me rest a minute or two."

The time stretched to nearly a quarter of an hour. Ryan recovered enough to look back down the crooked trail and see how relatively little distance they'd covered so far, and how the top of the sun-etched canyon still seemed impossibly far ahead and above them.

But the thought of failure—particularly in front of Trader—made him try again.

He stood. Trader had been flicking pebbles at a tiny emerald lizard that kept scuttling back and forth at a lower level of the path.

"Sure?" he asked.

Ryan nodded. His stomach was knotted with surging coils of sickness, and he felt freezing cold, despite the sweating heat of the morning.

"Going to try fifty steps, then rest a bit," he said. "See how that goes."

Trader looked at him. "Go for it." For a moment Ryan expected one of his old leader's familiar sayings, but Trader shook his head. "Go for it," he repeated.

Fifty paces, counted out slowly, took Ryan to where a section of retaining wall had crashed down from high above. He sat on the warm rocks, breathing slowly, watching a large turquoise butterfly feeding on the corpse of a tiny rodent. He decided that he maybe wasn't going to die, after all.

"How is it?" Trader asked.

"It's not too bad. No, not too bad."

After completing four sections, stopping each time after fifty steps and sitting down for two or three minutes, Ryan realized, to his enormous relief, that he could make it.

That he definitely wasn't going to die after all.

THE TOP OF THE CANYON was less than two hundred feet above them. The track here was better preserved, and there had even been a couple of stretches where the original wooden handrail remained.

"Odd how the mind can win out over the body," Ryan said.

"How's that?"

"Two hours ago I seriously thought that I was a candidate for the faceless guy with the black cloak. Haven't felt as rough for a long while."

"Now?"

"Now I still haven't had any water. Been climbing all the time. But I know I can make it."

Trader was sitting on a bench carved from the living rock, his long legs stretched out, admiring the view down to the bottom of the canyon and the slender white-flecked worm of blue-green that was the river.

"No sign of J.B. and Abe," he said. "Still, we don't know which rim of the gorge they're on."

During the long hours of the steep climb, neither Trader nor Ryan had mentioned the real possibility that both of their friends might have perished during the carnage of the powerful earthquake.

A PROTRUDING BLUFF had closed them off from any sight of the ruins for the past six or seven hundred feet. Now they were finally safely on the top of the trail, and the plateau was open, dotted with trees.

The old building was visible, a quarter mile away, with smoke rising from one of its chimneys.

Chapter Twenty

"Don't fancy it," Abe said.

"Looks safe."

"Looks to me like it's been made from last year's spiderweb."

The Armorer shook his head. "We have to get across the river, Abe. Last glimpse I had of Ryan and Trader was when they were under the cliff on the other side of the canyon. If they managed to get out of there, then they'll likely be over on the east."

"But suppose that bridge is wrecked when we get all the way down there?"

"Then we climb back up again. Or watch out for some way of taking to the water."

Abe laughed. "You sure got a hell of a nerve, John Dix. You can see the spray, and we've looked into the mouth of some of them rapids. No way anyone could have ridden the white waters. No way at all."

"So, we take the bridge. Difficult to see, with the sun rising over that side, but I'm sure I can make out a trail up to the top there."

Abe wiped sweat off his face. There was a livid bruise on his right cheek where he'd failed in his attempt to mount one of the fleeing terrified horses. It had been scant consolation that even the supercompetent Armorer had also been unable to stop any of the animals. They hadn't seen any sign of any of the horses since the quake.

"But what if we get down and across? Look, there's that side river we have to get over as well. Then you're wrong and there's no track at all? You saying we come all the way back up here, again?"

"If that's what it takes. Come on."

"How many rounds you got, Abe?"

"Full load and about a dozen spares."

"I got an extra clip for the Uzi and a few spares for the Smith & Wesson scattergun."

It was a source of wonderment to the little gunner how J.B. showed so few signs of their ordeal. His own clothes were covered in sandy mud, and he was a mass of bruises and cuts, as if he'd been dragged through a hedge backward.

But the Armorer somehow managed to look much like he always did: the fedora, admittedly dusty around the crown, perched solidly on his head; the glasses, admittedly a little smeared, high on the bridge of his thin nose; the coat pockets filled with all manner of esoteric tools and equipment; and the Uzi and the M-4000 shotgun, clean and oiled, immaculate as though they'd just been taken out of their original makers' containers.

"Well," J.B. said, interrupting Abe's thoughts, "let's go look at that bridge."

The track was steep, partly broken up, leading down from the rim of the canyon toward the side channel of the river.

It took over an hour to make their way through the growing heat. The sun, almost directly overhead, was filling the canyon with its bright fire.

It was impossible to reach the main channel and the skittering bridge without first finding some way over the slower-moving tributary.

Abe sniffed, looking down at the sullen, dark green water. They were less than a hundred feet distant, but a fierce thorn hedge blocked their passage, seeming to be impenetrable. "How we gonna get through that?"

J.B. studied it carefully. "See the tracks by the water's edge. Means animals come down. If they can get through it, then so can we."

"THERE," ABE CALLED excitedly. "Kind of narrow tunnel about the size of big possum. Can easy crawl along that if we keep low."

J.B. was a little behind him. "Might be a better way. I'm sure some of the tracks I saw from up yonder belonged to deer. They'd have opened up a wider path. We can check up and down stream."

But Abe was in too much of a hurry.

He dropped to his hands and knees, making sure first that his stainless-steel Colt Python was still in its holster. Then he lunged forward into the narrow tunnel through the sharp thorns. Behind him, J.B. had stopped, crouching and looking intently at the maze of tracks in the soft earth.

"Come on, J.B., it's fine. Get a few snags but it's gotta be close to the other side. Can't see the..."

The Armorer looked up, as if he'd been struck by an apocalyptic vision. "Dark night!"

Abe hesitated. "You call me?"

"Tracks. Abe, get out of there!"

"Why?"

"Main tracks here. Leading in where you've gone. They're made by a skunk."

"Didn't quite..." His conversational tone raced up to a scream. "No! There's a skunk in here and..."

The Armorer began to back away, seeing the hedge erupt into violent life. Branches waved, shook and rattled. And above it all came the horror-struck babbling and yelling of Abe, trapped inside.

The wind was blowing strongly down the side canyon, toward the main river. But enough of the skunk's foul spray filtered back to J.B. to make him turn and gag, doubled over, retching in the dirt.

"CAN I COME OUT?"

J.B. was sitting on a large rounded boulder, cradling the Uzi. He had gone only forty yards or so upstream, finding that the deer had picked their own wider path through the jagged thorns of the tall hedge. He had simply followed them, keeping to leeward of the hapless Abe.

The skunk had vanished into the brush, but it had left its mark.

Abe had eventually emerged onto the gently shelving strip of beach, his face as green as spring grass, his chest and pants slobbered with his own puke. When he saw the Armorer coming along the side of the river, he made a move as though he were going toward his old friends, stopping when the muzzle of the Uzi came up to cover him.

"One more step and I blow you in half, Abe," J.B. warned. "I swear I'll do it."

"What can I do?"

"Predark remedy was tomato juice," the Armorer offered. "We don't have any."

"So?"

"So." He gestured with the blaster. "So, get in the river and strip off, Abe. Best you can do."

URGED ON BY J.B., Abe had scrubbed at his clothes with handfuls of the fine silver sand that lined the river, scraping at his skin and hair to try to remove the insidious miasma that clung to him like a discarded lover.

"I can't tell whether I still stink or not," he complained. "I reckon it's gone."

J.B. sighed. "Wish I could agree with you. Truth is, you're still no bouquet of violets. Give it another half hour and then try again."

"I'll have turned into a pink prune by then."

"Half an hour," J.B. insisted.

THE BRIDGE WAS MORE SOLID than it had looked from the top of the cliffs. The wires that had originally held it together had largely rotted and corroded, but they'd recently been replaced and strengthened by long cables of hand-spun rope.

J.B. went first, the Uzi and shotgun both across his shoulders, testing each step of the way, hanging on to the handrails on both sides.

Abe followed him, breathing an enormous sigh of relief as he reached dry land on the eastern shore of the main river. "Best moment for a few hours," he said.

J.B. held up his hands. "Can you still keep a way clear of me, Abe? Just for a while longer."

The Armorer had been correct.

There was yet another narrow trail, this time winding up toward the rim of the gorge.

It was a hard climb, but J.B. kept Abe plodding on by pointing farther south along the vast waste of the canyon. "See the way the cliffs get higher a few miles that way?" he said. "Lucky we aren't trying to scramble out there."

"Bad enough here," the gunner panted, sitting down cross-legged in the dirt, sweat trickling down his pale face, dripping off the drooping ends of his mustache.

The Armorer was scanning the land around them, concentrating on a heat-hazed blur, about five miles to the south, right on the edge of the sheer drop.

"Some kind of redoubt or something up ahead," he said. "Seems like I can see smoke coming from it."

"We going there or going around it?" Abe asked. "Food and drink'd be good."

"Hemp rope around the throat wouldn't be so good. Who knows? Let's take this journey a single step at a time. And start by reaching the top."

Abe groaned. "You're worse than the Trader, J.B., you know that?"

He got a short, terse laugh in reply. "You think that, Abe? After your time with him? The one great truth about Deathlands is that nobody, repeat nobody, is worse than Trader."

NEAR THE TOP, the trail began to widen out. The crest of the climb was barely a hundred feet above them, and Abe had become far more cheerful, ignoring J.B.'s warnings to slow down and watch where he was going.

"I can see clearly now," he claimed.

"You said something like that when you walked into a backfiring skunk, Abe. And I tell you what—roses and violets you still aren't."

The gunner grinned, hesitating only to wipe perspiration from his eyes. "Jealous you can't keep up with a lively stud like me? That it?"

J.B. didn't bother to reply. He could already see the spiked tops of a thick grove of pines on the plateau above the canyon. Another four or five minutes and he could relax, sit down and take the weight off his legs. The muscles in his calves had tightened during the climb, and he had a ferocious headache from the dazzling sun.

The trail seemed to have almost disappeared, but the way was obviously straight ahead, down for fifty yards or so into a shaded dip that was filled with miniature piñon pines, no more than six feet tall, then up the last stretch to the top.

For the past hour or so they'd been kept close company by a number of brightly colored wild birds, redwinged jays and mutie crows with brilliantly iridescent chest and wing feathers. But now, oddly, they had all vanished and the morning had become totally still and silent.

J.B. stopped and eased the Uzi off his shoulder, feeling a sudden profound disquiet.

"Abe, stay where you are for a moment."

But the warning was too late. The little gunner, in the sunbaked hollow, had felt something brush against his ankle and was standing very still, looking around him with paralyzed horror.

Chapter Twenty-One

Doc Tanner had picked up a fair bit of first aid over the years, and he hastened to put into practice what he could remember.

"Shade. Check not swallowed tongue. Head to one side. Nothing blocking breathing. Pulse steady. Loosen clothes. Leave that for a moment. Then look at wound. Nasty. Lot of blood. What in perdition can have happened to the lady?"

He kept up his muttered commentary as he carefully lifted the unconscious woman from the dirt, wheezing at her weight, feeling a stab of pain in the small of his back from the effort. He struggled to carry her and lay her gently down in the shade of a nearby fallen ponderosa.

"Why, I do resemble poor mad Lear, holding his dead daughter enfolded in his arms."

Doc rather liked the fantasy, and struggled to recall some of the lines from the Shakespeare play. But all he could remember was rather a lot of roaring and thespian bellowing and spraying of actorplasm. He decided that this wouldn't be of much help to Sukie Smith of Hildenville.

She was breathing in a rather shallow but reassuringly steady fashion. Doc turned her head so that her cheek was in the dust, making sure she was out of the direct heat of the sun. That done, he felt able to move his attention to the bloody wound.

It had obviously been caused by a knife of some sort, though Doc's combat experience was too limited for him to make much of a guess at what kind of a blade had been used.

He fetched some water and soaked his favorite swallow's-eye kerchief with it, knelt down with much creaking of knees and began to mop away the blood. The cut was very recent, still weeping a copious amount of blood. But as he worked at it, Doc realized that it wasn't too deep or too serious.

The wound ran from the left collarbone, diagonally down, across the sternum, disappearing under the collar of the blouse, over the swell of the right breast.

Doc cleared his throat, peering intently at the woman's face, trying to see if she was showing any sign of recovering from the faint. Close up, he could see that she had spent much of her life in the open air. Though he was aware of how lacking in skill he was, Doc figured her age to be somewhere in the late thirties or the early forties.

Nervously, fingers trembling, he began to unbutton her blouse, opening it up, seeing, as he had suspected, that she wore no sort of undergarment.

He ignored the slight feeling of tightness and discomfort at the front of his breeches, concentrating on cleaning away all of the blood.

Judas whickered quietly, just behind him, but Doc ignored the animal.

A wide trickle of crimson filled the valley between the woman's breasts and Doc slid his kerchief into the canyon, wiping away the blood as best he could.

The voice, right in his ear, made him jump so much he nearly dropped the wet cloth.

"You don't have to make too much of a meal of it, Doc."

"I was... I mean to say that... It was not my intention, madam, to interfere with..."

Sukie Smith laughed. "I can see that. I journey all the way from wind-washed Wisconsin and end up being cut across my tits by a rabid dwarf. And then I pass out, come around to find I'm being groped by some goatlike animal beater."

"Goatlike!"

She patted his hand. "Sorry, Doc. Tongue runs away with me sometimes."

"Dwarf?"

"What?"

"I bethought that I heard you say that you had been attacked by a dwarf with rabies."

"Yeah. Called himself the best guide west of the Pecos, or some such cheap-vid nickname."

Doc sat back on his heels, absently squeezing the pink water from his kerchief. "Some wretch that you had hired as a guide did this to you? By the Three Kennedys! But if the running dog were still close by I would take the greatest pleasure in teaching him a lesson he would never forget."

"I did."

Carried away by his own anger and oratory, Doc didn't hear her speak. "I would have him whipped at the tail of a cart, clean back to his birth parish. Have him branded upon the shoulder. Nay, the forehead, so that all might witness his roguery. Perhaps he should also be—"

She laid a hand on his forearm. "Doc."

"Yes?"

"He's deader than last year's hopes."

"Dead?"

She drew a finger across her throat. "Kneed him in the balls. Grabbed his knife. Opened him up from ear to shining ear." There was a silence. She smiled at the expression on Doc's face. "Like to get on with mopping away the blood from where he cut me? I was kind of starting to enjoy it."

THEY FINALLY AGREED that the wound wasn't deep enough or serious enough to need stitching. Doc had an old shirt in his pack, and he tore off strips to make a rough bandage for the injured woman.

"I heal well," Sukie insisted. "Not much risk of infection. Funnily enough, his knife was about the only clean thing about the sick little runt. Never saw him wash, all the days we were together."

Doc had lighted a small fire, suspending a can of water over it, ready to brew up some coffee sub. Judas was eating quietly in the background.

The old man had given the woman a drastically edited version of his own life, omitting all mention of time-trawling and Emily and the children, not quite sure why he'd done that. He simply told the woman that he lived with Jak and some friends, describing the ranch, but not going into much detail. He explained that he'd felt he needed some time on his own and was intending to return in another couple of days.

"When you got your head together, Doc?"

"My head together? I fear that I am not familiar with that saying, Sukie."

"Heard it from my grandpa. Grandpa Polissar that is, on my mother's side. He was real old. Remembered predark. Used to talk about it." She laughed, wincing a little as the makeshift bandage tugged at the cut. "Fact is, he didn't talk about much else. Specially in his late days. Memory went walking about a lot. Nice old guy, though."

"The coffee will soon be ready. Do you wish to tell me something about yourself? Other than coming from Wisconsin and being attacked by your stunted guide."

"We got all day?"

"Indeed we do. Company is welcome, ma'am. We have all day and . . ." He hesitated.

"All night, you were going to say, weren't you?"

He felt his cheeks grow warm. "Now you make me blush, dear lady."

"Listen, you sort of saved my life, Doc. Now, we're both a little past the first flush... I'm forty-three if you want to know. So we don't want to go rushing our fences, do we?"

"No."

Sukie Smith's life story wasn't particularly interesting, and was fairly typical of what it was like to struggle for a living in Deathlands.

She'd been born and raised near the ville of Rice Falls, Wisconsin, and married at thirteen to the oldest son of the local baron. "He was fifty-one years old, Doc. One leg, one hand and no dick. The man was dickless. I was widowed at fourteen. Best you don't even ask, Doc. Can't say he died happy."

She married again at seventeen. "Lasted a short while longer. Wheelwright. Got to wear my widow's black at nineteen. Husband was a nice enough guy, but he had a gross rad cancer. Got me pregnant. Miscarried. Sort of lost some of my plumbing to a butcher doctor. Couldn't have any more kids after that. They hacked a tumor the size of a grapefruit out of my man's jaw."

The day was passing, but Doc felt no urgency to cut Sukie short. There was no need to move on, nowhere special that he really had to be.

Sukie married again at twenty-two, but by then Sukie had moved into Kansas, to a sodbuster's shack with their nearest neighbor more than thirty miles away, and a wind that blew for three hundred and sixty-five days a year.

"He was kind enough, Harry was. We lived there for six years. God knows how! Every single hour was an eternity. Boredom became a kind of art form, all on its own. Piece of tumbleweed blowing by was a real event. Weeks might go by and we'd never say a word to each other."

Harry had gone out early one summer morning and hanged himself in their barn, using his own belt.

She smiled at the memory. "Truth is, Doc, I didn't miss him for two weeks. I could smell him, but I kind of ignored it. Know how it is?"

Her last marriage had been six months later, in the pesthole ville of Mason, Iowa. Truman Shelley was a widower with six children, the oldest of them just turned nine. Their mother had been crushed by an overturning wag in the spring rains.

"Truman had a dream of heading west. Heard about the orchards of California. Oranges and lemons."

Their odyssey had ended in the mud of Deadwood, at the heart of a raging cholera epidemic.

"You ever been there, Doc?"

"Once. Rained."

"It was a beautiful morning when I buried Truman and all the little ones."

"All?"

"Sure. Hardly time to turn from putting a copper coin on the eyes of one of them before another tiny heart had given up the struggle."

"There was a cemetery up a hill. A steep, steep hill. It was as though one were already halfway to heaven. I disremember the name of it."

"Mount Moriah."

"Yes."

There, among the tall trees, looking westward to where the land was bright, Sukie Smith had overseen the interment of her entire family. "There was a little jack left. I raised a stone. Least I could do. 'I really miss them' was what I had carved on the square stone."

"You have a great deal of ill-fortune in your life, Sukie. What were you doing in this blistered wilderness with a murderous person of restricted growth?"

She laughed, lying back, with her knees slightly parted, showing several inches of firm thigh. "I needed a guide. Had a sister. Last I heard from her was around ten years ago. Thought I'd pay her a visit. Seemed to be a good idea at the time. Still does. She was living with a miner, out in a frontier ville called Hope Springs."

"Eternal," Doc said.

"How's that?"

"Nothing, nothing. You must forgive my wandering mind, my dear."

"Anyway, that's why I was out here. Fell in with a small family group going my way. Found a haven. Canyon with sweet water. They decided to stop. Just me and their oldest boy went on. He was the little fuckhead who sliced me. Been trying to get inside my honeypot for three days. And nights. Lost patience this morning and did... Well, you saw what he did."

"So what now?" It was beginning to get dark.

She smiled at him, her teeth white in the gathering gloom. "Now, Doc? Now I show you how grateful I am for your help."

Chapter Twenty-Two

A narrow stream tinkled its way toward the rim of the canyon, tumbling over moss-slick pebbles through a series of tiny green pools. Ryan lay flat and buried his dry, crusted face in the icy coolness, closing his eye, feeling the strength flowing back through his tired, dehydrated body. He had an almost overwhelming temptation to suck in the delicious elixir, fill his mouth, throat and stomach again and again. But he was too aware of the danger of such stupidity.

He hadn't been there himself, but he remembered J.B. telling him of the occasion. A young woman from War Wag Two had wandered into the desert. When the search party eventually found her, she was almost off her head with the heat, her brains broiling in her skull.

It had been close to nightfall and they'd made a camp, sponging down the woman's body with tepid water, allowing her only small sips, despite her desperate protests that she wanted more and more to ease her thirst.

In the night she'd crept from her sleeping bag and crawled to the drinking supply.

The rescuers had been awakened, only seconds later, by the noise of her dying.

The effect of the sudden vast intake of cold water had sent her whole body into shock. She had vomited, copiously and violently, her arms and legs thrashing at the darkness until her heart failed.

Ryan sipped a few blessed mouthfuls, then sat up, allowing the drops from the stream to trickle over his neck and chest. He cupped his hands to splash more over himself.

"Easy," warned Trader, who had knelt on the other side of the pool, lapping at it like a thirsty dog.

"Feel better already." Ryan tried to stand, but was surprised by a wave of dizzy nausea, making him stagger a few steps to one side. He steadied himself with a hand on one of the grove of tall pines.

"Yeah, you look a potful of fucking jack. Sit a spell, friend."

RYAN FELT FOR THE PULSE at his wrist. "Steadying down to normal," he said.

"Then we can start moving again. You young men, Ryan. All spit and no balls."

"Take you any day, Trader. With both hands tied behind your back."

"That'll be the day, pilgrim. Way you looked back there on the trail, you'd have struggled to punch your way out of a wet paper bag."

"What are we going to do about that place?" Ryan pointed beyond the trees toward where they could still see the column of gray smoke climbing from one of the chimneys of the building at the edge of the canyon.

Trader slung the Armalite across his shoulder. "Take a recce for starters. Then, if they look like they got some serious power, we might ask them for food and stuff. If they look like they don't have no power, then we can go in and take some food and stuff. How's that sound, John Dix? Fuck! I mean, Ryan?"

"Sounds good."

A SMALL SIGN was set by the side of the narrow, over-grown path that had led them within fifty yards of the side of the building. Even after a century of weathering, the words were still very legible: Open to Residents of Hightower Only.

"What's that mean?" Trader asked.

Despite all the long years that they'd known each other, Ryan had never been entirely convinced by Trader's claim not to be able to read or write. Yet he'd never quite managed to catch him out.

"Place must've been called Hightower. Mebbe some kind of rooming house. Hotel. Motel. Something like that. Sign means only people living there can go on this trail."

"Predark, isn't it?"

"Sure looks like it."

"I don't see guards. Doesn't seem much like a strong ville to me."

Ryan looked around. "I don't see anything except the big house, and a part of that's in ruins. Could be nothing for a hundred miles in any direction.

"One way to find out. Get in closer and keep our eyes open and our asses shut."

There was a row of neglected yews that had probably once been a neatly trimmed hedge. Now they were over six feet high, ragged and yellowed.

From behind them, it was possible to see that the ruins had once been a resort hotel. It must have been a marvelous location, close to the edge of the high canyon, with a wonderful view across its own grounds.

But the nukes and the quakes had combined to change all of that.

There had been major subsidence and the long, two-story building was now a lot closer to the brink of the chasm than it had originally been. In fact, the whole of its south wing had fallen in, decades ago. The rest seemed to be teetering drunkenly on the brink, and it looked as though a single sparrow fart could push it into oblivion.

The roof had gone from most of the hotel, as had many of the elegant wooden balconies that had decorated the canyon side of Hightower.

But there was clearly life.

As Trader and Ryan crouched under cover of the line of yews, they saw several men and women, coming and going. And a gas truck, its exhaust belching blue fumes, drove away from the front of the building.

"Could use that," Trader commented.

"And it figures they've got supplies of gas as well," Ryan agreed.

"Not many weapons on show. Just some rebuilt handblasters and one sawn-down."

"We going for friendly first?"

Trader nodded. "Sure. Got your honest, steadfast and true smile ready in place?"

"Here it is."

"That it? Then we should forget friendly. Go for terrifying, Ryan. For fuck's sake, bro, you can do better than that teeth-bared leer."

"Let's go, okay? And forget jokes. Travelers south from Seattle. Lost our horses and supplies in the quake last night. Could use a meal and mebbe a bed for the night."

"Sure," Trader said.

A YOUNG MAN in high-cut shorts left the front entrance and walked past them, waving a casual hand. "Hi, there. You come to see Baron Torrance?"

Trader answered. "Sure have. Hear that Baron Torrance is a good man to help someone with troubles."

"No, I wouldn't have said that. We hardly ever see any outlanders, in trouble or not." He shrugged his broad shoulders, smiling a broad smile. "Fact is, I wouldn't mention being in trouble to the baron. Best just kind of be passing by. Still, got to be going. I look after the gardens here." He grinned. "Only part of the ville that's in good shape. If you don't look too close at the hedges."

He gave them another friendly wave and went on his way, whistling to himself.

Ryan sniffed. "Not used to outlanders. Place is a total shithouse tip, Trader, but he still calls himself baron. Don't like it."

"Lot of men and women have ideas above their reality, Ryan. All we got that they might want is our blasters. Take some spilled blood to get at those."

"Plenty of barons could chill you for less. Remember that fat son of a bitch up near—"

He was interrupted by the appearance of a tall man in stone-washed denim jeans and a patched shirt, stained around the collar and ragged cuffs.

"Saw you come up out the canyon." He was holding his hand over the butt of a holstered handblaster. It was difficult to see, but it looked like a rebuilt .32 of unguessable manufacture. "Saw you from the tower window." He pointed to the four-story turret at the one end of the building. It was leaning sideways at so sharp an angle that you wouldn't have placed any jack on it being there in six months' time. Or six days.

"We come from Seattle. Got caught in the big quake." Trader shook his head sorrowfully. "Lost all our goods. Horses. Couple of friends." Ryan had learned the lesson early from the older man that the best lies were those that stayed close to the truth. Just nudged it a step sideways.

"What did you trade in?" the man asked.

"We deal in lead, friend."

The hand twitched and dropped onto the butt of the blaster. "How's that?"

"Ammo. Made and traded in ammo. Most common calibers. Lost the lot."

"Shame. Baron Torrance could have been interested in doing some dealing. Still, he'll like to see you. Few outlanders get this close to the canyon."

Ryan gestured toward the tumbled wing of Hightower. "Looks like your ville's getting closer to the canyon all the time. Last night's quake do any damage?"

"Some. Few more rooms went in. Health club annex dropped over. How did you get down the river?"

"Luck," Trader replied. "Managed to catch a fallen tree that took us through the rapids."

"Why didn't you take the old bridge, three or four miles upstream? Easier way to the top."

Ryan and Trader looked at each other. "Bridge?" said the one-eyed man. "Didn't see that. Then again, we were kind of busy hanging on."

The man nodded. "Best get in. Baron Torrance can be a tad antsy if you keep him waiting. Him and his daughters both. You two got any names?"

Ryan answered for both of them. "I'm Danny King and this is my father, Willard."

"Father!" Trader snorted, controlling himself with a visible effort. "Danny's little joke. He's my young brother. You got a name, mister?"

"Yeah. I'm Andy Arkadin. Sort of run the sec side of things here at Hightower."

A minor tremor rippled the earth, making them all sway a little. They turned to look at the tottering tower. A single pane of glass cracked noisily, but there was no further damage.

"Aftershocks," Arkadin said, grinning nervously. "Can finish off what the big quakes start."

"Looks like it won't take that much to topple the rest of the wreckage into the canyon," Trader commented.

"One day. Yeah, one day. One day. Mebbe I'll be gone from here by then."

"Not happy?" Ryan asked.

"Not like other villes. See that for yourself. Like a clock that's nearly run down. Twenty years ago Hightower was a place that counted. Baron Torrance lost his wife when his second daughter was born. Kind of old, his wife, by then. Lost interest at the same time. Only hope now is that his 'little girls' will get married and carry on the ville. Sort of restore it to the former glory. Know what I mean?"

Trader nodded. "Way the place is sliding into oblivion, I guess he's hoping for a quick marriage."

"You could say that," Arkadin agreed. "But you couldn't possibly expect me to comment on it."

They went inside the lobby of the predark hotel.

It had a faded grandeur that both Ryan and Trader had seen in other, similar buildings. There had been one set by a beautiful lake, among the glaciers of Montana, another overlooking a winding pass in Colorado. This one had to have been up there with the very finest.

But not now.

Arkadin led them in, stepping over the corpse of a dog that lay across the front step, flies gathering around the sockets of the opaque eyes.

Apart from the stench of the dead animal, Ryan wrinkled his nostrils at the stink of decay—sweat, urine, wet clothes and rotting food.

The lobby was in semidarkness, its furniture tawdry and filthy. The floor was so dirty that the soles of their combat boots stuck to it as they walked after the sec man. Their heels crunched among splinters of shattered glass.

"Christ on the cross!" Trader exclaimed, stopping to peel a sheet of greasy paper from his foot. "I never saw a place so triple unclean and unsanitary. Your baron ever think about getting some people with brooms and pails of water?"

Arkadin spun, finger to his lips. "Quiet, Willard! Baron Torrance can be friendly. Certainly used to be that way. Lately he... But it's better not to say anything kind of critical of the place. Much better."

"Sure. Get the picture."

"Just follow me. Best keep both your eyes open and..." He trailed off, suddenly aware of Ryan's condition. "Sorry, Danny. Kind of forgot you lost an eye."

"Mebbe if we keep all three of our eyes open," Trader suggested.

A LOG FIRE SMOLDERED in the hearth, the damp wood spitting and cracking. A boy of about ten was sitting by it, poking at a large spider with a long meat skewer, trying to pin down one leg at a time. He didn't look up as the sec man led the two outlanders past him.

"Bastard kitchen-bred brat," Arkadin said quietly. "Got all his father's gentle charm and all his half sister's kindly ways with living creatures."

"Where is the baron?" Ryan asked, looking out of a smeared window that opened across the dizzy red-orange expanse of the canyon.

"Probably on the top floor. Named it the games room up there. Likely with the 'little girls,' too."

"Why do you call them that? The 'little girls'?" Trader stopped, wiping dog shit off his boot on a piece of ragged carpet. "Some sort of joke?"

"No. Not a joke, Willard. One thing that the Torrance ladies aren't is a joke. Quickest way to reach the fucking river in twelve seconds flat is to laugh at them. Remember that, both of you."

"You fetched them, Arkadin?" The voice was like hydrogen sulfide bubbling through warm nitric acid.

Ryan glanced at Trader. "Mebbe we shouldn't..." he began.

"Yeah, agreed. Too late now."

Chapter Twenty-Three

The grass in the hollow was damp, with long, thick tussocks. A narrow stream flowed over the top of the cliff, turning the area below the rim into a swampy morass.

Abe stood in it, aware of the wetness, aware of the bright sun that glittered down on his head and the beads of sweat that had been trickling off his mustache, aware that J.B. wasn't all that far behind him.

But, overwhelming all other sensations, he was aware of the cottonmouth that was coiled around his feet.

A normal cottonmouth, or water moccasin as some people call them, would probably grow to six feet in length, its body not much thicker than the forearm of a muscular adult male. Though not as lethally poisonous as the desert rattler, the cottonmouth has a bite that could kill.

The snake that lay basking there, in the warmth of the hollow, lazily enjoying the remnants of its last meal—a full-grown wild burro—was at least twenty-five feet long, with a body that was as big around as a beer cask.

It wasn't taking much obvious notice of Abe, its head turned away, its eyes hooded, its mouth slightly open. The tip of its tongue was in constant, flickering movement, tasting the air around itself. But the last six or seven feet of its powerful body had lazily encircled the man's ankles, clamping them together.

"J.B.," Abe said, finding that the air had been sucked from his lungs and his tongue had become dried and swollen all in less than ten seconds.

"I see it." The Armorer's voice was calm and reassuring, coming from a dozen yards behind Abe.

The huge mutie snake responded to the sounds, opening its mouth wider, making a faint hissing noise. Abe stood perfectly still, not daring to go for his blaster. He could see the curved, hollow teeth, knowing that they would act like hypo needles, pumping poison into his flesh.

The thought of how virulent the venom would be from such a gigantic reptile made him feel sick. The day seemed to darken and he swayed, closing his eyes.

"Don't faint on me, Abe," J.B. warned, pitching his voice as low as he could. "Can't risk a shot at it from here. Got to move around or wait until it moves."

The cottonmouth was becoming uneasy. The mangled remains of the burro, one bloodied eye staring up at the sun, were completely forgotten. Another layer curled about Abe's legs, squeezing more tightly. The head of the enormous snake was sliding toward him, the incurious little eyes staring blankly at its prey. The hissing grew louder.

Abe felt utterly frozen, as if he had been soaked in a deep dark pool of Sierra meltwater. It was only with the greatest effort of will that he managed to stay upright.

Out of the corner of his eye he could just make out the blurred shape of the Armorer, sunshine flashing off his glasses, sidling around to the left, lower on the slope, the scattergun held at his waist.

Now the snake was rearing up, holding itself erect, so that its swaying head was almost at the same height as Abe's face. The mouth was less than a yard away, and he could taste the carrion corruption of the creature's cool breath.

"Can you move your feet at all, Abe?"

He was too petrified to answer, contenting himself with the slightest movement of his head, from side to side, hoping that J.B. had spotted it.

"All right. When I say to move, then I want you to try and throw yourself onto your back. Only chance I'll have of a good clear shot at it without taking your head off as well. Just sort of nod if you understand me."

Abe nodded. To his mounting horror he realized that the mutie cottonmouth was actually hypnotizing him, the rhythmic movement of its head and upper body making him feel utterly helpless, lulling him, so that he no longer felt too worried about being killed by it. The snake was also aware of J.B.'s slow, cautious flanking movement, its eyes following him.

It made a feinting lunge toward the Armorer, causing him to react instinctively, stumbling away, boots slipping in the muddied grass. Abe realized that if J.B. hadn't managed to recover himself, he could easily have tumbled five hundred feet down the steep wall of the canyon.

"Dark night!" J.B. nearly dropped the Smith & Wesson M-4000 in the dirt, the Uzi dangling from its shoulder strap.

Abe became aware that he'd been holding his breath for so long he was in danger of passing out. He sucked in some of the moist air, tasting the closeness of the great snake. Its patterned scales were rustling around his legs as it moved still closer to him.

"Ready, Abe. Any minute."

Now the Armorer had worked his way around so that he was almost directly behind the mutie creature, bringing the scattergun to his shoulder and bracing himself in the soft ground. If J.B. pulled the trigger before Abe had thrown himself flat, then the murderous little fléchettes would rip his head off his shoulders.

The cottonmouth was becoming more and more agitated. Its shovel-shaped skull swayed faster and faster, eyes blinking, its forked tongue darting in and out more quickly. Its jaws gaped open only inches from Abe's face, and he could see the tiny translucent pearls of poison clinging to the tip of each of the two large, hooked teeth.

"Now, Abe!" The sudden shout made him start, jerking him from the submissive paralysis.

The tight coils of the snake, wrapped around his ankles, made any sort of movement difficult. But Abe managed it, throwing himself clumsily backward, breaking his fall with his hands.

His vision was filled with the great head of the cottonmouth, looming over him, striking down toward his face.

The thunderous boom of J.B.'s powerful shotgun echoed across the wide canyon.

Abe closed his eyes, arms raised in a futile attempt to deflect the attack. There was a sudden spray of warm liquid, and he screamed as the muscular coils about his lower legs contracted with unbelievable force.

The shotgun boomed again.

The first round from the 12-gauge had very nearly missed the lightning-fast strike of the mutie killer. Of the twenty Remington fléchettes in each of the eight shells, only four had actually struck the snake, a hand's span below the skull. The inch-long needle-tipped darts sliced a chunk from the scaled flesh, making the cottonmouth rear up, hissing furiously. It turned toward the source of the noise and the pain, its helpless prey temporarily forgotten.

One of the most important things that Trader had drummed into all of his crews was never to make any kind of assumption in a potentially life-threatening situation.

J.B. had actually been working on the expectation that his first set of fléchettes would totally miss the rearing snake. He levered in another round and readied himself to fire immediately, giving himself just that vital splinter of a single broken second that would have been lost if he'd paused to check the result of his first shot.

He fired from halfway between hip and shoulder, bracing himself against the kick of the Smith & Wesson. The range was so close that it seemed as if the muzzle of the M-4000 were touching the dusty, blood-speckled scales.

There was no time for the darts to star out, striking as a compacted mass of slicing, piercing death.

J.B. took a half-dozen rapid, careful steps back, making sure that he kept his footing in the slippery mud. He brought a third round under the hammer, watching the pitching agony of the giant reptile. The darts had torn out a huge wound, much larger than a man's fist, about four feet below the questing head. It had broken the endless spine and opened up the breathing and digestive tracts of the creature.

For Abe, still pinned and totally helpless on his back, there was a moment of dreadful crushing pain, and the thought that he would have his legs pulped in the cottonmouth's death throes.

But the coils relaxed and he managed to scrabble away, splashing through the narrow stream.

"Again!" he yelled. "Give the fucker another couple rounds, J.B."

"No need. Done for." The Armorer watched the serpent in its thrashing, ruined ending, stepping farther to one side. "Just keep clear of it."

There was terminal brain damage as all the neural lines of communication went down for the cottonmouth. It was kicking up a great spray of wet mud and grass, biting itself, the poisoned fangs snapping off short, spurting the venom in a glittering arc of blinding beads.

J.B. turned away, feeling a few tiny spots land on the skin of his face, patterning his spectacles. The ichor burned like acid and he stooped, cupping water and splashing it on the poison, diluting it and washing the worst of it away.

The snake had plowed up the hollow, turning it into a quagmire of soft mud. Gradually, as its movements began to slow, it started to slide down the hillside toward the brink of the steeper drop high above the distant river. Bright blood still gushed from the two wounds, and its jaws were opening and closing in a series of mindless spasms.

"Going over!" Abe yelped, struggling to his feet, slipping and nearly falling. "Bastard's goin' right over!"

The gigantic cottonmouth was failing, its jerking and twisting getting more sluggish. There was a moment when it seemed that, despite its devastating injuries, it might still come back at them. J.B. had started to reload the scattergun, and he stopped, knuckles white on the pistol grip on the folding butt, moving the muzzle to cover the mutie reptile.

Then it was gone.

Both men stepped carefully and looked over, watching the last moments of the creature as it dropped several hundred feet, finishing in a cloud of dust on a ledge close above the river, where it lay quite still.

"That's it," Abe said. "Thanks a lot, friend. Thought I was an ace on the line for snake supper."

The Armorer touched his face. "That poison stings like a bastard," he said. "Let's get up on top and try and find some good water. Could do with a proper wash and something to drink. Dry as a scorpion's stingaree."

Patches of thick conifers rimmed the canyon, mainly spruce and larch, with a number of taller ponderosa pines. There was no sign of any real trails, though it wasn't difficult for the men to make their way southward along the edge.

"There's that ruined building," Abe said, stooping to rub at his sore ankles. "Smoke out the chimney. Could mebbe go and take a look."

"Why not?"

J.B. FOUND HIS WATER a quarter mile along, where the trees had thinned out, showing the glint of a large, reed-lined pool. A heron, disturbed from its fishing, flapped its stately way into the air, flying away inland.

"Could've shot it," Abe said.

"With the scattergun or the Uzi? Can't say either of them are the best weapons for going wildfowling. That place is occupied. Don't want to let them know we're in the area. Not until we're ready for that."

Abe flopped down and drank from the cool water, cupping it to his face, splashing noisily. The Armorer was more cautious. He stood still and took a good three-sixty look around the open clearing before taking off his stained fedora and placing his glasses neatly on top of it.

"Skin flames where the poison got sprayed on it," he said. "Come out in a rash."

Abe turned and stared at it. "Yeah. Kind of little whiteheads, with sore, red places around them. Give them a real good washing, J.B."

The Armorer winced as the icy water bathed the spots, running down his neck, inside his collar. "Better," he said. "Cooled them some."

He was kneeling down, leaning over the small lake, when he straightened. "Black dust!"

"What?"

"Look. The surface of... It's another..."

The pool was rippling, as though a strong wind had gusted across it. But there wasn't more than the lightest breeze. Abe, standing up, felt the earth begin to shift beneath his combat boots.

"Quake!" he shouted.

"Could be an aftershock," the Armorer said, snatching up his spectacles and his beloved hat. He straightened, rocking to his left at a severe jolt.

They heard the same rumbling noise, far below them, like a procession of subterranean war wags.

Somewhere on the far side of the lake they saw one of the tallest of the pines suddenly start to fall, crashing down, its top splashing into the water.

A beaver broke from cover, under the bank to their left, and started to swim across the rippling pool. There was an explosive gout of mud and bubbles and it vanished, giving a desperate cry, disturbingly like a terrified child.

J.B. and Abe looked at each other, waiting for the quake to subside.

Chapter Twenty-Four

Baron Torrance was everything that his ville of High-tower would have led you to expect—disgusting, run-down and filthy.

He was lying on a mattress on the floor, in what looked like it might once have been the main restaurant of the sprawling resort hotel.

Ryan guessed his age would be around seventy. Thin strands of white hair were pasted across the top of a yellowing skull. It was difficult to calculate his weight, but it was certainly the wrong side of three hundred pounds. His little eyes glowered piggishly up at the two outlanders from their wrinkled beds of layered fat. The baron's lips were thin, peeling pettishly back off the yellowed remains of crooked teeth.

"So, these are the men who have been sent by my enemies to assassinate me, Arkadin?"

"They lost their horses and trade goods in the quake, Baron. Managed to climb out the canyon. Came here looking for some kind of help."

"Help? What sort of help would someone of my rank and dignity offer to a pair of murderous wolf's heads?"

"Bed for the night, Baron," Trader said. "Little food to see us on our way in the morning."

"Do we know you?" Torrance asked, leaning up on one elbow, wheezing with the effort of moving. His clothes were just as baggy and shapeless as the man himself, looking like they'd been hastily tacked together from the stained and worn-out curtains of a pesthole gaudy.

"We?" Trader looked across at Ryan. "Something wrong with my old glims, is there, brother Danny? I don't see any 'we' in here, do you?"

They all heard a burst of muffled giggling, coming from behind a curtained doorway at the far end of the shadowy room. But Torrance ignored it.

"A sense of humor can be a fine way of talking yourself onto the gallows, outlander." The baron looked at his sec man. "Do they have names, Arkadin?"

"Danny and Willard King, Baron. Traveled with ammo. Lost the lot."

"Still got pretty blasters there. Managed to hang on to those during the shaky last night? Perhaps you might like to give them to us."

Ryan couldn't tell whether it was supposed to be a joke or a threat. Or just the idle, vacuous suggestion of a sick and bored madman. In terms of giving up their blasters, it didn't much matter which.

"No, Baron. You can try and take our blasters, but we don't give them up."

Again there was sniggering from the far end of the chamber. This time Torrance turned around, the question of their guns seemingly forgotten. "Oh, stop that rad-blasted noise, children." He returned his attention to Trader and Ryan. "You can meet my little girls, outlanders." The baron raised his voice. "Come out!"

"Well, I'll be hung..." Trader stopping his exclamation when Ryan nudged him hard.

Baron Torrance's little girls came simpering out of their hiding places like a pair of overdressed spiders, sidling across the room, hand in hand, pushing and pinching each other, giggling and blushing.

The baron looked around. "For heaven's sake. Behave, girls."

Andy Arkadin stared fixedly across the room, taking care that his eyes never quite focused on anything. Or on anybody.

"Cissie and Bessie Torrance. These are two brothers, my cherubs. Danny and Willard King. They deal in ammo for blasters and got caught in the quake."

Trader seemed quite paralyzed by the sight, but he followed Ryan's lead and offered a small bow. "Good to meet you, ladies," he said.

"Yeah. Best of the day," Ryan added.

Cissie looked to be around fifty, with bubbly curls that had been dyed the color of Kansas wheat. But the coloring had been done several weeks earlier and the roots all showed a clear, strident silver. She was around five-six, looking as if she'd tip the scales a little over the two-fifty mark. Her face was set in a simpering mask that went well with her cupid's-bow mouth, which had been carelessly daubed with scarlet lipstick.

The odd feature was her eyes, out of kilter with the girlish mask. They were a watery gray, like a dead cod, and they had fixed on Trader like a pair of homing missiles.

Bessie was clearly the younger, by around twenty years. Her hair was extremely long, hanging to her waist, colored an indeterminate midbrown. Ryan stared at it, unable to overcome his belief that he had seen any number of tiny insects moving amid the greasy locks.

Both women wore a bizarre mix of clothes. Cissie had a flowered skirt over a pair of torn jeans, tucked into a pair of rubber galoshes. One green and one black. Her upper half was shrouded in what looked like a tablecloth, crudely embroidered with garish flowers.

Bessie, fifty pounds lighter than her older sister, wore a dress made from dozens of pocket handkerchiefs, cobbled together with strands of multicolored silk. Her feet were crammed into golden pumps with high heels.

She was smiling at Ryan, her mouth smeared with purple lipstick, surrounded with a positive viper's nest of septic cold sores.

"Can they stay to supper, Dadsy?" Cissie asked. "You know we never get to see outlanders these days."

"They begged on their knees for the honor of sitting at a meal table with my little girls," the baron replied. "Did you not?" He glared at Ryan and Trader.

It was a painless lie, as long as it was going to lead to a free meal. Ryan and Trader nodded. "Sure did," said the older man. "Be a particular little booger of a pleasure. Won't it, brother?"

"Sure will," Ryan agreed.

The statement sent both sisters into another clinging paroxysm of tinkling laughter.

Torrance looked at his sec man. He wheezed as he tried to speak, but he was overtaken by a coughing fit. His eyes protruded like grapes in an egg custard, and a line of pink spittle drooled from his parted lips. His red complexion shaded gradually to an interesting purple hue. Nobody moved, and after several seconds the fit passed and he was able to speak.

"Arkadin?"

"Baron?"

"Show the outlanders to the . . . guest wing."

"Fell in, Baron."

"Fell in!"

"In the canyon."

"When?"

"Six months ago."

"That was the health-club annex, stupe!"

"No. That went more recent, Baron."

"There's that balcony room with the picture of the owl on the wall. Along from us," Bessie said, her colorless eyes still fixed on Ryan.

"Owl picture fell down, Miss Bessie," Arkadin replied.

"Well, a big poo to you," she said, stamping her foot hard on the wooden floor.

"Yes, sure thing, Miss Bessie." His lips clamped into a straight line. "But I guess I know the room you mean."

He turned to the baron. "That one?"

"Yes, yes." He waved a pudgy, beringed hand at Arkadin. "Be fine. But as soon as you seen them settled, I want you back here faster than a turd down a greased pipe."

"Sure thing."

"Can we go with them, Dadsy?" Cissie asked, clapping her hands together.

"No. Me and my little girls got some talkin' to do before the meal."

He dismissed them with another wave, watching as Arkadin led them back to the door and out into the lobby.

A FADED PICTURE OF AN OWL leaned up against the wall of the room.

Arkadin waved a hand. "No running water in the bath or the shitter. Went a long ways back. And I wouldn't be happy stepping out on that balcony."

There were two beds, one with worm-eaten legs that lay at a crooked angle. Ryan walked past it and carefully opened the double doors onto the oak balcony. He felt the floor creak and noticed a wide crack along the wall at his side.

"Fireblast!"

Trader crossed the room to stand by him. "What ails you, brother Willard?"

"You're Willard. I'm Danny," Ryan said, grinning at Arkadin. "Got a big rock on his head when he was a boy. Still gets a bit scrambled." He turned to look out the window. "I was just thinking that if all three of us jumped up and down at the same time, I reckon this whole place could end in the river."

The view was staggering. The first sensation was of amazement at the optical illusion that the balcony actually hung over the edge of a thousand-foot drop, sheer down to the glittering bracelet of the river.

The second sensation was the sick awareness that it wasn't an optical illusion.

The balcony really did hang out over the edge of the undercut, eroded canyon.

Trader whistled. "I want a piss in the night, I'll find somewhere else to go."

Ryan swallowed hard. Vertigo wasn't normally any kind of a problem for him, but their bedroom in Hightower was something else.

Arkadin slapped him on the shoulder. "Look like you just seen the ghost of your death."

Ryan managed a sickly smile. "That drop is... Yeah. How long before we eat this supper?"

"Time enough. I'll call for you. Food's better than you'd expect from the rest of the ville. Baron Torrance values his meals above all. All except his little girls."

Trader sat on the edge of the unbroken bed. "Yeah. His little girls. Shit, Andy, the one could be my mother. What goes on with them?"

The sec man paused at the door of the room. "Like I said before. Careless talk can easy buy you a ticket on the last nuke out of town. Keep your mouth buttoned tight, Willard. Baron's not a well man. Terrified about swimming the black river and leaving his little girls helpless and the ville unprotected. Doesn't trust any of us from Hightower. Been sending out trailers all across the land. See if there was any wanted the job."

"Job?" Ryan asked, not understanding.

"Yeah. Trailers asked for husbands for Bessie and Cissie. Never got the right reply. Oh, plenty of men turned up. Doesn't matter how poor a ville is, there'll always... But the girls never seemed to take to them."

"Long as they don't take to us," Trader said, lying back, crossing his legs, wincing a little at the pain from his bruised thigh.

The sec man opened his mouth, as if he were going to say something. Then he changed his mind and closed it again. He waved and went out, closing the door firmly behind him.

Ryan looked across at his former leader. "Try and remember what our names are."

"Guess those two pretty little fillies drove all that clear out of my mind, Ryan. Boy, they are triple something, aren't they?"

There was no reply. Ryan had gone across to stand near the balcony, looking out along the rim of the canyon. "Just wondering what happened to J.B. and Abe."

"They'll be out there, someplace," Trader said confidently. "Out there."

Chapter Twenty-Five

The food was about adequate. There was trout, the skin blackened, some of the flesh too pink, oozing a clear liquid, but parts of the fish were excellent; creamed potatoes, well prepared, with a sweet mixture of apple and pink cabbage; some duck, too greasy for Ryan's palate, with wild rice and a mix of thinly sliced peppers, covered in a fiery sauce of green chilies.

The beer was good and cold, served from misted pitchers by a couple of silent, dark-skinned women.

There were only five people at the meal.

Ryan and Trader sat opposite each other at the low table, both freshly shaved and washed.

Baron Torrance was at the head, looking a little less filthy and disgusting than earlier in the day, wearing a green-and-orange kaftan, belted across his capacious belly.

His daughters sat next to him, Cissie alongside Trader, Bessie close to Ryan. Very close to Ryan.

Too close to Ryan.

The sisters wore nearly identical outfits—white blouses, cut low and tight across the tops of their nearly identical breasts, and loose black skirts of antique cotton. Both wore tan sandals, with straps that laced up to the knee.

They both sported an extraordinary amount of jewelery, mainly turquoise and silver. They were cheap pieces that had seen better days, though Ryan spotted one or two quality items, including the heavy squash blossom, in solid silver, that dangled around Bessie's wattled throat.

The other thing that Ryan noticed about Bessie was the smell of her body. Overlaid with cheap soap and scent, there was a strange odor of musk and mold, as though a dead bird had become trapped in a box of face powder.

Her chair was so close to his that he couldn't move without brushing against her. While they ate bowls of pumpkin soup, the girls kept up a flood of chatter about clothes, food, hunting and how great Hightower had once been.

And how great it could be again.

Baron Torrance half lay, half sat on an overstuffed sofa, picking and slurping at the meal, using his ringed fingers rather than any of the costly jade-handled cutlery that was at everyone's places.

He contributed little to the evening, only showing any enthusiasm on the subject of how strong and influential the ville could be.

"I have been a sick man these many years," he said, "and my little girls are not skilled in the ways of the cruel and cunning world. But with the right sort of help, they can rule when I am gone."

Ryan spotted the dilation of the pupils of his eyes and the brittle urgency of his words. Catching Trader's attention he traced the single letter *j* on the linen cloth, without anyone else noticing.

Trader nodded his understanding and his agreement. The baron was fast in the relentless claws of the coke and mescal mix commonly called jolt.

During the first course Bessie Torrance twice dropped her napkin, refusing to allow Ryan to pick it up for her, making much play of reaching below the table for it. Each time her right hand settled on Ryan's thigh, well above the knee.

Each time a little higher.

The same thing happened three times during the fish course of the meal.

It wasn't the first time that Ryan had been felt up by a woman. But they were generally gaudy sluts after a purse of jack. It wasn't all that often you found the daughter of a baron groping at your jewel casket.

He considered shifting his chair, but a leg of the long table had been artfully placed to his side, blocking off any movement. Across the table he had noticed that Cissie's left hand had also vanished and that Trader was breathing just a little more quickly than usual.

The old man used to say that if you were going to get fucked up the ass and there was no way to avoid it, then you should try to lie back and accept it.

And, of course, make sure you chilled the sodomite at the very earliest opportunity.

Bessie was gentle in her ministrations, and he found himself starting to respond.

The dessert, placed in front of them all, was a baked sponge cake, filled with slices of fruit and served with chilled cream.

Halfway through the course, Bessie's napkin fluttered floorward again. She tutted at her carelessness and slipped once more under the table. But this time she didn't reappear. Ryan felt her fingers butterflying at his crotch, and he saw that Cissie had also vanished out of sight.

And, at the head of the table, Baron Torrance was sitting bolt upright, his eyes flicking between his two outlander guests and the half-dozen armed sec men that had been standing, silent and patient, around the walls of the dining room.

"Fine little girls, are they not?" he asked suddenly.

At that moment of realization, Ryan had his semierect cock deep between the warm, sucking lips of the younger of the two "little girls."

Trader was already halfway to his feet, a hand pushing the graying head of Cissie from his lap, his right hand reaching for the Armalite that hung from the back of his chair.

Ryan pulled his chair back, ignoring the disappointed snuffling sound from under the table, and went for the SIG-Sauer, holstered at his hip.

But they were both too late.

Behind them they heard the familiar flat clicking of blasters being cocked, every one aimed at their backs from less than six feet away.

"Be a crying double shame if my little ones lost their husbands before they even gotten themselves married," Torrance said very quietly.

"Husbands." Ryan took a slow breath, catching Trader's eye, seeing from the tension in the older man's body that he was about to take terminal action, all combat sense blinded by the sick intensity of the betrayal. He was going to grab for the Armalite, regardless of the armed men behind them.

"No," Ryan said. "You do it now and they'll take me along with you. Don't want that, brother. No blood on the floor. Take it easy for now."

To his relief, he saw the brittle, broken-glass intensity seep away from Trader, who relaxed and sat back in his chair, making a casual gesture of surrender with both hands.

"Good, good. Wise move, outlanders. Come out from under the table, my little doves."

First Bessie, then Cissie came giggling into the open, both wiping their mouths.

Ryan started to eat his dessert, using the act as a way of keeping himself calm, knowing that this wasn't a time for violence. They'd been caught cold. All they could do was wait and see what happened.

And hope that it wouldn't be too bad.

BESSIE WAS an enthusiastic lover, working herself into a sweat to try to give her husband-to-be the best possible time.

But Ryan found it difficult to keep his mind on what was going on under the blankets. The fact that Trader was receiving similar service in the same room—they'd propped up the broken leg of the bed—didn't help much.

Nor did the four armed sec men, including the grinning Andy Arkadin, who stood guard by door and balcony, do anything to increase sexual enthusiasm.

Before leaving the dining table, he and Trader had been forced to strip naked, submitting themselves to an intimate body search. The fact that it was carried out by Cissie and Bessie didn't make much difference to the humiliation and indignity.

The Steyr in the bedroom had been retrieved by a sec man, and all of the other weapons were taken from them.

"Get them back one day," the baron promised. "Can't have the husbands of my little ones going around Deathlands with no weapons."

Cissie had reached out and grabbed Trader by his cock, leering at her sister. "My husband's got a real good weapon, here."

Bessie had responded, claiming that her husband was even better equipped.

Ryan had stood quite still during the ordeal. There wasn't anything that he and Trader could do. For the time being. But from what he'd seen of Hightower ville, it wouldn't be all that long before a chance appeared to escape.

Trader used to say that a chance around the next bend in the road was always worth waiting for.

EVENTUALLY IT WAS OVER. The women, sated by their pleasure, had gathered up their clothes and left the room. Three of the guards had also gone, with only Arkadin remaining behind.

"Want some water brought in for a wash?" he asked.

"Go fuck a dead stickie, you grinning bastard!" Trader was sitting on the side of the bed, peering at his lower stomach and groin, wiping away a thin smear of blood.

"Words don't do no good, old man," Arkadin replied. "Trying to help is all."

Ryan stood, wincing at the stickiness that held him to the blankets, stretching to get some of the discomfort out of his body.

"Sure. Water'd be good. Hot if you got it."

"We got it." He turned toward the door. "Listen, all you have to do is sit quiet and do like the little ladies tell you. Baron can't live forever. I don't want to take orders from them two. So... you could be barons here."

"Not what we want!" Trader had the chilling light in his eyes, and Ryan worked to calm him.

"Could be right, Willard," he said. "Let's just take it easy. Get cleaned up."

"Take a blowtorch to get me clean of that triple slut." He punched his right hand into his left palm. "All right, all right. Get us some hot water and soap, sec man."

"No point trying the balcony," Arkadin said. "And there's men at the door all the time."

"What've you done with our blasters and knives?" Ryan asked.

"You'll get them back, in the baron's time. Until then they stay in his room."

"Gettin' dark," Ryan said.

"Lamps on that table. I'll send in some extra oil for them with the water."

In the background they heard the shuddering cough of a gas wag starting up."

"What's that?" Trader asked.

"Evening patrol." Arkadin paused with his fingers on the handle of the door. "These bad quakes mean some changes to the land. Baron likes to know what they are."

The door swung open, and they could see the instant attention of the four armed men outside.

"One thing, sec man," Trader said.

"Sure."

"This bullshit about husbands and weddings."

"It's not bullshit. You still don't believe it?"

"Those women want to marry us?" Ryan laughed. "Why us? Fireblast! Doesn't make sense."

"Does when you realize we don't see many outlanders. Mostly poor trash. Times are getting hard, boys, and husbands are real scarce."

"So when are we all going to enjoy this happy event?" Ryan asked.

"Didn't the little girls tell you?"

"They were much too busy fucking to do much talking," Trader snapped.

"Day after next. Be a rehearsal noon tomorrow. Then it'll be all systems go."

Chapter Twenty-Six

As he knelt down, Doc's overwhelming fear was that he wouldn't be able to get it up, or he'd get it up and not be able to keep it up, or that he'd get it up, and then come in three-eighths of a second.

He was also conscious of the cold northerly wind blowing up his bare ass, his boots creaking in the sand and the shuffling of Judas in the undergrowth.

Most of all he was aware of the attractive middle-aged woman who lay spread and waiting for him.

As though she sensed his doubts and fears, Sukie reached up and gently cupped him in her hands, smiling up at him. "All right?" she whispered.

"Oh, indeed, yes," he replied, feeling himself full and hard. "Oh, yes."

"OUT BEYOND THE DARKNESS there are no stars."

"How's that, Doc?"

"Forgive me, my dear lady. I was not aware that I had put my thoughts into words."

"Sounded like a poem."

"My poor brain is so filled to overflowing with half-remembered quotes and memories that I can no longer distinguish one from another."

"It was lovely."

They were lying under the blanket, spoon-fashion, her buttocks pressed against him. To Doc's bemused amazement they had already made love three times.

The first had been hurried and intense, both of them clinging together like drowning sailors, snatching at the moment with a fierce passion.

The second time had been slower, the movements gentler. Doc had been aware of the wondrous feeling of her body enclosing him, warm, moist and firm, sucking him deep inside her. Her voice whispered in his ears, telling him to go faster or slower, controlling it so that they both reached a thundering, trembling climax at the same moment.

After that Doc seemed to recall that they'd both slept for a while, wrapped in each other's arms.

He'd awakened to feel Sukie using her mouth, lips and tongue on him, bringing him to an unbelievable hardness for an incredible third time. He had lain back and watched the shape of her head, bobbing up and down under the blanket. Reaching down he'd tangled his fingers in her long blond hair, holding her still while he began to move against her.

But she had judged when he was coming close to his climax and wriggled back up his body.

"Gentleman doesn't finish his dessert before the lady has her soup," she said.

"But that was wonderful. I've never known such..."

"You got a lady here can suck the inside out of a grapefruit at twenty paces, Doc." She smiled at him. "Your turn now for a little eating out."

"I was always considered a cunning linguist," he said, but he saw she didn't get the joke. "Going down." He slid lower, kissing her breasts for a while, bringing the nipples to cherry-stone hardness, before she pushed gently but firmly on the top of his head, spreading herself to receive his attentions.

He could still taste her on his tongue, the rich, feral scent of her arousal. As he had pressed his face into her body, Sukie had closed her thighs around him, shutting out all sound and sense. Doc had quickly found the center of his interest, sucking it between his lips, making her moan with delight.

She stopped him only when she knew she was hovering on the brink of her climax, the muscles of her stomach fluttering. She pulled him back up to the top of their makeshift bed and slid him quickly inside her.

"Together, Doc," she whispered.

And that had been the third time.

Now, with the pressure of her body against him, Doc could feel a fourth miracle beginning.

She felt it, too. "You never get tired, Doc," she said, letting it lie somewhere between a question and a statement.

"I can't recall being in such stimulating company for many a long day, dear lady," he said.

"Flattering old dog."

"Flattery, they do say, will eventually get you everywhere, madam."

"And look where it got you. Save the life of a poor, frail traveler. Lost and helpless in this burning wilderness. Couple minutes later and you're dipping your beak in the honeypot like it was going out of fashion. You been in the sexual desert awhile, Doc?''

"Awhile."

"Guessed it. You not had anyone steady for a few weeks? Is that it?''

"Weeks! I would that it were only weeks, my dear Sukie. I cannot truly tell you how long it must have been since I have enjoyed satisfactory congress.'' There had been one or two isolated examples since he'd been trawled. Lori Quint, he recalled, had been a beautiful, wild child.

"How about gaudy sluts? You never gone with whores, Doc? Never?''

He hesitated for several beats of the heart. "Some time ago," he said cautiously, not wanting to give the woman too much information about himself too quickly, "I was most cruelly plucked from my home and my loved ones and taken to a strange place, many miles away.''

"Slaved? Heard of that, Doc.''

"The men who had taken me wanted me because of some knowledge I had. It doesn't matter what that was. But they tried to keep me happy in my imprisonment. Like offering a sweetmeat to a caged songbird. They took me out, under the most careful supervision, and allowed me to respond to the come-ons of whores working down on Seventh Avenue.''

Sukie squirmed a little, reaching behind her to see how his interest was going and found that it was rising. "Go on. Where's this Seventh Avenue ville?''

"New York, that most toddling of towns.''

"Thought it was totaled. Just ghouls and a shit-lot of nuking left."

"Ah, this was...in another sort of place." He pressed on before she began to question him again. "Anyway, these whores on Seventh Avenue. I must confess that there were odd occasions that I took some comfort there to ease my loneliness." He coughed. "But it was a poor comfort indeed."

"Well, it feels to me like you're ready for some of my own home-cooked comfort again, Doc?"

"So I am, my dear madam, so I am."

After that they slept together, most comfortably, secure in the knowledge that Judas would give them ample warning of any dangerous intruder.

For the first time in a long while Doc Tanner relished a gentle and dreamless sleep, free of the hag-ridden nightmares that normally plagued him.

BY THE TIME HE WOKE, the fire was burning brightly, and Doc could smell sausages frying in the skillet. Coffee sub was boiling and, most amazingly, Sukie was standing next to the mule, gently stroking his neck.

"Watch him, dear lady," Doc warned. "He can be trusted as far as a politician's promise."

"Seems sweet enough to me, Doc. Guess he's like a lot of men. Handle them right and they'll just eat out of your hand." She turned and walked toward him, smiling. "Though it wasn't exactly my hand that you were eating out of last night."

To his great embarrassment, Doc found that a rosy blush was spreading up his neck and across his cheeks, suffusing his entire face with bright crimson.

"I did not think that you . . ." he stammered.

Sukie laughed and sat down by him, leaning across, one arm snaking around his neck. She kissed him softly on the cheek, then tousled his hair. "You're something else, Doc, you know that? Really something else."

"I'LL CLEAN UP the pans, Doc."

"No, I would not dream of . . ." He shook his head. "Not with you injured."

She held up a hand. "Hell, that feels a sight better than last night. The exercise must've helped it. I mean it. There's a triple-big debt between us."

"Firstly there never was a debt, as well you know. If a gentleman cannot assist a damsel in distress without some expectation of recompense, then things have come to a sorry pass. And, secondly, if . . . That is . . . If a debt had existed, then last night's . . . activities would have more than wiped the slate clean between us."

She kissed him again, then left him to clamber slowly out of the bed. He headed to the nearby stream for a wash, taking care to give Judas a wide berth. Doc gasped at the icy chill of the bubbling water.

It was a wonderful morning, with the cool freshness in the air that is so typical of the Colorado Plateau. A large bird flew way above him, riding the thermals, but Doc couldn't make out what it was.

Peering into the bright sky made his eyes blur, and he rubbed at them.

He looked out across the flowing ridges of the foothills, way down to the open expanse of the desert. Somewhere down there was the homestead of Jak Lauren. Down there would be Krysty, Dean and Mildred. Maybe Ryan and J.B. returned, during his absence.

A dust devil skittered across the gray-yellow land. Or was it smoke?

"Smoke," Doc muttered. "By the Three Kennedys, but it looks uncommonly like a plume of smoke. I trust that all is well with my friends."

But, even as he looked, the wind rose and the thin pillar of smoke was blown away. Though he watched for another couple of minutes, it didn't reappear.

"Everything all right, Doc?" Sukie called from near the embers of the dying fire.

"Indeed, yes, my dear lady. I believe that everything is quite excellent."

Chapter Twenty-Seven

Dean's morning bonfire had gotten just a little out of control. It had started well enough, when he'd risen very early from his bed, before anyone else was stirring, intent on finishing the job of clearing old straw out of one of the smaller barns. It had been dry, mixed with ancient horse manure, and he'd shoveled and barrowed it outside.

Jak had told him to take it out well beyond the corral fence, past a patch of dry scrub, along the flank of an old wall, to the edge of an arroyo. He wasn't to start burning it until he'd found a safe place.

But that meant negotiating a narrow, bumpy section of the path, between piles of stones.

Nobody else was up and around, and Dean had decided to take a chance. He filled the straw against the ruined remains of the wall, with patches of adobe still covering it, then looked toward the house before lighting the fire.

The self-light had caught quickly, the wispy flame almost invisible in the startling brightness of the dawn sunrise. Then there had been a little feathery smoke, and a sound like a faintly indrawn breath.

The next moment the eleven-year-old was up on his feet, sprinting as if the hounds of Hades were at his heels, yelling for Jak and the two women.

The fire had blazed up, a few clumps caught by a gust of wind from the west, and carried into the dry scrub, which ignited instantly. Only then had Dean spotted the danger. Tufts of grass ran all along the low wall, which connected to the larger barn, where some of the livestock was kept.

It would only be a matter of minutes before the tongues of fire raced along the lee of the tumbled wall and reached the dust-dry timbers of the barn.

THEY STOPPED IT only a couple of yards short.

The thin column of smoke that had been rising into the still air was choked off and died.

Krysty threw down her scorched broom, wiping sweat from her sooty face, pushing back her fiery hair. "Gaia! Not the kind of start to a day that I like."

"Me neither." Mildred held a flat piece of leather nailed to a broom handle to make a fire-beater. It had worked effectively on the grass blaze, but would have been useless if the flames had traveled six feet farther.

Jak had been using a long-hafted spade to beat out the danger. Now he threw it down in the sand and wiped smudges of dirt from his white face. His snowy hair was matted with perspiration and flakes of charred grass. His eyes were as red as the pit when he turned to look toward Dean, who had dropped to his knees, fighting for breath.

"Well?"

"Not my fault, Jak."

"Not?"

"No."

"Krysty's fault?"

"Course not."

"Mildred? Me? No?"

"I didn't know it was going to set the grass alight. It was a kind of fluke of the wind, Jak. Honest."

The albino took three menacing steps toward the boy. "Honest! Not honest, kid! Not honest. Where did I tell light fire? Not here."

"Not exactly. You said to take the straw and stuff over to the edge of the draw and set light to it over there. It was hard so..."

"So took easy way. Could've burned barn. Lost animals. Know that?"

The boy stood, looking at his feet, not meeting the teenager's angry glare. The two women watched in silence. "I'm sorry, Jak. It was triple stupe. And I'm sorry."

"Ought to beat your ass black and blue."

"Sure. Make you feel better. But it won't make me feel any more stupe than I do now."

Jak nodded slowly. "Right. Make sure all sparks out. Then come back house and all get cleaned up."

Krysty looked toward the distant mountains, already shimmering behind heat haze. "Sure hope Doc didn't see the smoke from up there. Wherever he is."

Mildred nodded. "Right. It would worry him a lot. Probably spoil his trip. Send him rushing back down here to see what was wrong."

DEAN KEPT HIMSELF out of everybody's way for the rest of the morning and the early part of the afternoon. He was furiously angry with himself for having come close to causing a disaster by his own laziness and lack of foresight. If he'd been concentrating on what was happening, he would have felt the breeze and seen the threat to the outbuildings.

He had gone out alone to the edge of the ranch's land, finding a grove of flowering cherries that stood around a muddy waterhole. Dean lay flat on his stomach and flicked pebbles at a group of red ants that were laboring together to dispose of the carcass of a scorpion.

"Hurry up home, Dad," he said. "Been away long enough. Come on home."

It had never occurred to the boy, for even a splinter of a second, that Ryan wouldn't eventually return safely to rejoin them.

He stood and looked back toward the distant house and to the hills beyond.

It wasn't quite clear to Dean just why Doc had gone wandering off on this trip on his own. He wasn't much of a marksman, so it obviously wasn't for hunting. There'd been a conversation between Krysty and Mildred about it, part of which the boy had overheard.

They'd talked about "finding himself," though it seemed to the boy that the old-timer had more chance of losing himself up in the high country.

His keen hearing caught a sound behind him, and he turned, his fingers dropping automatically to the butt of his big 9 mm Browning.

It was the crack of a buggy whip. A couple of miles to the west, moving slowly over the trail between the dunes, was an old-fashioned canvas-topped wag, drawn by a pair of horses. It was what Dean knew used to be called a prairie schooner in the old times, even before predark. J.B. had told him that they were properly known as Conestoga wagons—after the ville in Lancaster County, Pennsylvania, where they were manufactured—and that the early settlers had ridden in them, with all their possessions, from the Sippi to the ocean.

Now one was lurching toward him.

Dean took a last careful look, seeing that there were two people sitting up on the box, and making sure there were no other wags or riders, before turning and starting to jog back toward the spread.

JAK HAD WATCHED the approaching strangers through a pair of binoculars. "Look ill," he said. "Man and woman."

They had taken the usual precautions. Dean on the top floor, by the attic window, cradling his Remington 580. The two women covered the first story, with Krysty making an occasional check out back to make sure that the approaching wag wasn't part of an ambush. Jak sat on the swing seat on the porch, the .357 Magnum with the six-inch barrel in his lap.

The horses looked exhausted, their chests flecked with crusted sweat. They stopped about fifty yards from the house, as the driver tugged once on the reins. The canvas was lashed tight over the iron hoops, stained with the red-orange mud of the desert.

"Hi," Jak called, not moving from his seat.

The man was around fifty, shoulders stooped, with a dark beard, speckled with white. The woman who sat next to him seemed about the same age. Her hair was gray and looked to have been badly cut, with bare patches of skull showing through.

With a visible effort, the driver hauled on the brake, looping the reins around it. "We're tired out," he said, his voice barely carrying.

"Welcome water horses. Give you meal if you want. Stay night here."

The woman began to cry, her shoulders shaking. "You mean sleep in a bed?" she asked.

"Guess so."

The man climbed down, walking around the rig to help his wife off the seat. She was so weak that she nearly fell and hung on to his shoulder.

Behind Jak, Mildred and Krysty came out onto the porch, both holding guns.

"No need for them," the man said. "We don't have a bow and arrow between us."

"Mind showing us inside the rig?" Jak asked, standing and moving toward them.

"No!" The woman almost screamed.

Jak stopped, bringing up the blaster. Krysty and Mildred also covered the strangers while the barrel of Dean's .22 rifle poked out of the upstairs window.

The man waved his free hand, while struggling to support his distraught wife. "Don't chill us, folks. I'll explain a little more after we've taken a rest. We got something precious in the wag here. Something could make us a fortune."

"Don't tell them, Ronny," the woman sobbed. "They'll murder us for it."

Krysty spoke. "If we wanted to chill you, then we'd likely have done it by now, lady. You got something you figure's valuable, then that's your business. Be safe with us. But we have to look inside and make sure you don't have a dozen armed men there waiting to try and coldcock us. Understand?"

"Sure," the man replied. "Sure. Take a look. But the . . . thing we got. It's wrapped up. Please don't . . . You know?"

Jak called up the stairs. "Dean. Come down and have look inside rig. But don't go in and don't touch nothing."

"Anything," Krysty corrected automatically. She grinned at Jak. "Sorry. Used to that with Ryan."

"Name's Ronny Warren," the man said. "This is my woman, Raelene. Traveling from over White Sands way. Good distance. Found our treasure there. Taking it to find a real triple-powerful baron. Where's the nearest ville like that?"

Jak shook his head. "Don't know. One a ways east. Direction you're heading. But . . ."

"What, mister? Can't we get in and have a rest and some water, please?"

"Sure."

Dean appeared on the steps. He walked past the strangers, pulling himself up and unlacing part of the back of the canvas covering, peering in.

"Don't let him touch our..." the woman began, but her eyes rolled white back in their sockets and she slumped unconscious in her husband's arms.

Krysty and Mildred moved to help, while Jak stayed, watchful, on guard, waiting to hear what Dean reported.

"Nothing in here. Pots and pans. Clothes. And this thing they're so fired about. Looks around eight feet long. But it's all tied in rags. Want me to..."

"Leave it," Jak said. "Just leave it and come in."

The man looked over his shoulder. "Could the boy see to the team? Put the rig into your barn for safety?"

"Sure. I'll help him."

"Grateful, folks. Most grateful."

Jak nodded, his ruby eyes staring intently as Mildred and Krysty half carried Raelene Warren into the house. Though he said nothing, he was looking puzzled.

Doc's room had a big double bed in it, and the strangers were put there. The woman was moaning, tossing her head from side to side, almost delirious. Mildred fetched some cold fresh water and bathed her forehead, mouth and neck, cooling the fever. Ronny stood helplessly by, watching.

"Get her into bed. Take a rest yourself. Anything we can get you?"

"No, thanks, ma'am. Don't know your names. Should do so we can say a prayer to the Good Lord for sending us your way."

"I'm Mildred Wyeth. This is Krysty Wroth. Boy with white hair is Jak Lauren. His spread. Kid is called Dean Cawdor. Son of a friend who's away for a few days."

"I thank you. The Lord'll be certain to reward you for your Christian kindness."

KRYSTY FOUND MILDRED scrubbing her hands with carbolic soap in the kitchen sink, working at her nails with a stiff-bristled brush.

"What's wrong? You think they got a bad illness?"

Mildred dried her hands on a small towel. "Don't know, Krysty. Need to examine them more carefully. But I don't much like what I've seen so far."

Chapter Twenty-Eight

It was ten minutes off noon, and another of the brilliant, crystal-clear days with an untouched sky from horizon to horizon. Only a light breeze ruffled the sagebrush and swayed the stately tops of the ocotillo. A red-breasted jay was perched snugly in among the murderous spikes of a tall saguaro, only a few yards from the main doors of Hightower ville.

Ryan had moved as close as he dared to the brink of their tottering balcony, peering into the singing abyss at the snaking river far, far below.

"Don't know why I keep on doing this," he said to Trader, who was sitting on the broken bed, knotting the laces of his worn combat boots.

"What?"

"Looking over the edge."

"No hope of getting out there. Unless you stand on the balcony and jump up and down."

"Then you get all the way, no stopping."

The older man stood, testing his feet for comfort. "Don't feel even part-dressed without my blaster and knives. Those bastards!"

"Time'll come, partner."

"Sure. But how long? They won't give us blasters for a while. Even after this dark-nighted wedding."

"Probably folks'll find it sort of amusing. When words leaks around Deathlands."

"Think Krysty'll laugh in a bright and merry way, Ryan?"

There was no answer. Ryan was flexing his fingers, one hand against the other, just for something to do. The rehearsal for the double marriage ceremony was scheduled to take place at midday, in about five minutes.

"There's that land wag again," Trader said, head to one side. "Looks like there might be a gas supply around to the north of the ville. The wag's big enough to get us well on the way home. If we can steal it."

"They're watching us like hawks over rabbits."

"Wonder what happened to Abe and the Armorer?"

Ryan shook his head. "Can't bet jack on them turning up, Trader. Down to us."

"Always is."

There was a knock on the door of their room, and Arkadin called out, "Ready Danny? Willard? The little girls are waiting for the rehearsal."

"Coming," Ryan said. One of the lamps was still burning and he turned the brass wheel to extinguish it, nearly knocking over one of the spare cans of oil as he moved.

"SOME KIND OF CEREMONY," Abe said. "They got sec men all over the place."

J.B. checked his wrist chron. "About five minutes to high noon."

"Fine day."

"Sure."

There was an open space on one side of the old building, on the opposite end to the wing that had plunged into the canyon. It was crossed with a number of narrow stone-lined paths, some of them skirting the white picket fence that edged the drop. About a dozen armed men stood in a loose circle, as though they were waiting for something to happen.

The Armorer and Abe had made their way through the scrub and scattered trees that filled the area around the ville. They had seen a crudely carved sign warning them that they were moving onto land owned by Hightower.

Now they were lying in an ancient drainage ditch, about eight yards from the nearest point of the ville.

"Could get some food there." J.B. yawned. "Wait until dark. Doesn't look the tightest-run ship in the world."

"You don't think Ryan or Trader might be there?"

The Armorer considered the possibilities, weighing them up in his combat-computer mind. "Mebbe," he decided.

"Only a mebbe?"

J.B. ticked off the points with his fingers. "Firstly they might have been chilled in that initial surge of the flood after the main quake hit. Horses went under. I doubt they could have made their way out of the canyon at that point. Unless they crossed when we did, and I don't think they did that."

"No," Abe agreed. "Hey, there's a fat lady coming out the door. Means the show's goin' to start when she sings."

J.B. ignored him. "But we didn't see them anywhere caught. So, they might've made it onto a fallen tree or something like that. Enough shit going down the pike. No sign of anyone getting out where we did, on that bridge. Or tracks higher, where we ran into the cottonmouth."

"It's a man, not a woman. Old and unsteady on his feet. Got a scarf around his head. Way the sec men straightened up, I figure him for the baron."

The sun flashed off the Armorer's glasses as he glanced up for a moment. "Yeah."

Abe looked across at him. "I didn't hear you say anything to make you think that they probably got out. Just a lot of stuff about what they didn't do."

"This place can be seen from the bottom, by the river. Only one for miles and miles. If they came down on the flood, then this is where they would've made for."

"That the mebbe?"

"Yeah. That's the mebbe."

RYAN AND TRADER WAITED in the main entrance hall of the old resort hotel. Great timbers, hewn from the living forest, towered all around them. Andy Arkadin was standing with them, his blaster held very casually in his hands. They had watched Baron Torrance sweep past, his head swathed in a turban of vivid purple silk.

His thin lips had been moving, and his hoggish eyes twitched nervously from side to side.

He seemed totally oblivious to their presence, or where he was going. Or why he was going there.

A young woman servant stepped discreetly from the shadows and guided him out of the double door into the brilliant midday sunshine beyond.

"Where does he get the jolt from?" Trader asked.

Arkadin looked sharply at him and gestured with the barrel of his gun. "Being married to one of the precious ladies don't mean you can flap your mouth like that, Willard."

"Willard?" Trader looked puzzled for a moment. "Oh, shit, sure. Why not ask? I never seen a man so deep sunk in jolt and still moving around. I doubt he knows which end produces words and which produces shit."

The sec man shook his head at him. "I truly urge you to zip that tongue shut. Way the baron lives and what he does is in that part of the field marked off as his business. Best we all leave it that way."

Trader sniffed. "I always say that a man doesn't ask doesn't get."

"Say what you like," Ryan whispered, "but try saying it quiet."

"Your brides are coming, gentlemen," Arkadin announced. "Just think. This time tomorrow and it'll be all for real. Happily married husbands."

"Yeah," Ryan said. "I think of it constantly."

NOTHING MUCH SEEMED to be happening and Abe had rolled over on his back, absently plucking straggling hairs from his mustache and watching a small flock of unidentified blue birds swooping and diving across the lighter blue of the perfect sky.

"Sure I felt a kind of tremble just then," he said. "Another of those afterquakes?"

"Aftershock," J.B. corrected him. "Felt it too."

"Anything going down?"

"Fat guy's sitting on an old sofa. Can't tell where he begins and the furniture ends."

"Mind if I catch up on sleep?"

J.B. laughed, pushing the brim of the fedora back off his forehead. "Way you snored last night, I wouldn't have thought you needed any more sleep."

"Never get too much." Abe closed his eyes and folded his hands on his chest.

J.B. watched the tableau. It was an almost motionless scene. Every now and then one of the guards would shuffle his feet, or surreptitiously spit a dark stream of tobacco juice onto the watered turf.

He was particularly interested in the precarious state of the main building, perched on the very brink of the canyon. One wing had already fallen, and the rest squatted like a reluctant partner in a suicide pact.

"Hey," he said.

"What?" Abe didn't bother to open his eyes. "What is it?"

"It's either a couple of tubs of lard covered in yesteryear's curtains, or two women just moved out.

Could be the old man's daughters, way they're curtsying and stuff.''

Abe belched and rolled over, rubbing at his eyes. ''Finest gaudy sluts I ever saw. You reckon them as the daughters of a baron, J.B., then you've got to have a spent round under the hammer.'' He laughed. ''Daughters of a baron!''

One of the sec men closest to them half turned, as though he'd caught the snort of amusement from the little gunner. Then he turned back again.

''Quiet,'' J.B. whispered. ''Looks like they're all waiting for something to happen.''

THE SISTERS WERE DRESSED in identical costumes. ''Dresses'' certainly wasn't the right word for what they were wearing, Ryan thought.

In their brief stay as enforced guests in the old resort hotel, both he and Trader had noticed that some of the original floral furnishings still remained, though those exposed to the sun had faded badly. It looked like Cissie and Bessie Torrance had both found a closet somewhere that contained some of these fabrics and they had been cobbled together into bridal gowns.

Purple peonies clashed with orange tulips and electric-green lilacs with silvery lilies.

The two women swayed together through the hall, arm in arm, chins trembling, ignoring their bridegrooms-to-be.

Ryan and Trader watched them in silence as they vanished into the sunshine, following after their father. Immediately after them came a servant, trailing yards of cable, a microphone and a set of speakers.

"What are..." Trader began.

"Baron wants to make sure everyone around the ville can hear the ceremony," Arkadin answered.

"When do we get out there?" asked Ryan.

Arkadin glanced outside, waiting patiently for a signal from one of the other sec men. "Real soon," he said confidently. "Real soon."

"THAT SOMETHING happening yet?" Quickly bored with the lack of any movement in the proceedings, Abe had rolled over onto his back again.

"No." J.B. had removed his spectacles and was assiduously polishing them on a piece of clean cloth from one of his bottomless pockets.

"Why don't we—"

The Armorer interrupted him. "Rigging up some kind of PA system out on the grass. Even if we can't see properly what's going on, we should be able to hear it."

"Great." Abe mimed clapping his hands together. "Can't wait for the thrill."

J.B. replaced his glasses and leaned on his elbows to take another peek at the proceedings. "Dark night!" he exclaimed. "Will you look at that?"

RYAN BLINKED HIS EYE at the dazzling sunlight.

He and Trader had talked briefly during the night about their chances of escape from Hightower ville. Neither was keen to cut and run, leaving their blasters and knives behind. Trader, in particular, was extremely reluctant to abandon his beloved Armalite to Baron Torrance.

"Goes back to my days with Marsh Folsom," he'd said angrily. "Part of my fucking body!" He became so enraged that Ryan had quietened him, reminding him that they were supposed to be brothers, trading in bullets. Not the legendary Trader and his onetime first lieutenant.

Even so, it hadn't taken long for them to agree that they would still snatch any chance to get away from this absurd yet deeply menacing situation.

"Always come back for the blasters," Ryan said.

But it was obvious from the first moment they stepped out of the mustiness of the old hotel into the freshness of late morning that this wasn't going to be the time.

A rough circle of sec men, most holding either hunting rifles or rebuilt handblasters, watched them closely. Baron Torrance was sprawled on a long sofa, studiously picking his nose. The two women stood in front of him side by side, whispering and giggling.

"Who's going to perform the weddings?" Ryan asked.

"No problemo, friends," Arkadin replied. "Got us a whiskey priest coming in from a settlement about twenty miles off. They got a tie with the ville."

"Great," Trader snapped. "I wouldn't want this charade to be done unless it was all proper and legal."

The sec chief laughed. "Like your style, Willard. Really like your style. Now go stand by the ladies."

He pushed Trader in the back, making him stumble. The older man spun, his fists clenched. "Do that again and you'll piss blood for a year!"

"Sure, sure."

Ryan was pointed to stand next to Bessie, who took his arm, smiling at him and licking her lips. Trader's hand was gripped like a bear trap by Cissie.

"Tomorrow, my eagle's heart," whispered the younger of the sisters.

Ryan didn't reply.

There was a long pause, punctuated by fearsome shrieking and crackling from the loudspeakers. The man in charge of them kept tapping the mike, then stooping to make minute adjustments to the controls.

Finally Baron Torrance hauled himself upright and lumbered to the servant. "What in the blood of the martyrs is going on?"

His voice, vastly amplified, boomed out over the ground of the ville, echoing across the canyon.

"WHAT'RE RYAN AND TRADER doing?" Abe whispered. "Is it an execution?"

"Don't think so. It hasn't got the shadow of death lying there."

But he had readied the Uzi.

"We should get closer if there's going to be some chilling, shouldn't we?"

J.B. didn't answer for several moments, concentrating on the scene ahead of them. "We move closer and they see us. No way around that. Wait for night. You don't broadcast it all over the canyon if you're going to take someone out."

They heard the fat man roar in anger.

"Holy shit!" Abe exclaimed. "That the baron, you reckon? Sounds pissed."

Torrance had grabbed the unlucky servant by the front of his shirt, gripping so hard that a strip of the material peeled away. With his free hand he punched the man so violently in the face that even J.B. and Abe heard the sound of his nose breaking.

RYAN WINCED at the ferocity of the blow. Blood spurted and the servant rocked on his heels, eyes closing. He would have fallen if Torrance hadn't been holding him up.

"Get this garbage out of my sight," the baron yelled, letting the man fall into a crumpled heap. He kicked him twice in the ribs, pettishly, almost as an afterthought.

Cissie and Bessie sniggered, perfectly in unison, like separated Siamese twins.

Torrance snatched at the microphone, making it howl and whistle. "Will someone get here who knows how to work this fuckin' machine?" he roared. "So we can get this bastard wedding rehearsal on the road?"

"WEDDING?" J.B. REPEATED. "Did he say 'wedding,' Abe?"

"Yeah. That's what he said."

Chapter Twenty-Nine

"You both got to read this and remember it, ready for the ceremony tomorrow." Arkadin handed each of them a piece of ragged paper, torn from the back of some predark book. "You both got reading?"

Ryan nodded. "Sure we do. Don't we, brother Willard? Got the reading."

Trader scowled. "Course we got fucking reading. Think we're stupes?"

The sec man smiled. "Marrying the little girls tomorrow? Course you aren't stupes. Likely the best thing ever happened to you two."

Trader had been staring out of the window, across the soaring deeps of the canyon, now tinted deep crimson and orange as the sun began to set behind it. "Sure. Thanks a bunch."

"Welcome. Make sure you get to bed good and early tonight. Want to be fresh and chipper tomorrow. Ready for the big dayo." He grinned. "And the big nighto afterward."

He closed the door behind him. Trader turned and threw a finger. "Can we fucking read? That son of a bitch has it coming when we get out of here, Ryan."

"Doing his job is all."

"Yeah. Sure. Like a dog does its job by eatin' its own puke." Trader looked at the piece of paper. "Come on then. Read it and tell me what it says."

"Sort of thing like swearing an oath."

"Read it."

"'I, Willard King, swear that—'"

"Hold it. If you're reading it, then how come it's got my name on it?"

"There's two of them, Trader. One with my name on it and one with your name. All right? Right. 'I swear that I will take the daughter of Baron Torrance, christened Chrissie'—mine'll say Bessie, Trader—'as my lawful wedded wife, from this day forth.'"

"They're serious!" Trader could hardly believe it. "Now it comes to the line, they're really goin' to get us to marry those scum-sucking sluts!"

"Goes on a bit about being loyal to the ville of Hightower and loyal to our wives in sickness and health. Until death parts us. Note that bit, Trader."

"Sure. If I have my way about chilling, this'll be one of the shortest marriages in the whole history of all Deathlands."

"Last bit is about us swearing eternal loyalty to the ville and to Baron Torrance. In the event of his death, then the little girls take joint control."

Trader sniffed. "You don't think this might be worth while taking over, do you, Ryan?"

"Take over Hightower ville, you mean?"

"Yeah." He pointed a bony finger at Ryan. "We can easy take the women and get us blasters from a couple of the sec men. Chill Torrance, if he don't drop dead and shit himself from fright. Then it's ours.''

"Trader," Ryan said, moving toward the window that still stood open.

"Yeah? Good idea, huh?"

"One thing is that I want to get back to Krysty, Dean and the others. Second thing is that this fire-blasted place is going to fall into the river anytime in the next few months. If I ever want to get to be a baron—which I don't—then I want to be the baron of something more than a rotting pile of waterlogged planks and buckets of broken glass."

Trader slapped himself on the thigh. "That's why you were so good as my Number Two, Ryan Cawdor. You stopped me from making a triple stupe of myself."

"I tried."

A small bat came flapping in through the open window and circled the room, its high-pitched cry barely audible to the two men. While they watched it, the little creature managed to gain control of its surroundings and flew back out over the balcony into the piñon-scented dusk.

"Way to go," Ryan said.

"LOOK AT THE BATS," Abe whispered.

"I seen them like this a lot of times, down toward the Grandee. Places they come boiling out of the caverns like steam out of a kettle."

J.B. and Abe had worked their way closer to the main building of Hightower ville as the light faded.

The sun had just gone beyond the western rim of the canyon, its shadows pouring blackly to lay across the tiny silver thread of the river, close to two thousand feet below.

"We have a plan?" Abe asked as they crouched behind a tall hedge of yew trees.

"Plan?" The Armorer turned his head, the scarlet glow from the far horizon burning in the lenses of his spectacles, turning his eyes to fire.

"Yeah. We just goin' to sail in, blasters going, like in the old days? Rescue Trader and Ryan from this fucking fate worse than death."

J.B. grinned. "It was Trader himself used to say that it was double shit to think that. Said that there really wasn't any fate worse than dying. It was the way you went that counted. Hard or easy."

He wore the scattergun looped over his shoulder, the Uzi ready in his hands. Abe had the stainless-steel .357 Colt Python unholstered.

"How about our plan?" Abe insisted.

"Sure. One thing we need is to try and find where they keep that land wag we saw. Plenty of gas if we can get it. Then we work out a way of getting inside. Find Trader and Ryan and all walk out together."

"That's the plan?"

"You have a better one, Abe?"

They sat where they were for several long minutes and silently watched the smoke cloud of bats circling the tall chimneys of the old hotel.

RYAN HAD TOPPED UP the three dirty brass lamps that stood around their bedroom. Using a self-light, he watched the steady golden flames flicker and grow, filling the darkness with their steady brightness.

There was still three-quarters of a gallon of oil left in the red metal can.

Outside the door they could hear the steady steps and the murmur of conversation from the three sec men that Arkadin had placed there to keep them safe during the long night before their shared wedding.

"Try and take them in the early hours?" Trader suggested, pacing up and down.

"Need a diversion. They won't come in just because I pretend you're sick or any old trap like that. No, I figure it might be a good wait, Trader."

They both heard the sound of high heels on the worn carpet outside and a woman's voice.

The sec men talked louder. Ryan moved quietly to the door and pressed his ear against it.

"What?" Trader whispered.

"Bessie, I think. Arguing she and her sister want to come in and spend a little time—a little loving time, she says—with their future husbands."

"I'll be hung, quartered and dried for the fucking crows! I could prefer rad cancer of the tongue to that, Ryan. Shout and tell them we're busy. Praying. Tell them that."

"Quiet, I can't... Ladies are getting their way, Trader. Be in here in a few moments."

The two men looked at each other, struck simultaneously by the same thought.

"Diversion," Trader said, grinning like a starved wolf. "Let them come."

THE SEC MAN LAY SPRAWLED in the deep pools of shadow at the rear of the garage. Blood seeped from his eyes, ears and nose and mouth, running onto the oil-stained concrete of the floor. There was a livid line etched around his throat where the thin wire garrote had choked him to death.

"Neat," Abe whispered admiringly. "Sure haven't lost your touch with chilling."

"It's a skill like any other," the Armorer replied. "Once you got it, you never really lose it."

The powerful land wag stood in the corner. It was a six-wheel predark Volvo that had been rebuilt so many times in the past century or so that there wasn't a whole lot left of the original truck. A flatbed had been added at some time, which had then been built up higher, as well as a makeshift roof and sides made from sheet steel to give it security.

"Check the gas in the tank." J.B. said.

He opened the double door and squinted out into the evening gloom. The guard had been patrolling the entire area around the flank of Hightower ville, walking slowly along, whistling to himself. J.B. and Abe had been watching him for more than twenty minutes, making sure he wasn't part of a team of sentries.

The garage hadn't entertained him for any longer than any other part of his beat, and he hadn't once even tried the bolt on the doors as he strolled by.

J.B. had slipped from the cover of the nearest hedge, standing still and silent at the angle of the garage, with Abe waiting as backup.

As the sec man passed the garage, something cold brushed against the front of his neck and then he was being pulled backward, with what felt like a knee rammed into the base of his spine.

"Bud," he tried to say, his face splitting in a grin, knowing that this was one of the practical jokes that Sec Man Emmons liked to play on the single sentries at night.

But the cold had turned to fire, burning into him, choking off both the word and the smile. There was a terrible pressure that stopped him breathing. The sec man knew he should be doing something to try to escape, but he was already much too busy with the limitless preoccupations of passing from this world to emptiness.

J.B. had given a low whistle and Abe had scampered out of hiding. He opened the doors and helped to drag the fouled corpse inside, closing the doors immediately behind him.

And it was done.

"Up to the brim," Abe reported from the rear of the big wag. "Any in the cans?"

J.B. nodded. "Plenty. Probably get us all the way back to the others. Get them loaded and I'll scout around. And be ready for some swift action, Abe."

RYAN KNEW THIS WASN'T going to be easy.

Bessie had on her golden pumps with the high heels.

Above that was one stocking and a pair of stonewashed denim shorts that were so brief and tight they looked like they were cutting her in two. Above a red leather belt was a torn bikini top in dark blue vinyl that barely contained what she obviously imagined were her outstanding attractions.

She was a poem in moderation compared to her older, larger sister.

Cissie Torrance's hair had been dyed since the wedding rehearsal at noon. Now it was a shrieking pink, from roots to tips, with a silvery net stretched over it. At first glance, as she swept imperiously into the bedroom, Ryan couldn't make out what was on the net.

When she moved into the aura of light from the oil lamps, he saw that a number of insects, like praying mantises, had been sprayed gold and tethered to the net around her hair with tiny golden chains, leaving them free to move around.

Two had obviously mated recently, as the large female was busily devouring the smaller male.

Ryan winced at the morbid thought that this might turn out to be symbolic of the coming wedding.

Cissie had on a short skirt that showed her enormous thighs, dimpled and quaking. The purple satin, dappled with orange sequins, was so skimpy that it did nothing to conceal her lack of underwear. Above it there was a diaphanous blouse of transparent white chiffon.

On her feet were a pair of mid-calf laced boots in patent leather.

"We are here, dear husbands," she cooed.

"Husbands-to-be, sister," Bessie corrected. "Best watch the legal shit."

"Of course. We thought we should have another little test, like before. Make sure that we're... What's the words, sisty?"

"Comparable, I think."

"Yeah." Her voice hardened. "So get the pants down and your cocks up and ready. Unless you want us to call in some help."

Trader looked across the room at Ryan. "I reckon now's as good a time as any."

"I reckon."

Chapter Thirty

Ryan had figured right. It wasn't easy.

They wanted to make enough noise to bring the sec men from the corridor outside into the room, so that they'd have a chance of disarming and overcoming them. The plan then was simply to get through the dark hallways of the old hotel to the quarters of Baron Torrance and retrieve their own blasters. Then they'd get outside to try to find the land wag they'd spotted earlier.

And away.

But they also had to make sure the women were no threat at the moment the guards came in.

So, timing was crucial.

Bessie strode toward him, like a ragged pirate galleon under full sail. Her heels clicked through the threadbare carpet and her hands were massaging her breasts, giving what she imagined was a tantalizing smile at Ryan.

"Let's go, lover," she purred.

When she was close enough, Ryan hit her once, a short stabbing punch that traveled no more than eleven inches. His fist buried itself in her stomach, just above the belt, sinking deep into the soft flesh. He twisted his wrist at the last moment to give extra impetus.

Bessie doubled over, her face purpling, and began to retch, hands clasping herself where she'd been struck. She drew in a gasping breath, unable to make a sound, winded by the savage punch. As she bent, Ryan brought his hands together and hit her on the back of the neck, harder than a mesquite war club, sending her unconscious to the floor of the room.

Trader was less successful with Cissie. The older, larger woman had been watching him with her cold, dead fish's eyes, and she saw the attack coming.

And got her retaliation in first.

She kicked at Trader, catching him a glancing blow on the shin with the chisel toe of her boot that made him whoop in pain. He hopped clumsily out of her way, nearly falling over the end of the broken bed.

"Help, murder!" she screamed. "Help!"

She turned toward Ryan and saw her sister lying on the carpet at his feet.

As Ryan dropped into a bar fighter's crouch, he felt a hand grip at his ankle, making him realize with a shock that Bessie Torrance had greater powers of recuperation than he would have imagined possible.

"Break him, sisty," she said in a sighing, choked little voice.

Like Ryan had figured, it wasn't easy.

And it had gone very wrong.

J.B. HAD MADE HIS WAY around the back of the ville, seeing how far he could go before reaching the point where the old hotel was toppling into the limitless canyon on his right. The first floor seemed to be totally unoccupied, but a few lights blazed on the top floor. One of them came from a room whose balcony was hanging so far over the black velvet abyss that it looked like a tug on a spiderweb would bring it down.

The Armorer froze in the shadows as he heard a woman's voice shriek out, just above him.

"Help, murder! Help!"

And, a moment or two later, Ryan, sounding strained and tense, shouted, "Come on, Trader! Now!"

After a moment's hesitation, glancing up to see if there was any possible way he could climb into the ville, J.B. spun on his heel and started to run back toward the garage, abandoning any pretense at secrecy.

RYAN STOMPED on Bessie's wrist, feeling bones snap crisply under his heel. By the time her yelp of pain had burst from her throat, he was already half-turned, kicking at her a second brutal time. He used the steel toe of the boot, feeling it thud under the angle of her fleshy jaw. There was the familiar click of displaced bone and her head flopped back at a weird, unnatural angle.

Trader was up once again, responding to Ryan's shout, grappling with the older sister, trying to get a grip on her enormously fat, sweat-slick wrists. But Cissie was far stronger than he had suspected, and she was still slapping hysterically at him. They were great, round-arm blows that rang off the side of his head, making him sway on his feet.

She had stopped screaming, putting all her energy into fighting. Outside, the group of sec men was still hesitating before entering, obviously terrified of upsetting the little sisters. One of the guards was shouting to the women, asking if they needed help or not.

Trader tried to knee Cissie in the groin, but her thighs were so fat that it was like kicking a soft cushion. Ryan picked up one of the brass oil lamps and smashed it over her head from behind. Colored glass shattered, cutting her on the side of the face, and the pungent oil ran all over her shoulders, soaking into the torn chiffon blouse.

"Bastard!" she spat. She gathered her strength and breath, and yelled out once more for the sec men.

Ryan stooped and picked up the can of oil, twisted the cap off and splattered it all over the woman, drenching her from head to toe.

Trader had managed to get in a good right cross to Cissie's jaw as her attention was distracted and she staggered sideways, waving her dimpled arms for balance.

"Door!" Ryan yelled, seeing it start to open.

He moved quickly toward the windows onto the balcony, snatching up another of the lamps as he did so, knocking the glass chimney off with his left hand.

His attention was focused on the surviving daughter of the ville, who was standing staring at him, like a fighting bull about to charge.

"Come on, bitch," he growled.

Three frightened young sec men stood behind her, jostling together for mutual courage, holding their blasters in nervous hands.

A maddened two-fifty-pound woman was out of the ordinary for Trader to handle, but the trio of guards was easy meat and drink to him.

He broke the nose of one of them with a fierce blow from the side of his hand, hitting the youth so hard that the nose was pulped and shards of needle-sharp bone were driven deep into the cavity behind it. Already dying, the sec man dropped his single-shot carbine.

By then Trader had, almost casually, snapped the wrist of the second guard, making him lose his grip on a rebuilt .32-caliber automatic. As the older man wrenched at the shattered radius and ulna, the agonizing pain made the sentry pass out.

The third man was panicked by the speed and efficiency of the attack and freaked by the sight of the woman's corpse on the floor. He snatched at the trigger of his revolver, sending a bullet into the plaster of the ceiling.

Trader kicked the man behind the knee, bringing him down, then struck him once just below the ear with his right fist, sending him into the dark.

Ryan was vaguely aware of the skillful mayhem being carried out on the far side of the room, but his attention was still centered on Cissie.

She seemed oblivious to the way that the balance of power had tilted away from her. The woman didn't even seem aware that her younger sister lay dead on the stained carpet, and she ignored the rancid lamp oil that dripped down her legs, gathering in a limpid pool around her polished boots.

"You're dead," she grated, spreading her arms wide and running at Ryan, where he stood with his back to the balcony.

"No, you are."

Ryan threw the lamp straight at the woman, striking her across her sagging breasts. The flame caught the oil, and she blossomed into red-orange fire.

For a heart-stopping moment, Ryan made a catastrophic error. He was hypnotized by the success of his plan, seeing her hair burst into flaring light, her chubby cheeks blistering. Despite her agony, Cissie was still determined on revenge, lunging toward the one-eyed man, trying to clasp him to her, so that he could share her burning doom.

Only at the last nanosecond did he realize his danger, and he dived to his right. He felt her hands brush against him, the sudden warmth of her passing. As he rolled up into a crouch, he saw the woman, unable to stop her murderous charge, reach the balcony beyond the bedroom.

There was the dry splintering sound of breaking wood, and Cissie was gone from their sight, leaving a trail of flames across the room, the curtains already ablaze, one of the beds starting to burn.

Trader rushed with him to peer out into the blackness, careful not to step onto what had been the hand-hewn balcony. Both men saw the falling star, trailing silver fire like a blazing comet, plummeting the hundreds upon hundreds of feet toward the distant, invisible river.

"There she goes, Ryan."

"Time for us to go, too. Noise'll attract some interest any moment."

"Yeah." Trader picked up the automatic and put bullets through the skulls of the two unconscious sec men, moving back as their heads bounced off the floor with the impact of the .32s. He ignored the one with the broken nose, who was clearly already sinking into his death throes.

Ryan grabbed the fallen revolver and quickly opened the door, bumping into Andy Arkadin, who had been running along the corridor.

"What's happening in there?" the sec chief panted. He was holding a small-caliber blaster in his right hand, down along the thigh.

"Both the sluts are dead," Trader said, appearing behind Ryan. "All your men."

"Don't shoot me. You know where your blasters are. With the baron. Take them and go. Won't stop you. Take them and get out of here."

Ryan nodded, pushing past Arkadin.

Trader also nodded, shooting the man once through the throat, following Ryan along the hallway.

"Didn't have to do that, Trader."

His feral smile brought back a hundred bloody memories. "Didn't have to do anything."

"WHAT'S UP?"

J.B. ignored Abe's question, as he tugged the rusting doors open. "Just get her started. Ryan and Trader could be in need of some transport in the next few minutes."

The land wag turned over easily, coughing into life, filling the garage with exhaust fumes. Abe was at the wheel, his blaster on the seat at his side. The Armorer stood on the step, holding the Uzi, the scattergun across his back.

"Where we goin'?" Abe shouted.

"Around the front, I guess. Park in sight of the main doors. Keep her running. Watch and wait."

"There goin' to be shooting?"

J.B. nodded, jamming his hat farther down on his head. "Guess so."

THERE WAS A FIREFIGHT at the top of the main staircase. A bullet peeled a neat strip of white wood off the balustrade close to Ryan's right elbow, and he returned the favor, shooting the crouching sec man through the top of the left shoulder, knocking him flat on his back.

"This blaster's shit," he said to Trader.

"So's mine. Still, should have our own back in a minute or so. Which way?"

"Left at the bottom."

A group of servants burst through the main doors, holding axes and garden tools, retreating as soon as Trader put a couple of rounds in their direction.

"They chilled the little girls!" someone bellowed. "Go and get them!"

Another voice, from farther down the lobby, shouted, "You want them, *you* get them!"

Ryan and Trader had paused for a moment, sizing up the extent of the opposition.

Behind them they could now hear the distant roar of flames, and the building shuddered. "Feels like the whole place might go over the edge," Ryan said.

"Yeah. Best we get out first."

Trader led the way slowly down the stairs, waving the blaster threateningly at anyone who appeared. No more shots were fired at them.

Just as they reached the first-floor level, Baron Torrance lurched into sight.

He held a gnawed chicken leg and a chipped tumbler of red wine in his left hand, sloshing it over the floor as he staggered toward the two outlanders.

"Smell smoke," he said pettishly, as though it were part of an unpleasant trick engineered at his expense.

There was a papier-mâché carnival mask in his other hand, a cockerel's head, with bright scarlet comb and curved golden beak. The paint was scarred and chipped.

"Come for our blasters, Baron," Ryan said.

"Who the fuck're you?" Recognition dawned. "Outlanders goin' to marry my little girls." He sniggered. "Husbands."

"Yeah," Trader said. "Only trouble is, it seems like we're widowers and not husbands."

"Didn't need to tell him that," Ryan chided. "Makes it harder."

"Who cares? Lot of times you find that hardest is really easiest, Ryan."

Torrance had placed his piece of chicken and glass of wine on a long table in the hallway. He pulled the mask on over his head. "What're you saying?" he asked.

The smoke was thickening. Ryan was aware that the cavernous lobby of Hightower was rapidly becoming deserted. Once it became obvious that a ship was doomed to sink, the rats wouldn't want to hang around.

"Let's get the blasters and hit the trail, Trader."

The bizarre figure with the cockerel's head moved to block their path. Torrance's voice was muffled and weak, barely audible. "You said about widowers. What's that mean?"

"Nothing," Ryan said.

"Tell me."

"We don't have time." Trader leveled his blaster and shot the baron once through the upper part of the mask, between the decorated eyeholes.

The man took three halting steps backward, arms flailing for balance. Blood flooded into the mask and began to drip through the ornamental holes at the end of the golden beak, pattering on the dusty wooden floor.

Trader headed past the tottering corpse, into the musty stench of the late Baron Torrance's quarters. "There." He pointed to the Armalite, the SIG-Sauer, the Steyr and an assortment of glinting steel blades, including Ryan's own favorite panga.

Above them they heard the deep rumble of shifting timber and crumbling walls, a sensation that felt as though it vibrated through the marrow of their bones.

"House is falling," Ryan said. "Beaten men come into their own."

Trader grabbed his Armalite, quickly checking the action. He stopped and looked around at his colleague. "What does that mean?"

Ryan grinned. "Don't know. Something I heard Doc say a couple of times."

"Sounds like a real triple-stupe old fuckhead."

There wasn't time to argue about it.

As they ran out of the main doors, past the sprawled body of the baron, the entire building seemed to be dying. Glass was breaking, and someone yelled for help. They could see the fiery glow of flames above them, and the lobby was thick with almost impenetrable smoke.

They paused for a moment, unchallenged, in the fresher air outside. Suddenly a land wag loomed out of the haze, with J.B. hanging on outside.

"Going our way?" the Armorer called.

Chapter Thirty-One

"Young Jak Lauren told me that this should be my destination. He says it is known as Bearclaw Lake."

"It's lovely." Sukie had been leading Judas and she stopped, one arm draped around the neck of the mule.

Her easy relationship with the murderous and untrustworthy animal was something that puzzled Doc. He felt vaguely aggrieved that the woman was so good with the vicious beast.

But that was about the only problem that he had with her. The past three days together had been among the happiest of his life. Doc quickly made a mental edit. The happiest *since* the white-coats had trawled him.

They had been content to talk and equally content to be quiet together. And the lovemaking had made Doc feel . . . well, nearly two hundred years younger.

"What're you smiling at?"

He jumped. "So sorry, my dear. My thoughts were such a long way off."

"Looked happy, Doc. Not to say a bit rude. You were leering into the distance like a bull who just spotted two hundred cows ready and waiting."

"No, no, Sukie. Not that sort of thought. Just that this is such a peaceful place."

He hadn't yet told the woman about his past. He feared that the idea of where he really came from would convince Sukie that he was either a stupe liar or a triple-stupe madman. Either way, it didn't seem like a good thing to do.

Not yet.

Soon, but not yet.

THE LAKE WAS AS CLEAR as the finest crystal, about two hundred paces across. It was surrounded by a bowl of low hills, dotted with clumps of young pines. There were also the blackened stumps of hundreds of dead trees, evidence of a major fire within the past ten or fifteen years.

Judas browsed contentedly among the bright grass along the edge of the water, tethered to a feathery tamarisk. Sukie sat on a long, flat boulder, her white blouse opened so low that Doc could see the dark rings of her nipples. The knife wound had almost healed. Her turquoise necklace glinted in the brightness of the morning sunshine.

Doc lay at her side, his head resting against the warm sandstone.

"This paradise, Doc?"

"Better than the Garden of Eden, Sukie. I haven't seen any serpents crawling around to spoil things."

"You know so much, Doc. About books and poetry and stuff like that."

"Mostly useless baggage, my dear. That is one thing that my time here in Deathlands has taught me. Ryan Cawdor has very little of what one used to call 'book learning,' yet he is one of the finest, wisest men that I have ever met.''

A fish jumped from the center of the lake, its scales sparkling, the water like rainbow mist as it splashed back out of sight.

"Trout," Sukie said.

"Very likely."

"You aren't hunting, Doc?"

"No. My talent with a long gun or a rod is about the same as my skill in speaking Mandarin Chinese."

"But you said something about leaving Krysty and the others to come up here and do some hunting."

He was holding his sword stick, poking with the ferrule at the tiny pebbles by his feet. "Did I say that? No, not quite a hunt. Perhaps a hunt for myself."

"How's that?" She lay flat on her back, revealing more of her breasts to him.

"Seek first within yourself. I've been feeling a little less than happy for a while now. I decided that I should take some time alone to try to discover what was wrong. And what I should do about it."

"Have I fucked that up for you?"

Doc sat up so sharply he strained his neck. "Ouch! Did you . . ." He fell silent for several hearbeats while he considered what she'd said. "I think that what you did was put a lot of things into perspective, Sukie."

She reached out for him, and he grasped her hand tightly. "You mean I helped some?"

"Indeed. I believe that I would like to return to the spread, bring you back with me to meet my friends."

"I still got this idea that I'd like to track down my sister. In Hope Springs."

"Of course. I would not wish to hinder that for a moment, Sukie, my dearest. But would you like to come back and meet my companions? Mayhap even Ryan and John Barrymore Dix will have returned during my absence."

She sat up again, fastening one of the carved bone buttons on her blouse. "I'd like that. You don't think they'll sort of resent me?"

"By the Three Kennedys! Why on earth should they? I think that I should be proud to go anywhere with you upon my arm. Anywhere!"

"But you still didn't say whether you've kind've cleared your mind, Doc."

He looked out across the magnificent view. A pair of ravens had appeared and were swooping low over the far side of Bearclaw Lake, etching their shadows against the still water.

"As we make our way back, there are some things I must explain to you about my previous life. Things that may prove difficult for you to believe."

"What sort of things?"

He patted her hand. "Nothing criminal, my dear. Nothing of which I feel the least ashamed. But a strange story, I promise you that."

"Tell me now. Or we could have a cuddle and a kiss and then you could tell me after that."

Doc smiled, showing his set of perfect, strong teeth. "You tempt an old man, my sweet one. But the day is passing. If we set off now, then I think we should be safely back at the ranch before sunset tomorrow.''

"Oh." Sukie sounded disappointed. "If you say so, Doc."

"I do. And I have a fine wide bed in my room at the house. But I will tell you, before we set off, that meeting you has quite changed my perspective on life. I had begun to think that I was walking a lonely path. Never daring to turn and look behind for fear . . . That is not to say Ryan and the others are not good, good friends. They are the best. But when I tell you some more about my past, you'll understand. Like you, Sukie, I have lost a marital partner.''

"I didn't lose my four husbands, Doc. They all just up and died. If any of them had just gotten lost, then I could have searched for them.''

He laughed, making Judas look up suspiciously. "Upon my soul, but you are a treasure, ma'am, you are indeed. I meant to say, in my clumsy fashion, that I am a widower.''

"Children, Doc?''

"Two. A little girl and a baby boy.''

"Dead?''

"Oh, yes. A long while ago. Since I have been traveling here in Deathlands, I have never for a single hour been able to forget Emily and the children. And I have spent futile times in working out ways of trying to rejoin them.''

"Top yourself, you mean?'' Her fingers tightened on his comfortingly.

"Not exactly. But I know that there have been times that my mind is not... What is the expression they use? An ace on the line! My poor befuddled brain has rarely been able to have an ace upon the line."

"Times I been crazy, too, Doc. Times when a good day was when I sat and thought how times used to be."

He nodded vigorously. "I know what you mean, my dear. Indeed, I do."

"So?"

"So? I fear that I have mislaid the thread of my discourse. What was I saying?"

"How I'd made you feel a sight better."

"Yes! The truth is, and I would probably never admit this to another living soul, but the idea of suicide was on my mind. Now, I think that it is not. Now you have helped me see there are reasons for going on."

"Am I one of those reasons, Doc?"

"Of course you are."

"Truth?"

"Truth and consequences, my dear. I have come to appreciate that a man who dwells in the past will only have shadows for company. And that is not enough. The soul will sicken and starve, as I believe mine was."

"Starving?"

"Starving because it was shut off from all the things that matter in life. It had friendship. Without that, then I think I would probably have declined to carry on with living these many months since. But it was too much of a one-way street. Ryan, Krysty and the others have given me their trust and their love. I responded as best I could, some of the time. But I realize now that I didn't respond all of the time."

"You gave me love. Saved my life as well, Doc. That's two big debts."

He stood, smiling down at the woman. "Friends don't have debts, Sukie. You owe me nothing. Nothing at all. I hope you'll come with me. How long you decide to stay is entirely your business. You understand that?"

Sukie took his hand and pulled herself upright. She pressed herself against him and kissed him very softly on the lips, letting her right hand drift lower across his body. "You sure we don't have time for a little loving?"

"Perhaps a little..."

The little somehow became a lot.

"If we're starting off back to the spread, then we should be going, Doc."

He'd fallen asleep, his grizzled head pillowed on her breast, mouth slightly open, breathing steadily.

"Oh, what was... Emily, did... I don't..."

Sukie sat up, kissing him once on the forehead. "Small clouds on the horizon, Doc."

"Ah. Those are the shadows of angels' wings, you know. One of the greatest of the predark singers and writers, John Stewart, wrote that."

"It's lovely."

"Indeed it is. I know more of his songs. Perhaps I might acquaint you with a few as we pick our way back toward the desert floor."

"That'd be nice, Doc."

THERE WAS A SHORT SHOWER of light rain during the middle of the afternoon, just enough to lay the dust and bring a scent of freshness to the high country.

By the time the sun was setting far away across the plains to the west, they had reached a camping spot perched on the edge of the plateau, a shaded stream and good grass for Judas, and a sheltering wall of smooth rock for their blankets.

"Not much food left, Doc," Sukie said, rummaging through the packs. "If I hadn't come along I guess you'd have gone home earlier or else done some hunting."

Doc thought about the third option that had been closest to the front of his mind. The option that would have found him so deep into the nest of trails and passes that nobody would ever have found him. Would never have found his body.

Now all that had changed.

He stood on the lip of the tumbling drop and tried to locate the speck of light in the gloaming that would be the ranch where the others were waiting.

But he could see nothing.

Chapter Thirty-Two

The old Volvo land wag carried them along, south and east.

The engine started unhesitatingly every morning and ran steadily along, across passes and over rivers, past small frontier pestholes, where local vigilante patrols were out and cautious. They didn't hide their hostility toward the outlanders. But the array of weapons that the four men displayed was always enough to deter any assault on them.

In the several days following their departure from the crumbling, burned-out ville of Hightower, there was only a single attack made on the foursome.

Ryan was at the wheel, looking for a good place to hole up for the night. They'd passed a strung-out collection of shotgun shacks, with hollow-eyed women and silent, naked children playing with snarling mongrels in the dirt.

A toothless man had waved a Kentucky musket at them, shouting a stream of curses. And one of the younger women, who looked to be eighteen going on seventy, had run a few steps after them and thrown a couple of flints at the wag.

Banks of trees had lined both sides of the muddied blacktop, dolorous pines that still dripped from an earlier rain, standing shoulder to shoulder, without even room for a man to squeeze between them.

Ryan hadn't heard the noise of the shot above the pounding roar of the powerful engine, but he'd glimpsed the puff of black-powder smoke amid the shadows from the corner of his right eye, and caught the pinging of the ball as it hit the steel at the side of the cab, close by him.

Trader had been sitting with him and he'd immediately levered a round into the Armalite, kneeling and peering into the forest. But Ryan had simply pushed the pedal to the metal and taken them along out of range and out of danger.

"No point wasting a bullet," he'd said.

They stopped a couple of miles down the highway. There had been a bright smear of lead, denting the bodywork, twenty inches from the window.

"Close," J.B. said, rubbing at it with his finger. "Smoothbore homemade. Still, might have made a big hole if it had hit you."

Trader laughed. "Sure. And if the coon hound hadn't stopped for a piss it might've caught the rabbit."

Abe had looked around. "We stopping here for the night? Trees are near."

Ryan had answered the little gunner. "No. Just wanted to take a look at where the bullet hit. Go a few miles farther. Upgrade stops a mile or so along."

"How long before we reach New Mexico and the spread? We made good time."

"Way we're going, route through the edge of Phoenix looks best. Not all that far from there. Up on old Sixty and then we're almost home. Could do it in three days."

Trader grinned. "So far, so good. Reminds me, boys. I ever tell you—"

"Yeah," Ryan said. "Your friend up in Peoria. Caught by stickies on the thirtieth floor of a ruined department store. You told us."

But Trader wasn't listening. "Friend of mine, Crazy Dog Kalin. Was up in Peoria, working as a bounty hunter for a local baron. Got caught alone on top of the fortieth floor of a big old store. Bunch of stickies. Ran right out of ammo after he'd put half of them on the last train to the coast. Only way out for him was over and down. There were men on most floors, and they heard him falling. All the way to the sidewalk, old Crazy Dog kept on shouting 'So far, so good.' "

The other three echoed the repetition of the punchline. "So far, so good."

ALL OF THE ARMORER'S traveling maps had vanished during the quake and flash flood, so most of the journey was being reconstructed from memory. Trader had been for pushing east at an earlier point. But Ryan and J.B. had opposed him, pointing out that it would mean crossing a lot of totally arid desert with only the meanest pesthole for water.

Abe hadn't had any opinion to offer.

So, they'd chosen moving in a southerly direction as far as Phoenix.

That part of the predark United States of Americ had suffered mixed fortunes during the brief mega-cull of the nuke holocaust and the long winters that followed it.

Innumerable missile bases and scattered silos held all sizes and shapes of rocket-fired weaponry. During the last accelerating years of the "new" cold war, uncounted trillions of dollars were poured into research for ICBMs as well as the smaller defensive missiles. The new range of nuclear weapons were hidden all across the Colorado Plateau, backed up by new redoubts and storage bases and triple-secret research units.

As a consequence, the region had been blanketed by the enemy, mainly using offensive missiles designed to take out individual targets with a high ground-zero effect. Most of the fissionable material had a relatively low half-life, meaning there weren't all that many hot spots around the region. The idea had been to keep it safe for the invasion that never came.

The population centers were very scattered and made difficult targets, so neutron bombs were used, with a high-intensity seeding effect that took out ninety-nine-point-nine-nine human factors while leaving buildings largely undamaged.

A city like Phoenix, covering hundreds of square miles, had been hit like a patchwork quilt. Parts had been totally flattened while other parts remained untouched with their inhabitants slaughtered.

Trader had been there a number of times, dealing with some of the subvilles that had sprung up, each with its own baron, each in a state of grudging neutrality with the others. A neutrality that was frequently broken.

"Head for the part called Scottsdale," he suggested. "Was once triple rich. But there's no water there now or grazing land. So it's a ghost town. Reckon that it should be a good place to hole up for a night."

It lay to the east of Phoenix, on the flank of the city where they wanted to be, along the side of what had once been the Salt River Indian Reservation.

J.B. WAS DRIVING the land wag, cruising slowly up and down a checkerboard of little streets that wound around and twisted in on each other like a prairie-dog town. Most of the buildings had only a single story, built of weathered concrete overlaid with crumbling adobe.

Tumbleweed was piled high against some of the angled walls, and they saw a huge gray-green lizard making its unhurried way across one of the intersections.

Everyone was on full red alert, guns cocked and ready, but they had seen no sign of life since passing a large smoky camp a dozen miles to the north.

"There," Abe said, pointing to the left with his Colt Python at one of the crossings.

The Armorer pushed down on the brake, bringing the six-wheeler to a shuddering halt. "What?"

"Big wide bridge up there. Broken down. But it's a good clear space to camp. Lots of options if we need to get out of this part of the ville in a hurry."

Ryan nodded. "Good thinking, Abe. Still about an hour or more to dusk. Get set up. Wouldn't mind taking a look around this place. Anyone join me?"

Trader vaulted easily over the side of the wag, with a catlike agility that a lot of men a third of his age would have envied. "Sure. Could do with stretching my legs after all this sitting around on my ass. Got the most jolted set of hems this side of the great divide."

"We'll start a fire and cook a haunch of that goat you chilled this morning, Ryan," Abe said.

"Don't go too far," J.B. warned. "Time to worry about an enemy is when you don't see him." He deliberately quoted one of Trader's aphorisms, though the older man didn't seem to recognize the saying.

"YOU RECKON THESE WERE all real expensive stores?" Ryan asked disbelievingly.

"So they said." Trader was carrying the Armalite at the trail as they walked together through the long-deserted streets, the steel heels and tips on their combat boots the only sound in the evening quiet.

Ryan had left the Steyr rifle back in the land wag, contenting himself with the SIG-Sauer P-226, which rested in its unbuttoned holster.

"I can't believe it."

Many of the units were in good condition, though the glass had gone from almost all of the front windows, and doors stood gaping open. Protected from rain and wind, a lot of the signs still remained. Ryan read several to Trader. "Dina and Mo's Crystal and Tarot Emporium. Wicked Watches of the West. Tanks for the Memory—Military Memorabilia. Native American Art and Artifacts."

Ryan shook his head. "This is total shit. Total useless shit! Fireblast! I never seen nothing like this, Trader."

"Me neither. I can't see a single place that would've sold a thing you and me would've ever wanted to buy."

The shops seemed to have been stripped. Ryan walked into the crystal and tarot store, boots crunching through the shattered glass. Feeling something twist under his heel, he stooped to peer at it in the fading light.

"What is it?" Trader asked.

"Kind of toy." It was a pewter model of a winged lizard, holding a tiny purple prism between its open jaws. "Who but a little kid would want stuff like that?"

"Some more down that side street, past the abandoned fountain. Worth a look?"

"Probably not."

"Think I'll get back to the wag. Feel the old hunger pains starting up, Ryan. Backbone and belly rubbing together. You coming with me?"

"Yeah. Oh, wait. One place down there's got a sign says it was a bookstore. Might just stroll along to it and take a quick look. Coming?"

Trader shook his head. "No. Me and books never somehow quite got an understanding." He turned on his heel and began to walk briskly back toward the parked land wag, where a thin column of blue-gray smoke from a cooking fire was already rising into the still air.

Steins' Books, proclaimed the red lettering over the door. A poster pinned to the wall, just inside, stated proudly that the pen was mightier than the sword. Ryan had a feeling that he'd heard that before, probably from Doc.

When he saw that the store hadn't been totally ravaged like most of the others, he wished that the old-timer had been there with him. "Guess that nobody wanted books for anything," he said quietly. "Can't eat them and they don't burn that good."

The floor was littered with the desiccated remains of hundreds of volumes. He stepped inside. The setting sun passed a bank of low purple clouds, and the light dropped by three-quarters. Ryan hesitated, feeling suddenly uneasy. Though there'd been no sign of life around Scottsdale, you could never even begin to feel totally safe in Deathlands. His fingers brushed against the butt of the SIG-Sauer, but he left it undrawn.

He knelt and started to look at the hoard of old volumes, feeling the familiar sense of wonder that these books had all been printed during the year or so before skydark, close on a hundred years ago. Ryan knew how delighted both Doc and Krysty would be if he was able to rescue anything from this pile of crumbling paper. However, the darkness of evening was easing into all the corners of the rectangular store, making it almost impossible to read any of the delicate, faded titles.

As Ryan turned around, he noticed an enormous book, bigger than a house brick. He lifted it and peered at the title, finding it was a biography of a writer called Charles Dickens, by another writer called Ackroyd.

He doubted whether Doc or Krysty would have heard of this Dickens, as he seemed to have lived a very long time ago. Also, it was far too heavy to stick in a pocket. Ryan placed it gently down on a top of a mound of illustrated books showing the adventures of someone called Judge Dredd, who looked like he was a double-tough sec man in a big ville.

Ryan picked one of the comix up, angling its muted colors toward the open door of the derelict store to try to catch the last shafts of light. But it was much darker now, almost as though someone had crept in and was moving toward him, deepening the shadows.

Preoccupied by the treasure of the books, Ryan allowed his combat reflexes to operate too little and too late.

Even as he started to turn, he heard the hiss of triumph from the attacking stickie.

Chapter Thirty-Three

Ronny and Raelene Warren took to their bed and weren't disturbed through all the hours of darkness.

Mildred slept in the next room to Doc's, and she heard one of the strangers get up a couple of times during the night and make his or her fumbling way along the hallway to the back door, going to use the outhouse.

The black woman lay awake for an hour or more after the second occasion. On her back, the tiny beads in her plaited hair whispered as she moved on the pillow. The moon sliced through the gap at the top of the blinds, moving inexorably across the wall of the bedroom, flirting with the corner of an old steel engraving of a hunter confronting a grizzly bear on a narrow ledge, high in the snow-covered mountains.

Mildred stared at the picture, finding she could almost taste the hopeless horror of the man, trapped with no way back, only a flimsy dagger in his right hand, confronting the enormous beast, with a sheer drop on his right.

If ever there was a pictorial representation of certain doom, then it hung on the wall of her room.

Over the long weeks since Ryan and J.B. had departed for the far Northwest, on their quest to track down the legendary Trader, Mildred had thought a lot about her relationship with John Dix.

She tried to deconstruct it, then reassemble it, hoping that it would then make more sense. But all the thinking and agonizing had only blurred her feelings. The word that fluttered at the edge of her consciousness was "love." When she'd been a younger woman, in her previous life at the end of the twentieth century, Mildred had enjoyed at least her fair share of relationships with young—and not so young—men. But she couldn't recall whether she'd actually been in love with any of them.

Now she thought she was probably in love with John Barrymore Dix.

Was that a wildly foolish idea for someone of her age? An ancient country song floated unbidden into her mind, making her smile in the darkness. Something about closing on forty and still wearing jeans.

She felt slight pressure on her bladder and wondered about getting up and going out back. But the night was cold, and she resisted.

That thought took her once again to their visitors, Raelene and Ronny.

She had offered to examine them, pointing out that she was a real, qualified doctor, but they'd been evasive, saying that they just needed some rest, which was obviously true. But all her medical training told her that there was something seriously wrong with the couple.

Lying there, half-asleep, Mildred mentally ticked off the symptoms she'd been able to observe.

Both were exhausted and had sallow complexions, despite having been out in the New Mexico sun for days. She frowned as she realized how vague they'd both been about precisely where they'd been traveling and just where they'd originally located the treasure in their wagon that was so important to them.

Both had colds and running noses. Raelene in particular had a nasty rash around her mouth, scabbing all over her fried and crusted lips. Her hair looked thin and unhealthy. Ronny's hair also seemed to be in poor shape.

As Raelene had sipped at a beaker of buttermilk, she'd winced, explaining that her gums were sore. And the rim of the mug had been smeared with a film of blood when Mildred took it out to the kitchen to wash up.

Ronny's hand had been very sore. He explained that it came from driving the team when he wasn't all that used to the reins. That was why he'd lost the nails of three or four fingers.

Mildred was slipping away into sleep. She was sitting at a large round mahogany table with a heavily carved scalloped edge, with a huge jigsaw puzzle spread out in front of her. The title on the cardboard box was "Showing His Paces." A spirited stallion was being trotted up and down in front of a row of beaming, brocaded, pipe-smoking businessmen. Much of the puzzle was completed, but there were several pieces missing. Mildred was searching and searching, unable to find anything that looked remotely right.

If only she could get the shapes to come together, she knew that they would make sense.

But, in her dream, Mildred had a terrible sense of foreboding, that if she completed the puzzle, she was going to experience some terrible luck.

Someone was leaning over her shoulder. "Solve the puzzle and savor your doom," said a soft voice, like a feather stroking across black velvet.

KRYSTY WAS SHAKING HER by the shoulder, leaning over the bed. "Come on, Mildred. I need help."

"What?"

"Raelene's ill."

"What kind?" She sat up, rubbing the sleep from her eyes, seeing that there was a bright sunny morning making itself felt through the blind.

"Puking and shitting. Bringing up blood as well."

Mildred's dream came swimming back to haunt her and she took a deep, sighing breath. "I think this is going to be triple-bad news, Krysty."

The redheaded woman had moved back toward the half-open door of the bedroom. "I've had this feeling, you know, since they first appeared on the horizon. Bad feeling, Mildred."

"Yeah. Be right with you. Throw on some clothes."

RAELENE LAY ON THE BED, a crumpled sheet rucked around her bare feet. She wore a thin cotton shift, soaked with sweat across her wrinkled breasts, stained with yellow bile down over her scrawny belly. Her face was filmed with perspiration, and as pale as wind-washed bone.

Her husband sat on the floor by her, holding her hand. He wore a patched shirt that barely covered his shrunken shanks. As Mildred entered the room, she couldn't help noticing that his genitals were exposed, and that there were livid sores on his scrotum and a festering chancre on his penis. He was crying.

"Come on, hon," he said. "Be fine. Just hang on. When we sell the big one it'll be fine. Milk, silk, honey and jack all the way."

"When did she start being sick, Ronny?" Mildred asked.

"Don't know."

"This morning? Last night?"

"No. About three days, I guess. Mebbe two days. Been gettin' worse. I feel real bad. Got an ache across my head like someone's tightening a band of red-hot steel. And I feel like throwing up here and now."

"Should I get a bowl and cloth?"

Mildred turned, seeing that Dean was peering in through the doorway. "Yeah. Do that." She called after the boy. "Where's Jak?"

"Gone out the fields, someplace. Milking the cows, mebbe. Don't know, Mildred."

"Okay. Cloth and bowl and some fresh water." Gradually she was lurching back to full consciousness. "And put a kettle on for hot water, Dean." Mildred leaned over the moaning woman, peering at her eyes, seeing how bloodshot they were.

Raelene raised a shaky hand and touched her own mouth. "Hurts," she whispered. She reached between the sore, cracked lips and felt around, grabbing something and giving it a gentle tug. She pulled out one of her own front incisors, the roots of the pointed tooth bright crimson.

Krysty turned away. "Oh, Gaia!" she breathed.

Mildred felt a physical shock as all of the pieces of the jigsaw puzzle slotted into place at once. "Yeah," she said. "Rad cancer."

THE DOCTOR WASHED her hands in the kitchen, while Krysty buttered some toast. The kettle was whistling quietly to itself on the stove, and some coffee sub was brewing.

Ronny and Raelene Warren had both gotten into their bed, and the rumpled sheets had been straightened and tucked in around them. Both of them had fallen almost instantly into a fevered, exhausted sleep.

Dean had gone out to look for Jak and hadn't yet returned.

"How long?" Krysty asked.

"Hours at the shortest. For her. Maybe four or five days for him. Can't tell. Shit. I don't know. Cryonics was my specialty. Freezing people. Not diagnosing rad cancer and giving a probable time of death."

"How did they catch it?" Krysty was staring out the window, across the kitchen garden.

"Enough hot spots around the plateau to chill everyone left alive in Deathlands."

"Nothing you can do for them?"

Mildred's face was bleak, her mouth set in a tight line. "If I had access to my drugs I could probably make their passing a little easier."

"Nothing else?"

"Truth, Krysty, is that the best and kindest thing to do would be to simply put a bullet through each of their heads while they're asleep."

RAELENE HAD BEEN sick again, her whole body contorted, her eyes staring as she fought for breath. Blood-specked froth trickled from the corner of her mouth.

Krysty and Mildred did what they could for her, washing her again after the spasm had passed, talking quietly, holding her hand when she wept in terror.

There was still no sign of Dean and Jak.

THE TWO YOUTHS REAPPEARED about half an hour later, walking together in silence from the corrals, across the yard and up onto the porch.

Krysty met them at the door into the kitchen. "You been milking and taking care of the animals?"

"Yeah. That and other stuff."

Dean was more voluble. "How're the Warrens, Krysty? They still sick? We found something. That is, Jak found something and he wants you all to—"

"Quiet," the teenager said. His red eyes turned to Krysty and she saw the bad news written there as clear as on a highway billboard.

"They're dying," she said. "Mildred says they've both got terminal rad sickness."

"Know why," he stated flatly.

Mildred had gone into the kitchen, carrying a bowl of fouled water. "You know the source of their illness, Jak?"

"Yeah."

"What?"

"Come see."

He led the way out to the large barn where the Warrens' rig was stored. Their wag horses were in a small separate corral to the side of the building and Mildred looked at them, noticing that both animals looked conspicuously unwell. One was repeatedly rubbing its head against a fence post, and a large abscess opened by its left eye attracted hordes of flies. The other was trembling as if it had a feverish ague. Its hindquarters were streaked with a greeny-yellowish discharge.

Jak caught her look and nodded, his white hair blowing back in the light breeze. "Yeah," he said. "Them too."

One of the pair of double doors stood wide open, and they all hesitated on the threshold.

"Gaia! The taint of evil's so strong here I can hardly even breathe."

Jak took a couple of steps into the gloom then stopped. "We got to leave," he said.

"The barn?" Mildred shook her head. "We have to see what it is in here."

"No. Show you. Then all leave. Straightaway."

Nobody spoke. He moved toward the canvas-topped Conestoga wag, feet slurring through the powdery straw and dust.

Mildred kept thinking that what they were doing was madness. They should turn right now and run away as far as they could possibly go and never come back. Despite that, she allowed Jak to lead them around the rear of the rig, where the stained cloth had been pulled open.

He hopped inside while they gathered around, their eyes slowly becoming accustomed to the semidarkness. The treasure of the Warrens had been partly untied, a single layer of the wrapping keeping it hidden.

"There," Jak said, uncovering it.

The "treasure" was a little over nine feet long, in white-painted metal. It was scratched, chipped and dented. One of the four tail fins was broken off. The nose cone had a small split in it, showing a mass of colored wires, in a rainbow tangle of confusion.

Krysty felt a deathly cold sickness sweep over her. She could read the set of numbers and initials along the side of the ICBM, giving its provenance, its trade name, neatly stenciled in dark blue lettering: Custer.

Worst of all was the gash that had been sliced in the flank of the nuke missile, nearly eighteen inches long, revealing the leaking innards of its rad-potent warhead.

It was Mildred who broke the empty silence. "Let us go."

Chapter Thirty-Four

The force of the attack threw Ryan forward and to the side, and he landed awkwardly on his right arm. The weight of the stickie pressed him down into the turmoil of ancient books and magazines, and he felt them crackling beneath him. Dust rose in a thick cloud, almost choking Ryan.

Though he had been taken by surprise, the one-eyed warrior's combat training came to his aid. He managed to get his left arm up, parrying a slashing blow to his face. The hundreds of tiny suckers across the palms and fingers of a stickie meant that it could grip and tear off great slices of skin from a victim.

But the mutie was quick, trying to fasten its suckers to his head. Ryan felt a chunk of hair and scalp ripped away, and warm blood trickled down the back of his neck. He kicked out, feeling his boot connect with solid, muscular flesh. He heard the stickie grunt with shock, and the pressure eased for a moment.

Snatching the second's relief, he rolled to one side, slipping in the mountain of dust-dry paper. As Ryan snatched for the blaster, the gibbering mutie came at him again, its mouth open, showing him the double row of needled teeth, the stinking breath clotting in his face.

He had the SIG-Sauer in his hand, just clear of the holster, when the thing grabbed at the barrel. With the suckers, its grasp was unbelievably powerful and it simply tore the blaster from him, taking some skin from his fingers.

But stickies have no use for blasters. They love fires and loud explosions, but haven't mastered even the basics of pulling a trigger.

The mutie snarled in delight and threw the blaster away. Ryan heard it strike the ceiling and fall among the catacomb of predark literature. He knew not where.

"Norm bastard!" The voice was harsh, the words slurred.

The way Ryan was lying, on his back, his feet scrabbling for purchase, he couldn't get at the hilt of the panga on his other hip. For a moment the mutie grinned at him, crouched and ready to lunge, sensing how helpless he was, exulting in the bloody power it held over him.

Ryan's right hand fumbled in the rubbish, desperately hoping he might find a sliver of glass or a hunk of stone. But there was nothing. Just paper and more paper, and books and mags, and books and comix, and even more books.

A big book.

The book by Ackroyd about Charles Dickens.

The suckered hands were spread, like the obscenely flattened tentacles of a powerful octopus, the teeth behind the smile glinting in the last rays of the evening light.

Ryan gripped the book in his right fist, feeling the solid weight, and slammed it with all of his power, square into the middle of the mutie's face. It struck home just above the watery, bloodless lips, roughly where a norm's nose would be. Most stickies simply had a gaping buccal orifice, fringed with ragged porcine hairs, that dribbled wetly.

The force of the impact was not unlike being struck by a block of masonry and the stickie squealed in shock and pain, rolling backward, hands covering its face from a further, threatened blow. Blood trickled thinly over its mouth and down its scrawny neck.

Ryan dropped the heavy tome and slid sideways, reaching for the taped hilt of the panga, drawing it smoothly from its long sheath in a breath of murderous steel.

Out of the corner of his eye he caught a flicker of movement in the doorway of the bookstore, as a second stickie stuck its head inside.

But that was for then and this was for now.

The crouched mutie took its hands from its face, spitting a spray of blood at the norm. "Fucker..." it said, lips peeled back off its lethal teeth.

"Fucker yourself," Ryan growled.

The panga had a honed point and Ryan used it like a sword, thrusting it straight at the stickie's chest. The creature recoiled, saving itself from the worst of the lunge, though the blade penetrated a full inch, drawing more blood.

It cried out for help, seeing its fellow stickie standing hesitantly by the door.

But it was far too late.

The crushing blow with the book had bought Ryan that most valuable of combat commodities.

Time.

Trader used to say that having time in a fight was better than having a hatful of bullets.

Ryan switched the attack, leaning forward, battling for balance on the shifting slopes of torn paper, swinging the eighteen-inch panga at the side of the mutie's head. It raised a hand to try to fend off the blow, which was like trying to check a runaway war wag with a butterfly's wing.

The steel cut clean through the wrist, blood spurting ceiling-high, the severed hand dropping to the floor like a shell-less crab. The fingers flexed and grasped, the tiny mouths of the suckers opening and closing.

The ending was inevitable.

As the wailing stickie fell back on a mound of old *National Geographic*s, the yellow covers splashed with crimson, Ryan swung again, backhanded, opening a huge gash, eight inches long and four inches deep, across the front of the mutie's throat. The blade sliced through the windpipe and larynx, nicking the cervical vertebrae.

Ryan was blinded for a moment by the pulsing gusher of warm blood that jetted into his eye and face, with its peculiar bitter, fishy, oily smell, making him gag with revulsion. But he was aware that the second mutie was also inside the store, only feet away from him, menacing.

He quickly rubbed his sleeve over his face, clearing his vision, seeing the nearer stickie falling away, dying in the midst of a rotting pile of withered pulp Westerns.

The second stickie was coming toward him in a curious shuffling walk, holding a short steel blade in a clawed left hand. It brushed at the air with the knife, as though it were in total darkness instead of the dim half-light.

"Crorn?" it called. "Where you, Crorn?"

Ryan realized that the stickie was virtually blind, as well as being badly crippled. One shrunken leg dragged behind it, rustling across the steppes of ancient print.

For a passing moment he thought about sparing the mutie. It would be child's play to slip past it and escape out of the store, back safe to the others.

But where there were two stickies there might be more. This poor disabled creature could raise the alarm, bring others of its vile, butchering tribe.

"Crorn? Brother?"

Ryan waited for the perfect moment. He stooped a little and let the point of the panga find the mutie's heart, almost on its own, sliding past the questing little knife, through the ragged, buttonless shirt of patchworked cotton, angling the eighteen inches of honed steel slightly upward, between the fourth and fifth ribs on the left side of the stickie's body. Ryan twisted the hilt as he withdrew the panga.

"Gone, Crorn..." The voice was no more than a bat's whisper in the stillness.

Ryan watched him kneel, then seem to carefully select a spot to lie and die. The books beneath him turned soggy from the flowing river of dark blood. Some of it touched the dented edges of the big book on Dickens that had saved Ryan's life, staining the ruffled pages.

When the only sound in the bookstore was his own breathing, the tall, powerfully built one-eyed man found his blaster amid the clutter of books and picked his way to the door, pausing a moment to read the poster tacked to the plaster wall.

He grinned and walked out into the evening.

THE BOLT CLICKED on Trader's Armalite as Ryan neared the smoky camp fire, alongside the Volvo wag. "That you, friend? Sounds like your walk."

"Yeah, it's me."

"You smell of... Had a run-in with stickies? Shit on a shingle, you did! I can smell their corpse stink on you."

Ryan nodded. "Two of them in the bookstore. One came close to selling me the farm."

J.B. was poking warily at a chunk of meat over the flames. "You took care of them?"

"Yeah."

"Any more?" The Armorer had uncoiled with that effortless, economical fluid movement that characterized everything that he said or did, reaching out for the Uzi that was only inches from his hand.

"Reckon not. Couple on their own. But we could sure think about keeping a watch."

Abe walked a few steps away from the wag, staring into the gloom toward the collection of tiny stores at the heart of Scottsdale. "Could go and take us a look," he suggested. "Make double sure."

Trader spat in the dirt. "No. Divide a small force and you got no force at all."

"They didn't have blasters?" J.B. asked. "Don't see armed stickies very often, but when you do..." He let the words trail into the darkness.

"No. Ragged-assed pair of poor bastards. One little knife between them."

"How come we didn't hear the sound of your SIG-Sauer, Ryan?" Trader asked suspiciously.

"Used steel."

"Nothing better than cold steel," the older man agreed, nodding wisely.

Ryan laughed, suddenly remembering the way that he'd managed to save himself from the first, nearly lethal attack by the mutie. And the poster that had been tacked to the wall of the bookstore.

"Got a new saying for you, Trader. Explain it, mebbe, later tonight."

"What?"

"'The pen is mightier than the sword.'" He grinned at the bewilderment on everyone's faces.

Chapter Thirty-Five

Judas didn't prove so amenable when Sukie decided that she was feeling a little tired on the steep descent and wanted to ride on his back.

He twice turned and snapped at her arms, once nipping a fold of flesh just below the elbow, making her cry out at the unexpected pain.

"You ungrateful son of a bitch, mule," she yelled. "I saved you from a beating and then you do that to me, pretty up and biting good!"

"Perhaps I should venture to offer a small chastisement to the brute, Sukie?"

"Beat the tar out of it for all I care, Doc. Long as you don't get blood on me."

He drew the Le Mat from his belt and reversed it, gripping the ornately decorated barrel, his spread fingers obscuring most of the delicate golden lettering of GEN. J.E.B. STUART. Judas looked up at him out of his deep brown, mournful eyes, his long head drooping, braying quietly, scuffing at the dusty trail with one of his front hooves.

"Oh, look, Doc. I guess that this is his way of letting us know that he's sorry."

"I beg your pardon?"

She smiled and patted the animal on the side of its neck. "I guess we can forgive him just one little mistake, can't we, Doc, dearest?"

"One?"

"Well, he didn't actually manage to get his teeth into me the first time, so that doesn't truly count. We should show a little Christian charity to poor dumb beasts."

Doc shook his silvery head. Sighing, he lowered the big Le Mat and slipped it back into its holster. "You damnable denizen of the basest levels of great Dante's Purgatorio!" The mule whickered softly. "And if you should ever again do aught to harm the person of this great lady, then I swear I shall drive your brains clean out of your rectal orifice."

"You got such a fine, round way of saying things, Doc," she said.

"Why, thank you, my little chickadee."

They carried on, picking their way slowly across the flank of one of the nameless mountains, ever closer to the desert floor and ever closer to the ranch where the others would be waiting patiently for Doc's return.

AT LUNCHTIME they sat together and discussed places that they'd visited.

For Sukie, this meant talking mainly about frontier villes across the Midwest and up into the wildness of the high plains country.

Doc kept her entranced by his tales of other big cities around the world. He still hadn't broken the news of his being time-trawled, though he was going to during the afternoon, so he wrapped up his anecdotes as though they were things that he'd once read when he'd come across a substantial predark library, buried among some hidden ruins.

"There is a fabled city in Spain," he said.

"Where's that? Think I went there once. Pesthole in the Black Hills."

"No, this Spain was a country in Europe. Far across the mighty waters of the Atlantic Ocean. The Lantic as it now seems to be known."

"Is Europe like the home ville where those yellow slant-eyed people come from?"

Doc was puzzled. "Yellow? That would probably be either China or Japan, my dear. But however did you come to hear of Orientals? In my experience there are precious few of them in Deathlands."

She sniffed and wiped her nose on her sleeve, refusing Doc's automatic offer of his kerchief. "No thanks. Those yellow outlanders. Seems I heard some rumors of posses of them, raiding and raping and burning and all. Far west, they said. And right up to the north."

"Really? That is fascinating, my dear."

"But you were telling me about this place Spain and a story about it."

"Ah, yes. Mighty Valencia in the ancient days of glory that was Spain. Home of the leader known as El Cid. But it had its critics and its enemies."

Sukie nodded wisely. "Don't we all, Doc, dear? And ain't that the truth!"

"Yes, it is. Well, these men who hated Valencia created this little sort of poem about it. I'll translate it, Sukie, but first in its original. *'En Valencia las legumbres son agua, los hombres son mujeres y las mujeres nada.'* It means that in Valencia all of the vegetables taste of water and the men are all women and all the woman are worth nothing."

She threw back her head and laughed. "I really like that a lot, Doc."

At that moment he realized that he was in serious danger of falling in love with the woman.

AFTER A SPARTAN LUNCH of the last of the jerky, washed down with almost the last of their fresh water, they had decided to lie down and take a siesta.

But Sukie had other plans. She pulled off her worn riding boots and wriggled her toes in the sunshine. "That feels so good, Doc. Think I might take off a little more." She dropped the dark blue jacket and peeled her way out of the white blouse, leaving herself with just the turquoise necklace above the waist. The sun spilled fire across her breasts.

"Are you considering removing any further apparel, my dear lady?"

"You aiming to go delving in the root cellar again, then, Doc?" Sukie asked with a wicked grin.

"It had crossed my mind that it might assuredly help to enliven what could be our last private interlude together, before returning to the bosom of my friends."

Even as he heard the word "bosom" slipping from his mouth, Doc knew that Sukie would use it to open up some distinctly carnal negotiations.

As it turned out, he was right.

WHEN DOC AWAKENED, he saw the woman sitting cross-legged and naked, examining the inscription incised down the length of the Toledo blade of the sword stick. She saw him blink back toward consciousness. "Can't read this flowery writing on the steel. What's it say?"

"Very old, like the sword. *'No me saques sin razon, no me envaines sin honor.'* Want to know what it means, Sukie?"

"Course I do, you old stud. Sounds real pretty the way you set your tongue around it. Speaking of setting your tongue around something..." She opened her thighs a little to allow him a glimpse of the moist pearl within.

"No, no! Time passes. Listen, time passes. Bible-black evening will soon come rolling toward us, madam. The message on my rapier warns that the steel should never be drawn without reason, nor sheathed without honor."

"Hey," she said, shuffling toward him, laying the blade aside. "That's the kind of moral could apply to another, real different kind of weapon, Doc."

He sighed. "Yes, I suppose it might."

AFTER THE WHITE-COATS had selected Doc as a prime candidate for the trawling experiments known as Operation Chronos, his life had been a perpetual roller coaster of mental confusion, mostly dark and horrific, but with the occasional flash of brightness.

It had been a very long time since he'd experienced such dazzling brightness as he had since his lucky meeting with Susan Smith, and entered into an admittedly short-lived relationship that had already brought him much of what he suspected might be called happiness.

It was his turn to lean upon his elbow and gaze down at her sleeping face, which wasn't exactly what you would have called truly pretty. The Pre-Raphaelite painters that Doc so admired would not have turned their heads as she walked by them along Piccadilly, or called her a "stunner."

But the forty-three-year-old from Hildenville—the one-hoss burg in the middle of the plains—had a great quality of strength in the lines of her face, a mix of wisdom and experience that was undeniably beautiful.

"Well, Emily, my dearest," he whispered to himself, "for the first time since the unkind Lords of Chaos drove us apart, I think that I have been truly unfaithful to your memory. Not just a penny bunk-up in a dark alley or a knee tremble in the back of a hansom cab. I think that I may actually be falling a little in love with this lady."

THEY DRESSED, standing close together, both watching a bald eagle that seemed to have a nest somewhere a deal higher up the mountain and a mile or more away to the east of where they'd been camping. It looked like it was hunting some small rodent, constantly swooping low over the tops of the scattered pine trees, then rising a thousand feet in the air in frustration at its lack of success.

"Must be the most marvelous feeling," Doc said, tucking in the tail of his white shirt.

"Best fun you can have when you're not lying down," Sukie agreed, running her long-nailed fingers through her mane of silvery-gold hair.

Judas whickered softly and Doc turned to him. "Well, old companion. Not long now before you'll find yourself safe and snug in your familiar stable, with plenty of good straw and a bucket of sweet water as a reward for your faithful service. Reasonably faithful."

"It's made its kill," Sukie cried, pointing at the eagle, now making its way eastward, wings flapping slowly, moving with a deliberate calm. Something that might have been a rabbit dangled from its curved claws.

They both watched the bird for several minutes.

Had either Doc or the woman looked behind them, down across the desert, they would have seen a cloud of dust drifting across the baked gray land, showing that a small party was moving out along a backtrail.

But by the time they turned from staring at the vanishing eagle, the dust had also disappeared.

Chapter Thirty-Six

The Volvo stood in the lee of a high bluff that protected it from the worst of the midday heat. The metal ticked and clicked as it cooled a little.

"By evening?" Ryan asked.

"Should be," J.B. replied, lying flat on his back, fedora shading his eyes, his glasses folded neatly and stuck in the top pocket of his jacket.

Trader had been complaining of some stomach pains earlier in the morning, but that might have had something to do with the fact that he'd eaten a very large bowl of fiery chili beans at ten o'clock, at the kindly invitation of a pair of Navaho sheepherders.

Abe was under the land wag, working away with a length of baling wire to fix a loose part of the exhaust system that had been rattling for the past thirty miles.

"How's your guts coming along, Trader?" the little gunner called.

"Gettin' better, thanks, Lee. Damn it! I mean, Abe. Yeah, gettin' better after I emptied myself out in that ditch an hour back. But a clean bed and some sleep and home cooking wouldn't be a bad idea."

"Be there by evening," the Armorer repeated.

"Looking forward to it," Ryan agreed. "Lost touch with how long we've been away."

"Long enough." J.B. flapped a persistent hornet from his face.

Trader was picking at his lip, where the sun had started a small sore. "You men sure changed since you rode with me. All this talk of goin' back. Getting to a fixed place. Wantin' to stop the moving."

Ryan nodded slowly. "It's true. All those years with the war wags, we were always moving, weren't we? One day the Lantic, then a few days later in the bayous. Week later chilling stickies in the Shens and then a firefight with the baron of some pesthole ville in the Darks."

"Damn right!" Trader whistled between his teeth. "That was the life all right. Never a dull moment. Living on the edge. Fighting over the edge. Running, always running hard, crossing the borderline. We should get back to that. Get us all back to the real basics of life."

"Nobody stopping you, Trader." J.B. looked at the older man. "We heard you were living and we wanted to check that out. Now we know. You want to go back to that life, then we'll wish you all the best, Trader. But it's not for us anymore."

"Mean you got soft, Armorer?" He grinned wolfishly at Abe. "What do you say, Gunner?"

"I say that I'll sort of go with what other folks decide," Abe said quietly.

"Well, I guess I'll meet up with all these good folks at the spread yonder." Trader sniffed. "Then I'll decide what we'll be doing after."

"No." Ryan stood. "You decide what *you'll* be doing, Trader. We'll do the same for ourselves. I reckon we ought to get this land wag on the highway if we're going to get back by dusk. Let's move it."

"IT LOOKS real pretty, Doc."

They stood together, looking at the way the setting sun was throwing their shadows out ten yards beyond their feet. There had been a brief rainfall that turned the rutted dust to mud. Now the land smelled clean and good, purged of the heat of the day.

Somewhere, far behind them in the foothills, they both heard a coyote howling.

"Another quarter hour and we'll be relishing some soup and fresh-baked bread, Sukie. With some of the best souls in the whole world."

"I'm getting real antsy and nervous, Doc."

"Nervous, my sweet bird of youth?"

"Suppose they don't like me? I don't think I'll fit in with all of them. Them knowing you and about the time-trawling and all that stuff."

"What difference does that make?" Doc had found himself stumbling over the explanation of his bizarre past, and he had grave doubts that the woman had really understood too much of it, though she'd made a valiant effort.

"Old friends, Doc. And me bein' new and not their kind of caliber."

"Horsefeathers, madam! That is absolute tosh and complete balderdash!"

She pulled a face. "Sorry, Doc. But you and me have been getting on real well, haven't we?"

"Not even a house on fire could hardly have got on better than we," he offered gallantly, wrinkling his forehead at the sudden thought that there had been something not quite right with the sentence.

"Sure." She grabbed him by the arm. "I just wish it was you and me, Doc, together."

"Well, we shall have to wait and see what the future has to offer, Sukie. For now, we should step it out and get on to the house before dark." He looked around, hesitating and staring into the distance behind them. "Are my rheumy old eyes faltering, or can I make something moving out across the sands of the desert that are red with the blood of the square that broke and... I am so sorry, my dear. There goes my tripping tongue and my disconnected brain yet again."

She turned to shade her eyes and looked westward, toward the vivid coppery glow of the setting sun. "Yeah, there could be something. About ten miles off, though. Can't tell which way it's moving, Doc. Best we get to the house, I guess."

"Indeed, I cannot but agree with that. One small thing puzzles me, you know."

"What?"

"We have been in the clearest sight of the ranch for an hour or more, yet nobody has noticed us and come out to greet us." Judas tossed his head and tugged at the reins. "Yes, quite right," Doc said with a smile. "We should indeed stop the talking and commence the walking. There will be a perfectly reasonable explanation, I am quite sure."

RYAN WAS AT THE WHEEL, applying the brakes and going through the gearbox, bringing the land wag to a slow halt. He peered out through the shield.

"There she is," he said. "Little gray home in the west, like Mildred called it."

The sun was low on the horizon behind them. Visible in a slight dip in the land, about three miles along the narrow sandy trail, was the ranch house.

J.B. was in the cab with him. "I'd have thought someone would have been on lookout and spotted us coming a ways back. Though I guess that rainstorm must have laid a lot of the dust. But, even so..."

"There'll be a good reason," Ryan stated.

THEY HAD STOPPED about a dozen feet from the front door, which stood slightly ajar.

"Hello!" Doc called, his right hand creeping down to cover the butt of the Le Mat.

"Trouble, you figure?" Sukie asked.

"I fear that it is beginning to appear a distinct possibility. Perhaps you should wait here, my dear, and I shall reconnoiter."

"I'll come with you."

"Best you wait here."

"There's no sign of life, Doc. How about if I go around the back?"

He considered the suggestion. "Perhaps... You could go and keep a watch out, there. But I beg you not to go into the house until I have ascertained that it is safe."

"Sure thing."

He waited until the woman had walked around the side, then stepped up onto the creaking porch. Doc had often heard Ryan and Krysty speak about how they got a sort of "feeling" that something was wrong.

"Well, I confess that I have that feeling," he muttered.

The light evening breeze was moving the half-open door very gently to and fro, the hinges creaking with the faintest whisper of sound. The sun had almost set, and the hall inside was as dark as pitch.

"Hello," he called again. "Is there anybody there, said the traveler. No, I believe that there isn't."

The house was silent. Doc stood in the entrance and hesitated for a few moments. Then he heard the crunching sound of Sukie's boot heels as she walked around the side of the building, toward the back door.

THE LAND WAG WAS LESS than a quarter of a mile away, and Ryan had again brought the vehicle to a halt. The sun was so far down on the western horizon behind them that the truck was sitting in a bowl of deepest shadow.

"I thought I saw someone goin' in the front door," Trader called.

"Who?"

"Come on, Ryan. How the fuck do I know who it was? Just looked like someone."

"Go ahead on foot," J.B. suggested. "This one's got a bad feel to it."

Ryan reached out and switched off the ignition. In the stillness they all heard the far-off howling of a lone coyote, among the foothills.

SUKIE STOOD A FEW PACES from the kitchen door when it opened and Doc walked out.

"Made me jump," she said. "Anyone there?"

"I only walked straight through, but I called a couple of times. I did not look in any of the other rooms. Can't be anyone there. They would have answered me. I thought that there was the smell of..."

"What? Danger?"

"No." He holstered the big Le Mat. "Perhaps it was my imagination. You saw nothing? There wasn't a note left anywhere around?"

She answered him very quickly. "Note! Why should there be a note, Doc? If I'd found a note, I'd have given it to you, wouldn't I?"

"Yes, yes. Take it easy, my dear. You almost acted as if I had been accusing you of—"

"Well, there wasn't no note, all right? Means that we're here on our own."

The voice came from just behind them, making them both start. "Not alone. Hi, Doc."

Doc spun, his eyes widening at the sight of his friend. "Greetings, my dear Ryan. The best of greetings. How are you and did you find your old companion? There is something amiss here, is there not?"

"Time for all that later. How long you been here?"

"Five minutes. No longer. Is John Barrymore Dix with you? Abe and the Trader?"

"Covering the front of the house. All fine. Got a wag out front as well. Was there a note? And who's this woman?"

"This is no woman, this is my... my friend. Susan Smith, known by the diminutive of Sukie. And this is my truest friend, Ryan Cawdor, my dear."

She had been staring at the tall, powerfully built man with a horrified fascination, unable to keep from looking at the black patch over his left eye and the dull gleam of the automatic blaster held in his right hand. "Hi, there," she said. "Doc's sure talked a bundle about you and the others."

"Yeah." He turned from her. "A note, Doc. Was there a note? They could've gone away for some good reason. If they did, then they'd likely have left us a note. On the front or, more likely, on the back door. Sure there was nothing?"

"I saw nothing. Nor did Sukie."

"Right. I didn't see nothing, Mr. Cawdor. Though a note might not mean anything."

He ignored her, looking toward the main barn and the corral. "Livestock's gone as well. We checked for tracks, but that bout of heavy rain washed everything away."

They all heard steps, moving toward them. J.B. appeared around the one side of the building, raising a silent hand in greeting to Doc. Trader and Abe walked around the nearer wall of the house, both holding blasters.

The introductions took only a handful of seconds.

"It's Indians," Trader said vehemently, gesturing toward the shadowy outline of the mountains with the barrel of the Armalite.

"No bullets, no fire, no broken windows, no blood." J.B. ticked points off on his fingers. "I don't see it as a firefight or an armed raid, Trader."

"Gone out hunting," Abe suggested. "Mebbe following deer and didn't notice the time passing. Could be they'll all return in the next hour or so."

Ryan considered the idea for a moment. "Possible, Abe. Guess that's the best one yet. But they wouldn't have left all of the doors open like this. It's unthinkable, isn't it? Must fine-comb the place. Soon as possible. First, though, we'll just have to bring the land wag up to the house. Get it parked safely out back. Abe, you can do that."

"Sure." He vanished at a quick trot around the side of the building.

Ryan continued. "All the rest of us can move inside and get some lamps lit and take us a room-by-room look around. Doc, you and..."

"Sukie." Both her fists were clenched tight in the pockets of her divided skirt.

He nodded. "Right. You two best go and wait in your room, Doc. Rest of us can search carefully."

"I would prefer it if you ceased treating us like a pair of country clodhoppers. We can search for clues as well, Ryan. We are not totally stupid, you know."

"All right. Time's passing and the darkness is coming down on top of us."

The house loomed over them like a gaunt, ghostly sepulcher, the windows shadowed, blank eyes staring down at the small group.

He turned for a moment back to the stranger among them. "Sure about there not being any sort of message for us?"

"I said so."

"It is more than a remote possibility that Krysty or one of the others could have placed a letter for us, explaining precisely where they are, within the house, Ryan my old friend." Doc moved a pace to stand next to the woman and placed a protective arm around her shoulders.

"Sure. Sorry, Doc. Sorry, Sukie."

"We will go into my room and keep out of your way, Ryan," Doc said.

"Fine." He watched them vanish into the kitchen.

J.B. was about to lead the way inside the house when he stopped, his eyes caught by something. He peered down at the lapel of his own jacket. "Dark night!"

"How's that?" Ryan said.

"Rad counters," the Armorer replied. "Just look at your rad counter."

Ryan did so, angling it to catch the last fading rays of the setting sun. For a moment the rich crimson light confused him and he moved the little counter again, tilting it to make sure what he was seeing.

"It's right around into the red. That means we're all standing in one of the biggest radiation hot spots that I ever saw."

"Mine shows the same," Trader said. "Can't all've malfunctioned at the same time. Not even shading in the orange. It's way off the top of the danger scale."

For a few moments the three friends stood still, looking at one another, each trying to work out what freakish combination of circumstances could have brought what was known as the silent death to this secure, isolated place.

"Doesn't make sense." J.B. wiped a finger over the counter and shook it, checking it again. "Same."

Ryan looked around. "Fireblast! It's getting real dark."

At that moment they all heard the sound of a woman, from inside the building, screaming in blind terror.